Bayside Blues

Happy birthday, Gayle!
Just remember —
Choice _ it's what separates
the saints from the sinners.

Louise Gorday

LOUISE GORDAY

Bayside Blues

ISBN: 978-1512249910

Printed in the United States of America

FOR DAD

You never fail to make me laugh, make me think,
or warm the cockles of my heart.

Love you, moon pie.

Contents

CHAPTER ONE

Out of the Blue

Ryan Thomas plucked sapphire-blue strings tied to the handle of his best cup of coffee in recent memory. Three white balloons bounced and danced against the ceiling like levitating marionettes. *World's Greatest Boss.* Bennie and Van had done a stellar job of keeping the Phoenix going while he recuperated, and his faith in them had never wavered. Still, it was good to be back at work.

He reached up and checked his shirt pocket. *Still there.* That little robin's eggblue box was burning a hole in his pocket. He could take it out and risk losing it, or leave it there and have it constantly pulling on him, prodding him to action. He wasn't comfortable with either, but it was just a *thing,* after all—it could be replaced. His and Van's relationship was the real deal, and her marriage to Richard legally ended, but his ego wasn't yet ready to risk a pratfall by assuming she was ready to say yes. And when he was ready, he would ask just once. *Soonish,* he promised himself . . . perhaps when Bennie got back from vacation.

Ryan shook free the brass key on his ring and unlocked the bottom right drawer of the mahogany desk. Taking the box from his pocket, he shoved it as far back in the drawer as it would go—which was not nearly as far as he had expected. He fished around, and his hand bumped up against the gun-socked semiautomatic pistol. His fingers tightened naturally and comfortably around the grip as he took a bead on a spot across the room. He ran the sock up the barrel, polishing as he went. A good firearm was a thing of beauty . . .

"Ryan?" Van asked through the door.

He shoved the pistol into the center drawer. "Yes? Not locked—come on in."

She cracked the door and stuck her head in. "I'm out of here. You're leaving soon, right?"

"Yep, right behind you. Call you later. It's got to be slick out there. Be careful." As she closed the door, he pulled the drawer back out and slid the gun into his jacket pocket. The feeling of security it gave would be fleeting, though certainly a step up from a crossbow.

Fluffy clumps of snow were wafting down—a rarity in late March. The meteorologists were wrong. Again. First predicted as "light mixed precipitation," the forecast had changed to "substantial snow," reinforcing Ryan's theory that Maryland weathermen staked their reputations and ratings to a capricious rain-snow line. The town had reliably gone into panic mode, and Ryan sent everyone home early. He felt nostalgic—for what, he didn't know or, more accurately, couldn't remember. So many memories were lost forever to his strange set of circumstances. He didn't mind the big empty holes in his memory as much as the ever-present, nagging question of just what strings were tying him to this earth. Surely, there was a point, a plan.

Brandy snifter in hand, he settled in front of the stone fireplace with Hoffa sleeping at his feet and embraced the feeling, though not the reason, as the last of the fire settled into glowing embers. He was close to nodding off when the front door clicked open and a sudden draft of cold air swept into the room.

"We're closed," he called over his shoulder.

"I know. It's the weather."

Ryan started at the sight of a tall, pale, lanky man. His shiny jet-black hair curled in tight ringlets around a long face with piercing emerald green eyes. In spite of his black jeans and jacket, he seemed to brighten the darkened doorway.

"Can I help you with something? It's crazy to be out in this weather."

"I won't be out long. One thing to attend to; then I'm off."

"What do you need?" Ryan asked. He put the snifter on a side table and walked around the couch. "I can have you on your way in no time."

"I'm sure you *could.* Relax, I'm not worried, and I'm not in a hurry. I like a little difficult weather once in a while—spices things up, makes me feel alive."

Ryan's skin tingled, for no reason that he could name. "You should get along before the going gets too bad. What do you need?" he said again.

"I came to see *you.*"

Ryan felt the reassuring weight of the gun resting against his ribs. "We're closed and I'm locking up. Come back during normal business hours and ask for Bennie. He handles the day-to-day. What's your name? I'll tell him to expect you."

"Hamelin Russell, but you're the one I need to talk to. I think now's a good time, when it's so lovely and quiet." His smile reached his eyes.

"*Hamelin Russell* . . . I know that name. *Right.* Aren't you the . . ." Ryan stopped. Snowflakes clung to the man's coat, hat, and scarf in a delicate lacy pattern. He reached out with the tip of his finger.

"Don't," Hamelin admonished, backing up.

But Ryan couldn't resist the urge, and as the tip of his finger melted a snowflake, a bolt of searing pain shot up his arm and across his chest.

"Holy shit!" Recoiling, he tried to shake the pain out of his hand. "Who *are* you?"

"Hamelin Russell, as I said."

"Okay, then, w*hat* are you?"

"Like you, I work in acquisitions." He took a step closer.

"Stop right there. No closer."

Hamelin stopped as a thunderous boom rattled the pub's front windows. Ryan's eyes darted back to the visitor.

"Not me," Hamelin said, chuckling. "Thunder snow, and if I'm not mistaken . . ." He walked over to the windows and put two fingers between the blinds, prying them apart. ". . . heavy snow, couple of inches an hour. I can't take you out in that. Let's sit and talk for a while, shall we?" He rubbed his hands together and dropped down into the dark leather barrel chair in front of the fireplace. The orange embers burst into blue-tinged flames, their reflection dancing in his bright eyes. "Unbridled power. I love its unpredictability." He nodded toward the other chair. "Sit?"

Ryan shook his head, drew the pistol out of his pocket, and leveled it dead center at Hamelin. "I'm only going to ask you once to get out. Then I'm going to blow a hole through you."

"You're incapable of hurting me, Mr. Thomas. Put your finger away and come sit over here and talk with me."

Ryan looked down to find his index finger pointed at the visitor. He could feel the pistol, still tucked securely in his pocket. Against his better judgment, he eased the gun out and placed it on the table, next to the snifter. Then, without another word, he took off, tripping over his feet as he bolted into the kitchen. Stainless steel bowls and pans skittered across the prep counter, clanging onto the floor as his right hand swept them onto the floor. He yanked open the heavy oak-planked back door and darted forward. The door bounced off the wall and slammed into his shoulder blade, shoving him face-first into a head-high wall of snow. No exit. He expected Hamelin to be right on his heels, but to his surprise, when he hobbled around, he was alone. He crept back to the door and peeked around the corner. Hamelin was still seated on the far side of the great room, calmly warming his hands by the fire.

"Are you the devil?" Ryan blurted.

"Heavens, no! I'm nowhere near that important."

"But you *are* evil," Ryan said as he sidled toward a cutlery drawer behind the bar. "I *know* evil. I've worked with evil."

Hamelin shook his head. "I don't think my job is that black and white. I make no judgments. You can think of me as gray—neutral and unassuming."

"You are anything but unassuming."

"I don't understand the fear, Mr. Thomas. I've invited you to chat a while, and you act as if I were going to hurt you. This should be a bonding experience. We're a lot alike, you and I: both professionals—coldly so. Whatever needs to be done, we take care of it—no useless agonizing, questioning, or getting personally involved. This is just business between you and me. Come sit while we have the chance to bond. You'll appreciate it in the end." He reached down and pulled Hoffa into his lap.

Ryan hid a butcher knife behind his back and came closer. "No chance of that. I don't know you. What *kind* of business? I know you're not from HYA."

"Oh, but I know *you*. I'll admit, I had to hunt around some. A minor distraction threw my schedule off kilter. I get a little rogue when I'm bored—limits my career potential, but what can you do?" He wiggled his outstretched fingers in front of the raging fire. "When I got back to the task at hand, you weren't where I thought you'd be. No matter, we'll set things right soon enough." Hamelin pulled a small black notepad from his breast pocket and leafed through it. "Ryan Llewellyn Thomas, born in the Delaware Wedge, July twenty-first, 1977. Mother Ellen Marie Seagle, Father Edward Michael Thomas. Am I right so far?" He momentarily lifted his eyes from the pad. "I'll take your silence as a yes." He flipped to a tab in the back. "Hit by a bus on May seventeenth, 2010, resulting in injuries that proved fatal. That says it all." He flipped the pad shut.

"Wait. I was never struck by a bus. No, no, no." Ryan shook his head as panic set in anew. "That was *the* Ryan Llewellyn Thomas. I am *James Hardy,* death by drowning. Same date, different person. It's complicated. You have us confused. Who *are* you?"

"Since you don't want to sit, we'll cut past the small talk. I don't have a lot of time here. I either have to pick up the pace or skip a few people, and I'll catch hell for that—figuratively speaking, of course." He put the poodle on the floor and approached Ryan.

"I'd like to keep some distance here," Ryan said. He feinted left and tried to duck right under Hamelin's outstretched hand but wasn't quick enough.

When he straightened back up, Ryan was no longer in the Phoenix. The butcher knife was gone, and he was standing, empty handed, on a bustling sidewalk. He looked at Hamelin and blinked. "Whoa! Where the hell . . . ?"

"Baltimore-Washington International Airport," Hamelin replied. "I'll give you a moment to collect yourself. Relax. And stop overusing the word 'hell.'"

"No amount of collecting is going to help. What *are* you?"

"All you need to know is that everything will be fine. I'm here to make it all neat and clean. See that bus coming down the street?" He pointed to the red Long-term Lot A bus, lumbering down the busy access road toward them. "In exactly two minutes, that bus is going to round this corner, and I'm going to push you in front of it. You might consider a tuck and roll—a rather nice touch. But above all else, stay calm. I'm good at this, so there's nothing to be afraid of. Trust me, it'll be painless. Then I can tick you off my list, and I'm that much closer to being caught up."

"Like hell you are. If you think I'm letting you do that, you're crazy." Ryan begged his legs to take him somewhere else, but they felt like lead.

"Just as you didn't let me bring you here from Nevis? Breathe now . . . deeply . . . atta boy. The two-minute wait is the hardest part. Pain and suffering"—he waved his hand around them—"are fleeting. I'll ease you out of it. As soon as you die, you won't remember it, anyway."

Ryan heaved the contents of his stomach all over the sidewalk, liberally spattering his shoes. Pedestrians continued to stream past him, singly and in groups, humming, chatting, and ignoring him utterly. His feet were rooted to the sidewalk. "For God's sake, don't be hasty," he pleaded. "Check your book again. You have the wrong man. You're wrong."

"I'm a lot of things." Hamelin replied. "But wrong is not among them."

The bus was close enough that Ryan could hear the squeaking of its burdened suspension and smell the diesel smoke it belched as it slowed and rounded the corner. Ryan took in its change of speed, the subtle rocking from side to side. It seemed to move in slow motion. As he tried to make his feet carry him somewhere else, Hamelin caught him by the shoulder and launched him into the path of the oncoming bus.

Ryan hit the pavement, winced, and squeezed his eyes shut as he waited for the squeal and smell of burning rubber, and the impact of the bus's grill. To his surprise, Hamelin was right: his death was painless.

CHAPTER TWO

Square Pegs and Round Holes

Ryan pried his face off the gritty, oily pavement and opened his dust-filled eyes. His head was still attached, at least. He scrambled back onto the sidewalk and ran his scraped palms down his pants, to the rips in the knees. He didn't see any blood, but there would be plenty of bruises. His shoulder burned like the devil. He wiped the stinging tears away with his shirttail.

The Lot A bus rumbled on down the road, and the pedestrians kept walking right on past, seemingly oblivious to his near-death experience. On a hunch, Ryan reached out and took a swipe at one. A solid right hook that should have caught the guy square in the ribs . . . traveled through as if he were swinging at a hologram.

"This isn't real—not the people, not the bus, not the weather. I'm not dead, and we're probably not even here."

"Shush," Hamelin warned, and he turned his back on Ryan. He paced on the sidewalk, poring over the notes in his leather pad. He stopped suddenly in mid calculation. "The bus, it's a constant. It comes every day at this time. The people, weather—all variables. They come; they go; they change. They're incidental to what we're about—just for show, really."

"So that bus could have killed me?"

"*Should* have killed you," Hamelin corrected. He grimaced and returned to his calculations. "What *am* I missing?" he murmured.

"I told you, death by drowning," Ryan said, pointing to himself. He walked over to Hamelin and peeked over his shoulder. "If your book is so complete, look up *James Hardy*."

Hamelin ducked away. "James Hardy, Hardy, Hardy," he repeated, running his finger down the page. "Quite right. Death by drowning, Glen Burnie, Maryland, on May seventeenth, 2010." He paused and gave Ryan an appraising look. "You don't look anything like James Hardy. Still," he mused, "the stories do match up . . . and the bus didn't kill you. Maybe this does require a shift in paradigm. Let's suppose you *are* Hardy. *Hardy plus drowning* should successfully feed the algorithm. Right?"

"Right. No, wait—"

Ryan awoke to a face-full of salt spray, and the *whomp* of a Del Rey speedboat skipping across choppy water. He clutched the gunwale and jettisoned what remained of his stomach contents into the dark, churning water below. At the fore, Hamelin sat in the captain's chair, steering with one hand. A faint glow shimmered around him.

"Hamelin . . . why?" he gasped, shrinking back down onto the slick deck.

"Nothing personal," Hamelin yelled over his shoulder. "My job assignment is to put Ryan Llewellyn Thomas back on his appointed course. He's been judged. He needs to go to hell, and it's my job to get him there. You appear to be him, but certainly not a perfect fit. I can't account for the aberration. It's maddening, and I'm getting hopelessly off schedule. I suppose it doesn't matter who I take, really, although I do get more points for staying with the program. At the moment, I'm dead last—pardon the expression—and I do enjoy roaring back when the odds are heavily against me." He paused. "Since I was sent for you, *Ryan Thomas,* it seems most appropriate that you be the one I take back."

"You are the devil . . . taking me to *hell?* Damnation shouldn't be some kind of cosmic game. Check my bio, fact sheets—hell, report cards if you have to. I'm a good person. Wait—there are more of you?"

"Oh, there are lots of—*tsk, tsk, tsk.* You're the type I'm going to have to watch. You're stuck with me. I'll just say we like to make it interesting. Eternity can be long and boring. 'The devil,'" he repeated, rolling his eyes. "Why this need to *label* everything? You're so judgmental! Acceptance is so much easier."

Ryan pulled himself up from the deck and made his way forward, hand over hand, along the gunwale, to the bow. Ignoring him, Hamelin guided the speeding boat expertly around the buoys in the channel. The wind whipped the black curls straight back off his face to reveal flawless marble skin to rival Michelangelo's *David.* But, Hamelin's demeanor was no longer serene. He was wild-eyed, the intensity in his emerald eyes unnerving as they darted left and right across the water, seeing God only knew what, on a night hung heavy with fog and bellowed warnings from the Thomas Point Lighthouse down the coast.

"I didn't fall off a boat, you know."

"You'd prefer we walk?"

"Suit yourself, but you are not killing me. This is all more illusion. You came for Ryan Thomas, and as you've seen, I'm not your man. If I was, I would have died back there when you threw me under the bus.

He ain't me, pal. You have to stick with the program. Check with your supervisor. Do *something.* Otherwise, you're making a career-ending mistake here."

"Hardly. They're used to me screwing up, although I may have to go with plan B. Relax. We generally operate under a do-no-harm credo."

"What's plan B?"

"Oh, God in heaven, help me," Hamelin groused. "Why can't they let me handle things?" He threw his hands up in the air and motioned Ryan over to the wheel as the boat hurtled, unmanned, into the darkness. "Ryan Thomas, you're getting a reprieve because I'm needed somewhere else. I'm going to put you back where I found you, but I'll be back. Don't wander. I don't have time right now to go looking for you again. And relax. When I get back, I'll make sure you're a priority. It's the least I can do."

CHAPTER THREE

Sillage

Ryan stirred to the late afternoon light filtering in the windows of the Phoenix, and his neck jammed up against a red leather couch pillow. Apparently, he had spent the night here. He bolted upright, heart pounding. There was no sign of his strange nighttime visitor. The brandy snifter sat on the table to his left, the pistol right alongside it. He exhaled. Maybe he had dreamed the guy. Then he smelled his vomit-covered shoes and broke out in a cold sweat. The bastard could at least have left him with clean shoes.

Ryan didn't need a little leather notepad to tell him Hamelin Russell was bad news, a celestial screw-up trying to make up for poor decisions and lost time. He was definitely not human (or sane, for that matter). Immortal? Possibly, but not angelic—not with such a lack of compassion. Hamelin didn't appear to feel anything other than an urgency to get back on schedule. Maybe *all* his deliveries were to hell.

His cell phone buzzed, and he jumped several inches across the couch. He let it go to voice mail. Two missed and two placed calls. His pulse quickened. What the hell? When had he made these? If he had been foolish enough to put the numbers under "Contacts," he would have entered them under "T"—for "*Trouble.*" All were HYA executives. It was too much drunken dialing to be believable, even for a pub owner.

He eased his Top-siders off, tossed them in the trash, and went in search of clean clothes. The ones that hung on the wooden peg on the back of his door would do. He checked for the little box in his desk and, finding it undisturbed, pocketed it, along with the pistol.

The Phoenix was well into its afternoon rush. Nothing seemed amiss: every seat at the bar taken, Van in deep conversation with Jean, and Marla off pouting in the corner. He could set his watch by Chips, the curly-haired blond snack delivery guy, sipping Kendall Jackson Chardonnay as he scribbled away on a yellow legal pad. Van waved and held up her index finger. She'd be a minute. He desperately needed her, but she would never buy his wacky story. He had to settle down and break it out calmly because she had to be sick of all his drama.

He stuck his head outside and did a double take. The storm had died down to patchy snow, fast melting away in the bright sun. A whorl of yellow butterflies floated by, playing tag, and little rivulets of water snaked around the edges of the brick street pavers. Relief swept over him. He had dreamed it all. *Note to self: no more brandy before bed.*

He walked outside and, as minutes passed, paced up and down the sidewalk. He checked his watch. He was a stickler for punctuality, and he had never understood why women said they were ready when, in fact, they were nowhere close to being ready. A night on the couch was beginning to take its toll. He rotated his aching shoulder and flexed his legs to relieve the throbbing in both knees. He had no explanation for why his fingertips felt like 60-grit sandpaper.

"Where's your snow shovel?" Van asked as she joined him out front.

"What happened to all the snow?" he said. "And what's the deal with all the yellow butterflies?"

Van shrugged. "Snow, butterflies—everything's gone crazy. It snowed like mad for a couple of hours, switched over to rain, and then quit."

"But I opened the door—"

She mimed taking a drink. "Perhaps a little too much, eh? Give some thought to all those disappointed kids who turned their pajamas inside out last night to guarantee a day off from school. Only one weatherman got it right this time—point for Dave on Channel 7. He stuck to his forecast."

"Why'd you let me sleep the day away?"

"Aww, you looked so cute and tired after your all-night bender, we didn't have the heart to wake you up. I checked on you a couple of times to make sure you didn't aspirate your own vomit," she said, noting his clean shoes.

"There are worse ways to go, trust me," he said.

"I thought you'd be staying here to put in a few honest hours. You're leaving?"

"Can't get it in gear today. I'm going home to crash for a while, but I'll be back . . . back in when . . ." Ryan stopped, suddenly transfixed by something in the distance. The swarm of butterflies scattered, and Van turned around to see what had caught his attention. "Sorry," he began again. "Lost my train of thought."

"Sweet Jesus, hon, you look out of it! When's the last time you ate?" She surveyed his face. "I thought so. Walk home with me and I'll make you a tuna-fish sandwich. Or grilled cheese. You pick. You can crash there and then we can meet up again later. Or you can go home when you feel up to it, and I'll see you tomorrow. I'm not hanging around the house. I have to go work Jean over until she screws up and tells me what she's been working on. She's stoked but won't tell me about it. Friends should have no secrets."

"Uh," he said, shaking his head. "I don't know. Tuna fish sounds good, but I swear I might not make it through lunch. If I'm not good company, don't get mad, okay? I feel like I was up all night long."

"That'll teach you not to party hardy anymore. Come on."

Perhaps it was best to let her go with that, at least until he figured out last night. Maybe friends should have no secrets, but friends also shouldn't worry each other needlessly. He might have dreamed up his encounter with the spectral Hamelin Russell. The brightness of the day made it all seem unreal. If the guy did exist, what could Van do about it anyway? Hopefully, if it wasn't all a dream, and the specter did exist, he'd get distracted again, or given a time schedule that could easily spread over eternity. Come back in a couple of lifetimes. And she would be all over him if she found out about the HYA calls. She would see them for what they were: a sinister invitation to stop by and catch up on old times. Ryan hated to acknowledge it, but Van was right: everything, including him, had suddenly jumped the rails.

CHAPTER FOUR

Mayo, Hold the Crazy

Van pulled him into the house with little protest and shoved him toward the couch. "Sit. I'll be right back with some lunch."

As soon as she disappeared, Ryan scooted off the couch and headed for the window. He tipped the venetian blinds. His uneasy gut was right: there was Hamelin, three houses away, leaning against a utility pole, brown paper bag in hand as he held court over a flock of squabbling white seagulls. He didn't appear to have a care in the world, which was probably accurate considering the otherworldly nature of his mission. *Desperate.* Hamelin seemed reluctant to come inside the pickle boat house after him. Ryan Llewellyn smiled and closed the curtain. Nowhere near checkmate, but he was done being anybody's pawn.

How refreshing to surface and be in control again! Ryan Llewellyn breathed deeply as his eyes panned the room. It was always this way. He had no real idea what this house was all about. The moment his foot crossed the threshold, he had begun to lose what little dominance and control he possessed. There was no use struggling. In here, James

Hardy's persona had the upper hand. He would have to find another time, with better odds, to resurface and seize full control of his own body. This coexistence with Hardy had to end. *Squatter.* Hardy had gall and more control now, but that would soon change. The fact that *he* could enter this house today, with Van on his arm, showed that Hardy didn't have a lock on the situation. The encounter with Hamelin had changed something, and when he found out what, he intended to exploit it to the fullest and push Hardy someplace deep where he couldn't interfere. He would let Hardy sit and mildew in the dark recesses of the subconscious, as he himself had done for months. Even as his fury rose, Ryan Llewellyn Thomas was forced to give in to the insistent call of his body's subconscious. He relinquished control to his corporeal rival, Ryan James Thomas.

Ryan James woke with a start. He must have blacked out. He had no idea how he had gotten to the pickle boat house. The last he recalled, he was out on the street . . . with butterflies. He stood up and circled the room, picking up whatnots, expending energy. Something was very wrong. He and Van should talk. Impulsively, he swept his finger along the top of the massive rolltop desk.

"Ouch! What the . . . ?" Ryan reached down and picked up the roll of toilet paper unspooling past his feet. "Did you throw this at me?"

Van giggled. "Yes. What am I going to do with all the rolls that Jean talked me into buying? Milk, bread, and toilet paper . . . the three essentials. It's going to be a blizzard . . . milk, bread and toilet paper. I have enough to paper the *whole house.* Why do I listen to these crazy people? And yes, I saw what you were doing. There's no dust up there. What's wrong with you? You look like a caged animal, pacing about."

Ryan stared at his clean fingertips. What were the consequences of getting her involved? He had no idea. He put the roll down on the desktop and nodded to a montage hanging above the desk. "You've changed your pictures," he said, buying time. "Where's the skydiving one?"

"I thought I asked you to sit down."

"I know. I caught myself sleeping over there. Half of me's exhausted, but the other half feels ready to explode with pent-up energy."

"The skydiver's still on the table, but lots of new ones hanging. I like to switch it up a bit. Sit. Here's your tuna sandwich."

"That sounds good." Ryan ignored it and plucked the skydiver out from a group on the end table. "Strangely enough, when I look at this, I can relive the experience: my face flattened against the air . . . trying to pull my lips back over my teeth . . . the silence after the chute opens. Without the visual cue, nothing."

Van gave up. "Those two drawings there are from Mrs. Morton's daughter. The scruffy worker sleeping on the end of the caboose, and the carousel horse. I wouldn't be surprised if those go back to the early days of the amusement park. And there's a new one of you on the wall. Can you find it? Tell me if you remember that."

Ryan studied the half-dozen photos of various sizes, some in color, others black and white, searching faces and places as he moved from picture to picture. There, in the last color picture, a smiling little boy of about 6 stood in a crowd of full-size cartoon characters. "Me at Disney World? Oh, my God, that's cool. Doesn't ring any bells, though. That's really me? Wow. I never . . ." *There.* The face in the crowd was almost completely hidden by a baseball cap pulled down low over his face, but it was unmistakable. *Hamelin Russell.* Ryan almost peed his pants.

"What?"

"Here, in the baseball cap—who's this?"

Van walked over to the desk and leaned in for a closer look. "Hmm, no idea—not with us. I never gave anyone else in the picture a second glance. You were so cute at that age! I think you hugged every one of those characters." She looked at Ryan, and he could see the lightbulb go on in her head. "You *remember* this person?"

"No, but I thought you might. It's a cute picture," he said, turning to study Hamelin once more. Without a doubt, it was him, twenty years earlier but looking exactly the same. Even with the hat, he could never forget that alabaster face. But had he really met Hamelin again. Or was his brain playing tricks on him, merely piecing together newly unearthed childhood memories? Ryan scanned the other pictures. Was this the only other time he and Hamelin had been in close proximity, or could the guy have been stalking him his entire life?

Van walked up behind him and put her arms around him.

Ryan swallowed hard and pulled her around to face him. "I met someone . . . at the Phoenix. I'm not sure what to make of him. He's not from here, but . . ." He stopped and gazed into her soft brown eyes, so earnest and loving . . . so trusting.

"And?"

"Ah, forget it. If he's back in, I'll point him out and you can form your own opinion.

"Something's bothering you. Tell me. Is it Hector Young and Associates and the trial? It's open and shut—they'll convict Hector Young of attempted murder. They're sure. *You* should be sure. It's just a matter of time, and it'll be behind us. Am I right or not?"

"Of course you're right. You're always right. And I'll be glad when we're past it. I'm really tired of all this. I'd like a clean slate, that's all—blue skies and smooth sailing . . . On second thought, no sailing," he said with a shudder. "I'm beginning to wonder if that's too much to ask of life."

"No, it isn't," she said. "We both deserve a respite. There isn't anything we can't handle together."

"Absolutely," Ryan said. Except for the things he didn't feel comfortable telling her about. It always seemed to be that way. And from experience, he knew she would react badly if she found out. If he could handle it, she need never know. The little blue box in his pocket began burning away again. "You, me, open road. Let's run away together—no cares, just you and me."

"If I didn't know you better, I'd swear you were serious." She raised up on her toes, kissed the tip of his nose and pulled away. "I have to go next door and pester Jean."

The burning stopped, and he let her go. "Okay," he said. "I've decided to go home, so if you're leaving now, take a key with you because I'm locking the door behind you. He fumbled with the doorknob and avoided her eyes. "You do lock your door when you're alone, don't you, Van?"

"Look where we are, silly. Nobody locks their door here. You're acting weird, Ryan Thomas. Tell me what's going on and why you feel the need to carry a gun in your pocket. In Nevis! Did you really think you could hug me and I wouldn't notice it?"

"Nothing's going on, and I wasn't trying to hide it. I was going to make a bank deposit, but I changed my mind. I have a permit to carry, and do sometimes. Nevis is not the little paradise you'd like to think it still is. After all we've been through, why haven't you taken any of it to heart? Nevis has the same real-life dangers any other town has to deal with. Use some common sense and lock your doors. Be cautious for me; then I won't worry."

She studied him for a moment. "Yeah, sure, boss. I can do that for you." She pulled the house key from her purse and dangled it in front of him. "If you ever need it, there's an extra in the garden . . . somewhere."

She kissed him and slammed the door shut with a resounding thud on the way out.

Ryan walked her to the birdbath and waited until she disappeared behind Jean's house. The only threat he could see was Mouse, who intercepted them halfway across the driveway. He mewed and dogged every other step until Ryan stepped on his forepaw. Then he screeched, bolted underneath the nearest azalea bush, and resumed his watch from there.

Ryan turned and scouted out both ends of the street. Hamelin was nowhere to be seen, and Ryan would be perfectly happy never seeing him again. It could happen. By now he had probably realized his mistake and was off making someone else a priority—someone who actually *deserved* eternal damnation.

CHAPTER FIVE

Priority

Ryan hit the snooze button and flopped back down in bed, but there would be no return to gentle slumber. Even with his eyes closed, he could still see Hamelin Russell standing in the doorway of the Phoenix, softly illuminated by his own light, staring with those strange, ageless eyes. He burrowed back under the covers.

Every day, from the moment Ryan woke up until he nodded off at night, he jumped at every noise and scanned every face. And every day, nothing. Apparently, he wasn't on Hamelin's do-it-now list. And for this, Ryan was thankful, because life was filling up his day with other problems. He hoped and prayed that HYA had dismissed his late-night calls as a minor annoyance. He certainly wouldn't be making any more. And he couldn't face another day at work like yesterday. Not that the shine was wearing off the Phoenix. Stepping away from his previous employment at HYA, and all their shady activities, was the best decision he had ever made. The employees and patrons at the pub were like family—he just wasn't cut out to run it alone. He was counting the hours until Bennie's return.

Bennie was the drive wheel in the Phoenix machine, and Ryan would be hard-pressed to replace him. But he couldn't work the man around the clock forever. He had sent Bennie off on vacation with a promise to call him back if things began to fall apart. He had tried to get him to go for a couple weeks, but Bennie wasn't having it. The Phoenix was his baby. Ryan loved the place, too, but he didn't see himself as the paternal type. Once in a while, he had to get away. Not Bennie. He never took a vacation. His New York regulars made good-natured sport of him and gifted him with shot glasses from everywhere they traveled. He enjoyed the attention, displaying them all on a special shelf, but it never changed his mind about taking time off. The farthest he ever got from New York City was the occasional break to admire the cherry red glass with a polar bear glued to the side, extolling the natural beauty of Anchorage, Alaska.

Bennie was very much mistaken if he thought Ryan had any real intention of calling him. That would be admitting that he couldn't handle his own pub, which was unacceptable even if partly true. He didn't know all the ins and outs—just enough to keep things afloat, open his wallet for someone to fix problems. And he was smart enough to employ an old hand like Bennie to do the hard stuff.

The alarm buzzed again, louder this time, with a white pulsing light to up the ante. Ryan kicked the covers to the bottom of the bed and looked beyond to the cheesy pastel abstract clone bolted to the wall. He didn't give a fig about the tackiness. He had gotten used to the Bayside and didn't mind the months he had spent here. He could come and go as he pleased without drawing attention, and until a couple of days ago, he had still been haggling to buy the house he wanted: Ernest Pickett's, next to Van's place. The crotchety old coot had died with no apparent beneficiaries, and a will as old as the hills. The disposition of his estate had finally wended its way through the courts, and Ryan's offer to buy the house had been accepted. In a month, it would be his. With cost not a big factor, he had thrown a lot of money at the Pickett estate, and as he expected, they had jumped at it. Van was clueless. Even though he had bought her a ring, they never really talked about what the next level of their relationship would be. Both seemed content to enjoy what they had, and let the rest follow along as it might. He didn't mean to crowd her, but he didn't feel the need to discuss the sale, either. And right now he had his hands full just trying to keep up with the Phoenix.

Suddenly, for the second time in a week, it dawned on him that he had cut Van out of his life. Was he making her important enough? He wondered. But no, this was situational, not just a pattern he had fallen into. She would be pleasantly surprised.

He flipped his pillow over and rolled onto his side. After all, he was in Nevis to stay, so he had to find a place of his own somewhere. Pickett's house was as close as he could get to going home again. He closed his eyes, promised he would give her a heads-up next time he saw her, and rolled out of bed. All problems were finite. He just had to keep moving.

He grabbed a polo shirt and jeans off the stack of clean clothes in the chair, and fifteen minutes later he was headed out the door with a mug of stale robusta coffee and a pile of invoices he hadn't gotten around to paying. The Phoenix was within easy walking distance, but he was in no mood. Nature could take the hike this morning. His mood deepened, and he got his heart rate up just fine without the walk—the moment he saw Hamelin lounging against the fender of his black Carrera, a yellow and black tiger swallowtail perched on his index finger. He watched as Hamelin shook the creature free, only to have it flutter out a few feet and then return again to his outstretched finger. He turned it loose one last time and put his hand in his pocket, whereupon the butterfly joined a half-dozen more of its kind on the car's windshield wipers. Hamelin calmly opened the driver's side door, slid in, and buckled up.

Ryan halted, quickly weighed his options, and saw that he was fresh out of good ones. Without making eye contact, he got in on the passenger's side and muttered, "Don't come any closer than you are right now."

Hamelin ran his hand along the dashboard, under the steering column. "Keys?"

"Ah, hell no. I've seen you drive. Get out of my car."

Hamelin frowned and dropped his hand to the seat. "You look surprised. I told you I'd be back to take care of you."

"I was hoping that would be eons from now," Ryan growled. "I've spent the last week terrified of seeing you again, but right now all I feel is angry. Are you going to be bopping in like this all the time, or is this plan B? And if it's plan B, do whatever it is you need to do, and be done with it."

Hamelin ignored the question. "I promised I'd make you a priority, so here I am. But I've devoted far more time with you than normal, so we're going to have to wrap this up."

"Why didn't you tell me we'd met before?"

"Where do you *think* we've met before?"

"Disney World. I was six."

Hamelin smiled. "You're remembering things. Exciting, isn't it? Like living life all over again."

Ryan turned in the seat until he could look at him directly. "Nothing about you excites me, Hamelin. It's a blank spot like everything else. Van has a picture of me, and lo and behold, there's your scary mug in the background. Have you spent all my life stalking me? And why are you so thrilled that I'm remembering things? You've been studying up on me, and my story checks out. Admit it: there is no reason for you to be here. So go away and leave me in peace."

"Stalking? Heavens, no! Er . . . that is to say, only when professionally required. As I recall, the day was nicely planned. You were going to ride the gaily painted teacups, eat some expensive Disney chocolate ice cream, and hug a few gigantic underpaid, overworked cartoon people. Then a quick trip alone to the men's bathroom, where you would be secreted out a back door and murdered several hours later by a pedophile who liked to haunt bathrooms at the park."

"Oh, God. Van didn't—"

"Chill. Never happened. Your mother never wanted to send you in alone, and at the last minute, she dragged her humiliated and loudly protesting young son into the women's privy. Fate changed. My services weren't needed until the next day, with another little boy who wasn't so lucky. Terrible crime," he said. "Nice little boy."

"That never happened. You're energized by the dramatic."

Hamelin rolled his eyes. "Stop being such a naysayer. Accept these things. I'm not going to lie to you. Verify it. Jeremy Little. *Orlando Sentinel.* May seventh, 1992--page one above the fold."

"Was that the only time?"

"Just that once . . . before now. Of course it's all shocking, but mortals would be surprised how much of life is like that: right place, right time . . . wrong place, wrong time. People make decisions all the time that affect their fate and the fates of others. They never see the repercussions of a different choice. Now, move on and get this out of your head. You were better off not knowing. It's not necessary to know everything behind the curtain. Back to present business. I'm still here because I am. We need to address your current choices, many of which are questionable. Who are you calling yourself today?"

"We've been all over this. For the last time, I go by Ryan Thomas, but I'm really James Hardy."

"Okay, still sticking with that one." Hamelin consulted his phone, punched a few keys, and scribbled in his notebook. "Now that I've had a chance to step back and review everything, I agree. You're the mulligan."

"Mulligan?"

"The do-over. Or else, it's a clever ploy to avoid responsibility. Your *situation* is much more involved than I had anticipated. I don't get a clear reading on you. You are a contradiction, and *that's* your problem—a little good, a little bad. I have to figure out who you really are. Is it Ryan *Llewellyn* Thomas, a clever, atheistic sociopath, or Ryan *James* Thomas, a moralistic dreamer who loves his *mo-ther*?"

Ryan flipped the buckle on his seat belt and opened his door, but before he could get out, Hamelin grabbed his shirtsleeve and yanked him back in the car.

"Stay in the car. Don't make me follow you around. That would be infuriating, and you really wouldn't like that side of me. You're a little bolder today, I see—worked past upchucking on your shoes. Still, I'm not sure anger suits you."

"Do you realize just what a disgusting blowhard you are?" Ryan slammed his door. "Stay on your side of the car. It's not what you think it is. Van and I, we're strangers. There is no backstory if no one can remember it."

"As in the old conundrum about a tree falling in the forest? Blah blah, blah. Bottom line is, I don't get paid to think. *You* figure it out. In fact, I'll give you a month to get your act straight."

"You just said you were in a hurry to move on to other things. The quickest way to do that is to acknowledge you missed your window of opportunity to procure the soul of the original Ryan Thomas, and go on to the next unfortunate soul on your list. Other people's mistakes really aren't my problem."

"If you really are Ryan Llewellyn Thomas, they *are* your problem. And you'll need to get about fixing them."

"That is utter bull crap that you're making up as you go. For politeness' sake, I'll bite, but you're not giving me much to work with here. I may look like Ryan Llewellyn Thomas, but all I know is, he was a ruthless, conniving bastard who always came out on top, and everyone hated him for it. From your unbiased perspective, do I have that about right?"

"He was bright, very bright. A doer, leader of men.

"Good qualities. So why drag him off to hell?"

"They're all *natural* abilities. Let's just say he didn't apply them well. Ryan Llewellyn could be enchanting, but you never wanted to cross him. He was an idea person but a driven SOB who led by intimidation and used his intelligence to further his own interests—to the detriment of others, of course. But most of all, he was a solitary figure, an atheist who didn't believe in anyone but himself."

"Then how could you possibly talk about giving me the same fate? I'm not any of that. I *believe.* If you take me anywhere, I should be heading up, not down."

Hamelin slid his notebook back into the pocket of his black and orange Baltimore Orioles track jacket. "Don't berate the messenger. I don't mete out judgment; I merely carry out the decision. They say, 'Take 'em to hell,' I take 'em. And here I am."

"So the devil directs you?"

"Heavens, no! He doesn't have a say in who goes to hell. He's a receiver, not a distributor. And you, you don't get a passing grade. I must either take you or clean you up. I'll give you a fighting chance. And no, I don't do the heaven thing. Dreadful bore. Relax, I promised I'd take care of you."

"So you say, but you tried to throw me under the bus. That's not reassuring." Ryan studied the mass of yellow butterflies collecting on his side-view mirror. "Here's the thing," he said, tapping on the window glass at them. "I'm not going anywhere without a fight. That notebook you keep flipping through—there must be an appeals process in there. I demand a higher-level review. I've been sent back to this life for a reason, and by a higher authority than you. I'm pretty confident it's not in your job description to interfere."

"So much the lawyer," Hamelin said. "There has to be a process, one more chance." He shifted out of his mocking tone and said, "There is a time in life when each of us must pay the piper. This . . . is . . . your . . . time, James Hardy Ryan Thomas, or whatever you want to be called."

Ryan closed his eyes and took a long, slow breath. "*All* corporations have levels of review. Whistle-blower protection? You're so inept, whoever sent you here needs to know what a half-assed job you're doing. You can't possibly be legit."

"It's a corporate world, Mr. Thomas. Everyone has a job to do. I work independently, with only a cursory review of results. As long as I meet long-term goals and expectations, I'm good to go. Time is relative. By the time they post, my metrics will look the same as everyone else's. Averaging is a beautiful thing."

"Heaven is boring? Uh-uh. My guess is, heaven's a plum assignment. Trips to hell, that'd be the bottom-feeders that have no sense of humanity. You're a bottom-feeder, aren't you, Hamelin? The authority to give me a month? I don't think so. You're still off the reservation. Somewhere along the way, you screwed up so bad, they quit letting you take people like Jeremy Little to heaven. You're a screw-up—it's what you do best."

"Full authority," Hamelin repeated. "Show a little respect. I could call time right now and haul you off to where the sun doesn't shine. Here's the deal . . ."

"Yeah. See, that's what I don't get. At first, you were hell-bent. Now you're hesitant and offering me a deal. You said you don't make judgments, but that is exactly what you're doing. Don't you realize humans aren't perfect? There's good and bad in all of us. You're going to force me to do things I wouldn't do of my own free will. Maybe you can't—"

"Enough!" Hamelin's deep voice boomed across the parking lot. The butterflies flitted up off the windshield in a cloud of yellow and retreated to a nearby buddleia bush. "Again, here's the game plan, "he said, returning to his quieter, calmer voice. A few butterflies returned tentatively to the Porsche's windshield, wings batting warily. "I'm going to give you a chance to prove there's somebody good inside here." He poked his finger at Ryan's chest. "The question we need answered is, how much of you is pure-as-the-driven-snow James Hardy, and how much is black-hearted Ryan Llewellyn Thomas? Can you clean up your act and pass the test? Maybe I'll dish it out; see if you can take it."

"What's that supposed to mean? You're going to unleash demons from hell in the middle of the night to screw with me?"

"You're a haunted man, Mr. Thomas. The only demon I have to unleash is the one in your head. As interesting as it would be to leave you to your own devices and return once you've crashed and burned, I've decided to leave you with something that gives you a fighting chance." He leaned over the seat and pulled a tall hourglass from the floor in the back.

"That isn't mine," Ryan said.

"Now it is. This is an aurascope." Hamelin held it up and flicked the upper bulb, which was filled with cobalt-blue sand. Magenta sand began to sift into the empty bulb below. "My heavens, look at that! You are such a screwed-up mess of a man. The sand is color coded to reflect your aura: blue for benevolent, red for reprehensible. Your aura right now is magenta, an equal mix of both. Pay attention to the sand; it will give you instant feedback on how you're doing, maybe even promote some introspection. When you're behaving like a decent human being—good motives, serene life, à la James Hardy—the falling sand becomes blue, and the flow almost imperceptible, essentially an endless supply of sand. Engaging in morally objectionable behavior, after the fashion of Ryan Llewellyn Thomas, on the other hand, causes the sand to fall faster, and the lovely blue changes to red. Time is truly relative. Take stock of your life, and make it a good one. Get rid of the duplicity, the evil that lurks within. Stop your game playing, and foster a good-citizen image that is more than skin . . .

"Wipe that blank look off your face!" Hamelin snapped, scowling. "You know *exactly* what I'm talking about. I know everything, remember? Stealing files from HYA wasn't too smart, no matter what the reason. And if you love Ms. Hardy, treat her the way she should be treated. Be honest and open with her. You threw a wrench in her relationship with Richard Hardy. If you had not come along, they might have reconciled. They did have a solid marriage for many years. Think about whether she's better off with you. Stop to consider all the ripples you're creating, because if and when this upper bulb empties out, I'll be back for you. Be a good boy, I'll verify you're James Hardy, and you're rid of me for good. Not so hard, right?"

He handed the glass to Ryan, who promptly flipped it over. The magenta sand continued to flow at the same rate, though upward now, into the empty bulb, defying gravity.

"Where did you get this?" Ryan asked.

"Try altering the *behavior,*" Hamelin said, shaking his head. That's the only way you can affect the sand's flow and color. The aurascope is just a tool of the trade, and a great one for individuals who seem unable to grasp the consequences of their actions. Straighten up and fly right, Mr. Thomas. Everything has a ripple effect. You can't just go off willy-nilly, making ripples all over the place. There are too many unintended consequences. Much in your life is out of kilter. Now I have to get it all straightened out, and frankly, that wastes my time."

Ryan shoved the aurascope back at Hamelin. “You’re insane. Take your ridiculous toys and go someplace else. You have no idea what you should be doing, or the ripples *you’ve* created. You can’t come here and direct the decisions people should make. We have free will. This whole situation is entirely your fault. If you had collected Ryan Thomas on schedule instead of loafing, nothing would be ‘*out of kilter,*’ as you put it. Surely, you have other people, business to look after. Now, get out of my car. I’m late.”

Hamelin ignored the aurascope being thrust against his chest. He opened his door, tucked his hands behind his head, and closed his eyes. Immediately, the butterflies flew in and began fluttering around his head. The air surrounding him began to shimmer and glow softly.

“I don’t magically cease to exist when you close your eyes,” Ryan growled. “Look at me. Nothing I do will affect Van’s relationship with Richard. She chose to leave him. I had nothing to do with that, and she’ll never go back to him. My citizenship credentials have been impeccable since I met Van. You know *nothing.*”

Hamelin waved off the handful of butterflies clinging to his hair and shirtfront. The glow vanished. “With that attitude, you’re doomed,” he sniffed. “There are things in motion now that I have no control over. Take charge and change your life. And don’t go discussing it around—no chitchatting about this with other people. Dig in and fight, Ryan Thomas. When that sand empties out, I have twenty-four hours to come and fetch you. *Nonnegotiable.* If you can clean up your act, I might let you go. Remember, one chance. Your decision. Redemption or hell—it is and has always been your choice.”

CHAPTER SIX

Blue-eyed Blonde

Marla Fisher was almost past the last table, a tub of dirty dishes balanced against her hip, when the woman sitting at the end of the bar reached out and touched her forearm.

"Excuse me. I'm looking for Vanessa Hardy. Is she here?"

"Back table, red shirt." Marla pulled her arm free and kept going. She had already been fussed at three times for piddling around.

The woman didn't move from her place. Instead, she studied the back corner for several moments. Finally, as Marla was coming back out of the kitchen, she threw back the rest of her liquid courage, picked up her brown knockoff Coach handbag, and headed to the back of the room.

"Mrs. Hardy?" she asked the attractive brunette wrapped up in the gray cardigan sweater. "*Vanessa* Hardy?"

"Yes, that's me," Van said, looking up into the startling bright-blue eyes of a lithe, eye-catching blonde in close-fitting jeans and a cropped black leather jacket. "I'm sorry, have we met before?"

"No, never. I read the newspaper reviews about this place and recognized your picture in the paper."

Van frowned. "If we've never met, how did you know who I am?"

"It's a little complicated, but I'm here specifically to see you. Do you mind if I sit? I can explain if you have a few minutes."

"No. Of course, be my guest." Van pulled her scattered papers onto the top of her open laptop. "You have me at a disadvantage . . ."

"Sorry, I'm Livia Williams. I knew your son, James."

Van's head jerked up. "You knew James? Please, sit, talk." She took the girl's hand and pulled her down into a chair. "Where and when did you know each other?"

Livia sat down with her handbag in her lap, swallowed hard, and began kneading the leather purse strap in her hands. "James and I were friends. He told me a lot about you. He respected and loved you very much."

Van's stomach squeezed in on itself. "You were close friends, then?"

"We dated about a year before he di . . . passed. We . . . were close."

"I wasn't aware of James dating anyone then. Occasional dates?"

"No, we were seeing each other exclusively."

"Excuse me? The funeral—were you there?" Van stopped and shook her head. "Oh, God, that sounded awful. I'm sure I wasn't together enough to remember *that* day."

Livia's head drooped, and she fiddled with one of the charms on her gold bracelet. "I didn't even know. I was interning in London, and his e-mails and phone calls suddenly stopped. It was like he fell off the face of the earth. I'd never been broken up with like that before. It took three weeks for me to get back to the States, and I went directly to his apartment. Empty. His next-door neighbor found me sitting on the floor in the middle of the hallway, crying my eyes out. I thought it was my fault he'd left me."

The young woman stopped, seeming to relive the moment as she stared at the pub bar with unfocused eyes. "She was so consoling: hugging me, telling me how sad she was that my friend had died." She shifted her eyes back to Van again. "Imagine *my* shock. Being dumped—I could have eventually handled that." Livia studied her handbag strap.

Van pushed back in her chair a bit and shoved a loose strand of hair behind her ear. "I . . . I don't know what to say. I had no idea he was seeing anyone. I would have contacted you. James didn't tell me everything, but I would have thought he would mention a serious relationship."

"James was concerned about Natalie, his ex. He'd had a hard time breaking it off with her, and he wasn't sure how she would handle him having a new relationship. He didn't want her hunting me down to start trouble. We were going to tell everyone when my internship ended and I was back in the States." Livia's hands began to wring the handbag strap in the other direction, and her eyes welled up.

"Natalie took their breakup hard. She couldn't let James go. How close were you and James?"

Livia hiccupped, and the tears trickled down her flushed cheeks. "We had talked about getting married. We weren't together a long time, but I knew as soon as I met him that I would never meet another man like James. He was the one." Saying it, she nodded. "Everything he did, everything he said, told me he felt the same."

"I see," Van said, studying her. "Why did you wait so long to get in touch with me?"

"Couldn't handle it . . . I was too wrecked. I retreated to my apartment and didn't get out of bed for weeks. Talking about him was impossible.

I didn't know any of James's friends or family, and what did it matter anyway? He was gone.

"Every time I went out, I found myself wondering if everyone else was just going through the motions of living, too. Or was I different now, separate and apart in my own little hell? The thoughts were detached from any particular feeling—an outsider's observation of the world around her. I went through the motions, silently screaming for comfort that no one could possibly give me. There was no closure. And then I saw your name and picture in the *Post* when this pub opened. There was an uncanny resemblance to James. I had no doubt you were his mother. I wasn't sure I could handle meeting you, but I felt I had to come find you. I'm not even sure what I hoped to accomplish. I just had this driving need to come here."

"Aw, I know all about closure, hon—or the lack of it," Van said. She leaned over and gave the young woman a hug. "I'm not sure people like us ever truly find it. I do believe, though, that we will continue to try, because James was surrounded by strong-willed people who don't give up easily. Am I right?"

Livia squeezed tight and nodded as she cried. Van closed her eyes to the sound of quiet sobbing. It was haunting, familiar pain, and she was a little surprised to realize that some of the sobbing was her own. The girl's hug awakened memories, a lifetime away, when her own mother's embrace healed even the deepest wounds.

"Does this ever get easier? You look like you're keeping it all together."

"Some, Van whispered. "I think it gets buried, but it never goes away. If you really love someone, you'll always miss them."

"Mrs. Hardy, I can't seem to move on. I don't know how to deal with this."

"Listen, if you're still walking and breathing, you *are* dealing with it. It's hard to let someone go that you love. It took me a whole year to take the dirty clothes out of his hamper. His whole life is still stacked away in my basement—a life packed into a few cardboard boxes. My lovely boy reduced to *things*." She shook her head. "Yeah, it's hard. And no one has the right to ask you to move any faster than you're capable of moving. You're not ready." She pulled away. "Livia, all these new things about James . . . I'm blown away. It's hard to even wrap my head around it all. You seem like the kind of person I would have wanted in his life. You can't imagine what that does for me. Thank you for being brave enough to come here, to me."

Livia studied Van and then suddenly smiled—a feeble but honest, heartfelt smile. Van watched the pain in her face seem to dissipate, as if she had regained some control or perhaps even felt some comfort from what she had heard.

"Sometimes, I'm afraid I'll forget what he looked like, the sound of his voice. But when I look at you, Mrs. Hardy, I see him. I do. It's in your eyes and the way you speak. There's a quietness about you, too, that I loved about him. It makes my heart warm and breaks it, all at the same time. I want you to know, he got quite a kick out of you. He was proud of both his parents." She looked around. "Does Mr. Hardy come here often? He's handling . . . *things*?"

"He's not here, but he's dealing. It's a process, you know?" Van pulled a tissue out of her purse, to give to the girl. And then her heart skipped a beat as Ryan's car pulled into the parking lot. She jumped up, feeling an uncontrollable urge to hide the girl. "I've got to run," she blurted. "It's been lovely meeting you, Livia, but I'm afraid I have to go. Come on. Let me walk you to your car." She drew Livia out of her seat, put her arm around her shoulder, and maneuvered her toward the door. From the corner of her eye, she could see Ryan, still in his car, engrossed in something. "We should get together again, talk some more. You should call me. No, better yet, I can call you. If you have paper in your car, give me your number."

"I'd like that. Maybe include Mr. Hardy."

"We'll see," Van replied. When they reached Livia's car apparently unseen, she breathed a sigh of relief. Two minutes more, and this odd little experience would be history.

"Van, where you off to?"

Busted. A few steps past his car, key still in hand, Ryan stood staring at them. For the first time since she met him, Van tried to wish away that dazzling smile and the graceful way he carried himself. She waved him off. "Banker's hours are pretty nice. I'll be back in a moment. See you inside." To her consternation, he ignored her and sauntered toward them, smiling. "We'll talk inside about last night," Van shouted back.

He ignored her. "I think bankers get off while it's light out," he said as he got closer. "I didn't make it back until after you were gone. Marla told me I just missed you."

Van stepped in front of the car window, cutting off Livia's view. *Start the car. Start the car.* "Another bad night?" she asked as he leaned in and kissed her. "Go in and put your feet up. I'll be there in a minute."

"I'm bushed. I was here till one this morning." Leaning around Van to acknowledge Livia, he gave her a nod.

Van reluctantly stepped aside. "Livia, meet Ryan Thomas. Ryan owns the Phoenix. Ryan, this is Livia Williams. We just met. She saw the story on the tavern in the paper and decided to come down and take a look."

"Right," Livia said, giving Van a guarded look. "I wanted to see it in person. I wasn't disappointed—it's a fantastic place."

Van watched for some recognition to flit across Ryan's face, but to her relief, he seemed oblivious. Her relief quickly gave way to self-loathing at her own duplicity and dishonesty in holding Ryan to a much higher standard. He had become so honest and open. Thank God the girl would soon be gone. Then Van could go back to being honest and wouldn't have to address the issue of Livia at all.

"We've gotten a lot of mileage out of that story," Ryan said. "I'm happy it's played so well. If all you've done is look, you should come back in and have a drink. Really, it's on the house."

"I'd love to—"

"Why so late, Ryan?" Van asked, changing the subject.

"I was trying to unplug the drain in the back. Apparently, Marla thought there was a garbage disposal."

"Doesn't surprise me. That's what you get for hiring with your heart instead of your head," she said, teasing him. "You need to fire Bennie. He needs to train them right."

"My head instead of my heart? Sometimes I think my heart is the only thing I have going for me. Fire Bennie? Nope, no can do. Bennie does no wrong in my book. Marla should stick with hostessing. If we're shorthanded, I'll hire someone else for the bar. It'll be cheaper in the long run." Ryan looked at Livia again, apparently waiting for a reply to his invitation.

She hesitated. "I'd love to, Mr. Thomas, but I don't have the time. I might be interested in helping out at your bar, though—temporarily, until you can make permanent arrangements.

"I think Ryan needs someone with experience," Van interjected. "I—"

"I have experience."

"Van's right. It's a bad time to bring on a trainee. My partner's on vacation. It's a zoo with him gone." He paused. "What kind of experience?"

"I can do the job. I worked at a bar to pay my way through college. I can hit the ground running." Livia got out of her car, as if she planned to demonstrate there and then.

"Don't you have a regular job?" Van blurted out as she watched the interaction between the former lovers.

"We're in a slow cycle right now. I've been there a while, and they're pretty flexible. Besides, I have vacation leave coming to me. But listen, money isn't the overriding issue, if that's a problem."

"No, it's not a money issue," he said, studying her face. "I don't usually get involved in hiring decisions. That's up to Bennie; he's the one that's got to make it work. But unfortunately, he'll be gone a few more days."

Van put her hand softly on his arm. "You know how meticulous Bennie is. Might want to wait till he's back, Ryan. Keeping up with Marla can be a full-time undertaking."

Ryan continued to stare. "I don't know. If you have experience . . . temporarily . . . I have so much on my plate. You might be the perfect solution to a big problem here." He gave her a final once-over. "Done. If your references are good, I'll vouch for you. What's the worst that can happen? Bennie gives me the malocchio?"

Van's smile vanished, and she let go of him.

"Van, we need to talk, but could you excuse us for a bit?" Ryan said. "I'll need some references. Got a minute to come back inside, Ms. Williams?"

They left her alone in the lot. If James were alive, alone would have been okay. But James was dead, and life had long since repositioned all the players. Since Livia would be gone soon enough, did Ryan even need to know who she was? Should she tell him? Her gut told her there would be nothing but heartache coming from this newest walk-in addition to the Phoenix family.

The crunch of gravel behind her made her jump. She whirled around to find Marla, a few feet away, sitting tall in the driver's seat of a sparkling blue Dodge Charger.

Marla pulled directly up alongside and lowered the window. "What's wrong, Van? You look like you've seen a ghost."

"Christmas future," Van answered bleakly. She looked the car over. "You're driving a new car?"

"Present from Dad. Cool, huh? He's the best." She beamed as she rolled the window back up.

Great, thought Van. Nothing was better for a child of divorce than an absentee father suddenly trying to buy affection with expensive gifts. How was Jean going to compete with that? She pulled out her cell phone and reserved a table at Cap'n Mike's. Before the day was out, they both were going to need a drink—just not at the Phoenix.

CHAPTER SEVEN

Just Peachy

Redemption or hell—how had life suddenly narrowed down to such a stark choice? If thoughts of Hamelin's return had haunted Ryan before, they were nothing compared to the new warning and predictions that had been playing on a continuous loop in his head for the past few days. Hamelin was a force to be reckoned with, although Ryan wasn't sure where divine law stopped and Hamelin's own interpretation started. Ryan was now involved in some sort of cosmic game. He felt like a mere pawn on the board: useful in the short term, but totally expendable by the endgame.

He ran his hand around the case of the aurascope and watched the gravity-defying sand stream up from the bottom into the top. So all life was supposed to revolve around *this*? The base was intricately carved into curlicues, cherubs, and butterflies, all covered in cracked gilt and looking positively ancient. It wasn't helpful. The running deep purplish-red sand made him feel like as if he were bleeding out. And yet, he was afraid to ditch the thing. He had no real idea yet how to make the sand change color, but if it helped him get rid of Hamelin, he was all for it. He slid the thing out of view behind the desk lamp—everything in its own time.

Now that Hamelin knew where he lived, there was no way Ryan was going to stay at the Bayside. And the less time he spent alone, the fewer opportunities for Hamelin to get at him. Until the deal with Pickett's house went through, he had to find another place, preferably with a roommate. But in the end, there was probably nowhere he could run that Hamelin wouldn't eventually find him alone.

He put his head on his desk and thought about the one bright spot in his life. Livia Williams was proving to be an asset, and he wished he had run into her sooner. Things were going so well at the Phoenix that he could have cut out for a few days and taken a break, too, if he were so inclined. She was an anomaly in his carefully controlled existence, and he liked the spontaneity of hiring her and working with her. After years of having to watch his back in the cut-throat world that HYA created and promoted, he wasn't one to pull somebody in off the street. Best of all, Bennie would approve. What was not to like? Livia had class and just the right amount of sass, if he was reading her right. She was a good addition to their tight-knit little group. She was what an angel should be when you needed one: cheerful, helpful, and sweet. But most of all, Livia was pub savvy. He could hear her, out in the great room, finessing the latest patron to have trouble establishing sensible limits to his alcoholic intake.

"Okay, Joe, this is your last," he heard her say. "Giving you notice right now. You didn't drive, right? Because I can get you a ride. No? Okay, you let me know."

She was perfect, and that was exactly what bothered him. *Right place, right time.* Hamelin's words. Was her visit one of Hamelin's schemes designed to entice him and destroy his relationship with Van? An alluring siren set loose on him? Ryan wouldn't put anything past him, but

Hamelin could throw all the good-looking girls he wanted at him; it wasn't going to make him any less devoted to Van. Ridiculous. He banished it from his mind and tried to stop second-guessing all those decisions that had seemed logical and good when he made them. He hadn't made a mistake in hiring her. And when the time came, he would have no problem seeing her leave.

"Nice job," Ryan said, walking up behind her. "You sound like a Bennie Bertolini clone."

"See? Like I told you, I can do this. I used to work the late shift. We threw 'em out left and right. I can hold my own, trust me."

Ryan smiled, cleared his throat, and studied his shoes. "I do—which is unusual, believe me. One thing: next time, the distributor receipts go in the wooden box on my desk. That's the only way I can keep track. Okay?"

Livia nodded, and a pink cast crept up her neck above her collar. "That'll teach me to boast."

"Small thing. You're doing great, really." He watched her discomfort fade and the smile return. Bennie would like her. She could go a long way with a smile like that.

"You'll introduce me to this wonderful Bennie today?"

"Bennie? God, I hope so. The man is indispensable. Remind me to kiss the ground at his feet and never let him take another vacation."

"Just kiss my ring; that's enough," said a voice behind them.

"God almighty, Bennie!" Ryan whirled around to find the portly, balding bartender standing directly behind them. "I never thought I'd be so happy to hear that baritone again. How'd you get in here without me seeing you? Never mind, I don't need to know." Ryan gave the portly bartender a high five. "You're not schedule to work today, are you?"

"Vacation's fine," said Bennie, "but I need to get back to work. I really missed this place." He stopped to give Livia an appraising look. "I'm gone a week, and you've already replaced me?"

Livia's eyes darted to Ryan. "He's kidding," Ryan whispered. "Livia, as you might have guessed by now, this is Bennie Bertolini. He's all teddy bear. And no, Bennie, you're irreplaceable. This is Livia Williams," he said, with a grand sweep of his hand. "She's temporarily helping out. I told her you'd like her. Don't make me a liar."

Bennie offered a meaty hand. "Pleasure, Livia, nice to meet you."

"Where'd you go?" Livia asked.

"Here and there." Bennie opened a brown paper sack, pulled out a bottle, and held it to the light. "George Washington peach brandy," he said, caressing the label. "From his reconstructed still at Mount Vernon. Given that our peerless forefather blessed this town with his talents, I thought it appropriate to honor his memory in the Phoenix. Four hundred bottles, aged over the last two years, one of which is now mine. No one touches this until I say it's time." He pushed it up onto the top shelf above the bar, right next to the herd of long-horned steers stampeding around the rim of his *Don't Mess with Texas* shot glass. "Now, if that isn't my apron you're wearing, Ms. Williams, I'd like to get in the back, find mine, and take stock of the place. Any problems with that, Mr. Thomas?"

"Certainly not, as long as you drop the "Mister" thing. I'm ceding the whole operation back to you. I'll fill you in later on the finer points, but everything's pretty good, all things considered. Welcome back. We all missed you, especially Marla."

"Wha . . . Bennie!" Marla shrieked. "When did you get here?" She crossed the room in three bounding leaps, flung her arms around him, and hugged him as he sheepishly patted her back. "You are never allowed to go on vacation again. Ryan is *so* mean to me."

"No, never again," Bennie replied. "Working here is my vacation." He pried himself loose from the buxom brunette and went off in search of his apron. Marla avoided Ryan's stare and darted back out front.

"I could be *so* much meaner," Ryan murmured to Livia. "But no need, Bennie's back. One less problem in my little world. With him around, I never have to worry about the Phoenix."

Bennie reappeared, pulling apron strings around his ample middle as he went. "What's wrong with the security camera out back? Something knock it cattywampus?"

"Damn birds. They've built a nest at the top of the pole. Been trying to run 'em off before they lay, but every day it's the same: an up-close view of sticks and bird butt."

"Osprey?"

"Nah, thank God. Little chirpy things. I'll see if I can pull the nest down again."

Bennie nodded. "Okay, Ms. Livia, let's see what you've been doing back here. Ryan, go do whatever it is you do when I'm here. Give the man some room."

"I'm gone, man. If you need anything, ring my cell." Ryan made a beeline for the back door.

It may have been the speed with which he turned that made him light-headed. Whatever the cause, his vision filled with bees and faded to black. He fumbled for the door to steady himself but lost his balance when a strong hand clamped on to his shoulder and jerked him backward. In an instant, heart pounding, he snapped alert and his vision cleared. He lost his grip and fell, twisting and grappling with the hand that held him by the back of his shirt, choking him. His assailant fell with him, and they tumbled against empty crates and garbage cans that spilled their reeking contents everywhere. Ryan turned and yanked the pistol from his pocket, shoving the cold, dark steel against his assailant's ribs. "Talk fast."

CHAPTER EIGHT

Misplaced Loyalties

"Please, Mr. Thomas, don't shoot me. It's Meekae, Meekae Skalski."

"Mike?" Ryan leaned back into the stinking wet pile of crab innards, potato peels, and rotten tomatoes to get a better look at the skinny guy he now held by the nape of the neck.

"Please. You gotta hide me."

Ryan shoved the slightly built man off him and got to his feet, flicking a sodden lemon wedge from his hand as he stood. "What the hell are you doing here? You should know better than to sneak up on someone like that. You're lucky I didn't—"

Skalski gestured toward the door. "Can we talk in there? It's complicated. Not here. Please."

Ryan shoved him toward the door. "Get in there."

"Ryan?" Bennie yelled from the other room. "That you making all that noise out there? What the heck are you doing?"

Ryan shoved the kid toward the corner on the far side of the kitchen. "Fine. I'm good. Just got dive-bombed by an angry beak and backed into one of the trash cans. I'm on it."

He locked the back door. Satisfied that Bennie wasn't coming to check on him, Ryan joined Skalski in the corner and looked him up and down. "Christ! You look like hell. What's going on with you? Am I going to be sorry I didn't leave you out there?"

"No sir, please don't make me leave. I'm on your side."

"*My* side?" Ryan didn't like where this was going. Skalski's eyes were darting all over the room, and his sweaty hair was plastered to his forehead. "Let's talk in my office, huh? It's private. No one'll even know you're here. Come on, Mike."

The kid let his guard down as Ryan secured him behind another locked door. His shoulders and eyes drooped as soon as he sank into the nearest chair. Or maybe it was exhaustion catching up with him. He looked a far cry from the chipper 19-year-old computer geek Ryan had known in New York.

"HYA?"

Mike nodded and put his head in his hands. Loud sobs reverberated through the office.

"Ah, kid. What'd you do?"

Skalski pulled a flash drive out of his pocket and handed it to Ryan. "Now you have everything."

"You *stole files* from them*?* Are you nuts? Damn, Mike! I took you for having more smarts than this. What did you think you were going to accomplish? Didn't you hear? I'm not in the business anymore. *This* is my life now," he said, gesturing around him. "I don't have any files."

Mike shifted in his seat, and for the first time in the conversation, his head came up. He looked Ryan squarely in the eyes. "I know what you did. Computers are my thing, remember? I didn't tell them anything, but I wasn't the only one looking. I tried to cover up your trail, but they found out in spite of my attempts to hide what you missed. It was only a matter of time before they found what was left, so I took it. I figured you had your reasons. That was good enough for me. Fuck 'em all, right? I can help you. With what you know and I can do, we can do serious damage, *serious* damage. All the rest of it's on there." He straightened his shirt out and shifted his shark's-tooth necklace around until it hung properly in the front again.

"Holy shit. Seeing as how you're here, running for your life, they already know you took this, right? And you've led them right back to me. Swell." Ryan watched his life flash before his eyes like a 3-D Technicolor version of *The Godfather*. "Christ! What am I going to do with more?" He walked over and shoved the drive into his computer.

"I'm . . . not sure. I freaked out, so I looked you up. We're in this together now, so I thought you'd help me. Did I make a mistake?"

"No. You didn't make *a* mistake. Totally wrong. You made a *whole string* of them. And we're not in *anything* together. There is no 'this.' You've dumped a boatload of trouble in my lap because of some misplaced loyalty about *nothing*." Ryan grabbed him by the arm and hoisted him up. "Listen, hotshot. This isn't some video game you can shut off and walk away from. These are nut jobs with real guns, and they're going to plug you full of holes and leave you in an alley somewhere for maggot food. I should kill you myself and save all the drama."

Skalski blanched, and his eyes darted around the room like those of a wary animal looking for a place to bolt. Ryan gave him a shove that sent him tumbling back into the chair. He cracked his head against the wall, closed his eyes, and broke into more sobbing.

Ryan sighed and tried not to look at him. Playing the tough guy was going to solve nothing. "'S all right, Mike. Relax. I'm not in the mood to whack anyone just now. In fact, I've never whacked anyone. Does your family know where you are?"

"Of course not. I don't need their permission."

"Let's keep it that way. Your car out back?"

"Yeah."

"Show me where, and I'll cover it up with a tarp. You can stay in the Phoenix, out of sight, until the end of the week. No phone calls, no leaving the building. Even if the place burns to the ground, you don't come out till the ashes get too hot for your little keister to sit on." He studied the kid hard. "Ever been to Houston?"

"No."

"Didn't think so. HYA is strictly East Coast, which makes Texas a great place for you. When things have died down, we'll fly you out of here. For now, you just sit tight here. Are we clear? Because if we're not, you're on your own."

"Yeah, I've got nowhere else."

They sneaked back out and covered up Mike's black Honda Civic. It was a beater, and Ryan half wondered whether it might draw less attention uncovered, but right now the best action was quick action, and he didn't have time to noodle through all the scenarios. They would deal with the car later. He put the thumb drive in a plastic bag and shoved it down to the bottom of Hoffa's bag of kibble.

Nevis would soon be crawling with HYA. Unbelievably, life had just gotten worse. To all his other troubles, he could add a little computer nerd with no life and bad judgment, whose misplaced hero worship had inspired him to protect the back of someone utterly unworthy. Ryan hated being beholden to anyone. Now he was going to have to stick his neck out to keep Mike Skalski alive long enough to see Houston. How in the hell to do that and keep one step ahead of Hamelin?

CHAPTER NINE

Wouldn't Bet on It

Bennie shifted the phone to his other ear. "Somebody needs to explain why . . . That's not good business. Our account is in good standing, isn't it? . . . Right. And we were under the impression we had a good working relationship with you . . . Right . . . Then why aren't you renewing the contract? You're gonna just up and stop distributing to us? What's the deal? . . . No, I'm not finished. You're telling me you're shifting your delivery area, but we're in your backyard, for cripes sake! We've got big promotions coming up, and you're killing us . . . Bad business. Who's your boss? I want a call back from him . . . Yeah, same to you." He slammed the phone down and turned around—and bumped into Marla, standing right behind him. "What do you want?"

Nicky's back," she whispered. "He took the corner table and pulled out his little black book and phone. Can I run your little drill, pretty please?"

"*Phew,* I'm not getting paid enough," he muttered. "Sorry I snapped at ya, hon. Thanks for telling me. Nah, I'll run him off. He's just looking for bourbon and bonding—typical barfly. In Manhattan, whenever I changed bars, the regs would start showing up at the new establishment, regular time, as if nothing had changed. Our connection made life meaningful—one big, happy alcoholic family. Same here. I'll go talk to him."

Bennie sat down across from a gaunt, balding middle-aged man with a tad of gray in his sideburns. "Nicky J. Fincher! I've almost missed running you out of here. Where ya been?"

"My good man, Bennie! Oh, you know, here, there . . . around. If you'd treated me well, you could have been a rich man by now."

"Well, you know what they say. If you don't earn it honestly, it's not worth having. Nicky, I love you as much now as the last time you were in here. You don't look a day different, and you're running the same old game. Pick up your stuff and beat it."

"I'm sure I have something you're interested in. Good odds on Muckahoonie in the fifth, Aloysius in the eighth . . . How about winner of the All-American Soap Box Derby?"

"No, no, and no," said Bennie. "Out. I'm going to get my phone."

"Really? *None* of those? All great opportunities." Nicky flipped his book shut, shoved his pen in his breast pocket, and pushed his chair back. "Okay, you don't have to ask me twice. I'll be on my way. Guess you don't want to discuss the New York betting line on the Phoenix."

Bennie whirled around. "New York betting line? What are you talking about?"

"Five to one you're not here by the end of the year."

"They're betting on whether I'm going to stay at the Phoenix? Good Lord, the city's gotten boring!"

"Nah, not you, the *Phoenix*."

"They don't bet like that. Besides, nobody in New York knows or cares about a small bar in a two-street backwater like Nevis. Why would they care?" Despite his bluster, Bennie had a sinking feeling in the pit of his stomach.

"Compulsive people will bet on anything. Yeah, they have their favorites, but sooner or later they get bored or burned out losing all the time. Then it's time to try something new—something luckier—and bring back the excitement. Don't know where it started, man, but I've got takers. You cross the wrong people?" Nicky ducked his head and looked furtively around them to check out who was within earshot. "You know these money types. You can't screw with 'em." Anyway, don't kill the messenger. I'm just giving you an opportunity here. You think you're gonna stay, bet a few, make a bundle."

"What a buncha' crap. There's no connection between the Phoenix and anyone in New York. Quit spreading talk and enabling these needy people. You go tell 'em they're throwing away money. Now, get out before I give Officer McCall a detailed description of you. Out."

"I hear ya. Change your mind, you contact me. I'm around."

"Beat it while you can still walk out on your own. Ryan'll be here any minute, and he'll bounce you out on your ear."

"You might want to take a vacation of your own when I get done with you," Bennie said to Ryan. "Which do you want first: good news or the bad?"

"Good first—it'll cushion the bad."

"Nicky Fincher was in earlier today."

"The bookie? Thought we ran him out of here. Give up on the Sox, Bennie. They're a losing proposition."

"Yeah, well, he's back, and he's not peddling sports. It's us, the Phoenix. They're running odds on us in New York—five to one we don't make it to the end of the year. Heard that one?"

"Christ, Bennie, the man knows how to jerk your chain. Anyway, that's the *good* news?"

"You know we can beat those odds. As Nicky puts it, 'bet a few, make a bundle.'"

"Nobody in New York gives a rat's ass about us. What sense does that make? What's the bad news?"

"I know, but he's got connections, and he didn't sound like he was making it up as he went."

Ryan waved him off. "Okay, so the bad news?"

"The main distributors and a couple of the smaller breweries have cut us off. They're refusing to renew our contract. I've been on the phone half the day. And they all give the same bullshit reason. Wanna guess? They're all 'shifting their areas of distribution.'"

"Christ, they're all local deliveries. Butch and Lee have this whole region locked up. If they don't sell it to us, we ain't getting it anywhere else."

"Exactly. You know I make a practice of not getting deeply involved. You offered me a good job here, and I'm nothing but grateful. But with all this going on and Nicky's BS, too, I've got to ask, Ryan, is there money invested here that I should be worried about? You know what I'm asking. Have we somehow crossed the wrong people?"

Ryan looked him dead in the eyes and did what he did best: he lied. "Bennie, you're one of only a handful of people who could ask me that question and expect a civil answer. Absolutely not. We're good with everybody. The only money invested in this business is *mine*. I don't want any interference from anybody, especially north of the Mason-Dixon. That should be obvious from the company I keep now. Nicky's full of horse pucky, and this is all coincidence. Somebody's got their wires crossed at the distributorship. I'll get on the horn, straighten it out. It's as good as done. Trust me."

"I do trust you. You've always played straight with me. And I do the same for you. But I had to ask."

Ryan winked. "Good man. Now, if you'll excuse me, I need to go make a few phone calls. A pub with no beer—I don't have to tell you how that would play."

"You can try, but my gut is telling me a few phone calls from you aren't going to solve this. And we need it solved—soon. We can't have all these people coming in for promotions and run out of beer. This isn't the chardonnay-and froufrou-cocktails kind of crowd."

"I know. I'll go take care of the *conspiracy*. You just keep Mr. Fincher out of here."

CHAPTER TEN

Napoleon

Ryan wheedled, then threatened, then pleaded, but he couldn't persuade the distributors to restore the flow of liquor. He wanted to jerk a knot in Butch and Lee. The distributorships cutting them off made no business sense for either party. The Phoenix might be back in Bennie's capable hands, but it was foundering, and there was no way he could focus on cultivating a good-citizen image when business was close to bottoming out. They could go all-restaurant for a while, but a pub couldn't run forever without liquor.

Bennie was right, although he would never be so crass as to mention it. There were no coincidences here. Someone was screwing with them. If it was Hamelin, Ryan didn't get the lesson he was trying to teach. No matter how hard he tried, the sand in the aurascope continued to stream in a frightening shade of magenta. There had been no change since Hamelin gave it to him. The Phoenix was on the up-and-up—one of the few endeavors in his life that were beyond reproach. Driving the business into the ground would hurt good, innocent people and not teach him a damn thing.

Maybe he wasn't looking at things the right way. He tried to put someone else in his place and take a peek from the back of the room. It was hard because nobody was as screwed up as he was. What if his late-night calls and Meekae Skalski had set other things in motion? Was it HYA, and not Hamelin, who was screwing with him? What if he had extended some sort of invitation or threatened them? Maybe he had been cheeky, then blocked it all out. Maybe. But if it was HYA, he was better off. He understood what made them tick. Hamelin, on the other hand, couldn't even play it straight with his own kind.

If HYA was putting pressure on the distributorships, he could push back. There was one negative influence screwing up his aura that he could take care of. That would put HYA in its place and make Hamelin happy at the same time. Hector Young. And there were people who could help him without getting directly involved with Hamelin. He needed to put an end to the cat-and-mouse game. Then HYA would have to deal face-to-face.

Frederickton, the county seat, still had many of its original eighteenth-century trappings. It was bisected by a traditional main street, hemmed in at the heart by a cluster of lovely brick colonial buildings, originally built—and continuously maintained—for municipal affairs. It also had other sundry brick and framed structures that had been repurposed and remodeled so many times over the years that they had no character left.

Ryan studied the more modern court annex for a moment, tucked his shirt into the back of his pants and straightened his tie. Suits weren't his daily attire anymore, but he respected the system, and if you were going to play the game, you had to wear the uniform. He looked up at the flights of marble steps, with awkwardly sized rise and runs, between where he stood and the entrance. At just under six-one, he should be able to angle his size twelves diagonally and take them two at a time.

Midway up, he surrendered to the architecture, resigned himself to looking stupid, and plodded up like everyone else. There was no real hurry, anyway. The meeting with his lawyer wasn't for another twenty minutes. He had enough patience for that. But continual assurances that the attempted-murder case against Young was such a lock that not even a company like Hector Young and Associates could buy its way out of it were wearing thin.

Ryan winced and loosened the front of his shirt from around the scar left by Hector's gunshot. If he and Hector had brought their A game that night, they both would be dead, and their beef with each other over. He took no comfort in knowing that Hector was locked safely away in South Neck Correctional Institution, pacing and planning as he awaited trial. Ryan had to make sure the man stayed in jail where he belonged, and that meant letting HYA know he could up the ante.

An elevator door slid open, as if urging him to hurry it along. He walked in, pushed "3," and stepped back to the left corner. Only one other rider followed him in—an average-looking young gofer, white shirtsleeves rolled up to the elbow in a serious manner, toting a half-dozen coffees. He took the opposite back corner. They glanced at each other's shoes, but neither spoke. When the elevator stopped, Ryan got out alone on the third floor.

The State's Attorney's office had a waiting room full of people, but Ryan was barely in the door before Mike Flanagan intercepted him and shook his hand like a candidate stumping for office. The prosecutor was a man going places. Member of another old-boy network, he was a public servant by trade, but a politician at heart. From his tailored suits to his shiny black Ferragamos, he made it clear that he was a man who could get results. Ryan wanted to have faith in him, but he had little respect for a man who pumped his hand without ever mustering enough interest to look him in the eye when he did. Then again, maybe it wasn't disinterest, but an attempt to hide the burning ambition in his eyes.

Ryan took in the personal office decor: a giant blue glass crab, a miniature of Orioles Park, and picture after picture of Flanagan—at ribbon cuttings, kissing babies, shaking hands with all the right people, and in perfectly posed dynastic family portraits at various Maryland landmarks. Unlike Van's pictures, which captured the love and spirit of a family, these were coldly calculated images, created to convey a story that was both ill-fitting and fraudulent for the grandson of an itinerant tobacco farmer who had made his bones bootlegging hooch. If there was ever a man quietly running for office, it was Mike Flanagan.

"Coffee?" Flanagan asked as he poured a cup from a silver coffee urn behind his desk. "Brand-new pot."

"Nothing," Ryan said, shaking his head. He sat down in a chair facing the executive desk.

"So, Mr. Thomas, first of the month again? Seems like only last month we were meeting. How's my favorite star witness?"

"It was, and not well, thank you. Any movement in the case?"

Flanagan stirred his coffee for a moment before turning and commenting. "Uh, well . . . that is to say, no. But no news is still good news. Hector Young is behind bars, where he belongs. Don't be worried there—I got us an airtight no-bond ruling. It's only a matter of time before he's there permanently."

Ryan took a deep breath and placed his palms on the desk. "Mr. Flanagan, every day that he isn't tried and convicted is a day of worry for me. I don't understand the delay here. You people have been assuring me for weeks that this was going to be a slam-dunk conviction, and yet, here we sit, with no trial date and no hint of when this is going to move forward. I'm beginning to lose faith in the Maryland judicial system. If this were New York—"

"But it's not, Mr. Thomas, and with all due respect, we're right where we should be, given the circumstances." Flanagan pulled up a side chair and leaned forward, forearms resting on his knees, lean fingers intertwined confidently. "You know this is a difficult case. Nobody likes to admit it, but we all know there's an elephant in the room, and its name is 'Wealthy Connections.' Hector Young, with his smart *New York* lawyers, has been running us ragged with motions, delays, appeals—you name it. At some point, they'll run out of options and he'll realize the end result is the same: he's rotting in jail. As long as we can keep him behind bars, which we've done so far, and we have you to provide your testimony, everything's going to turn out right. Trust us. That's all you have to do."

Ryan stood up and looked down at him. "I am trusting you—with my life. The longer this goes on, the likelier he is to walk. They are going to force you into a mistake. You'll make a mistake. I know it. Please. Next time I come in, I'd like to hear something different. Can we try that on and see how it fits?"

"Absolutely," Flanagan said. "We'll keep in touch. Go on with your life and let us take care of business. It's what we do. I can assure you, I have never taken on a case that I didn't think we could win. You have my personal guarantee. We're expecting things to turn around shortly. Don't let the delays upset you." The intercom on his desk buzzed and he checked his watch. "Sorry, another meeting. Can I walk you out?"

"I'll be back next month. I can let myself out."

As soon as he cleared the revolving door, Ryan slipped his jacket off. *Another meeting, my ass. More like doughnuts and coffee and putting the moves on that cute paralegal.* He saluted the windows above with a middle finger. *Put this picture on your wall.* Movers and shakers—they were all the same. How a man in Flanagan's position could be missing the big picture was beyond him. Hector Young had few friends, but he worked in a buddy system of back scratchers, and none of *them* were rotting away in jail.

Halfway down the stairs, he stopped and fished through his pockets. Where was his parking lot stub? He had forgotten to get it validated. He contemplated the trip back up the marble stairs. Frederickton parking was expensive, but so was a knee replacement. And anyway, his stomach was grumbling to be fed. He could spare the few bucks for parking.

It was time to grab a bite, but whatever he scarfed down wouldn't compare to the napoleon being enjoyed by the dumpy lobbyist in the ill-fitting dark suit, sitting halfway down the stairs. His eyes were closed in near-orgasmic appreciation of his last bite of sponge cake, custard, and chocolate. He pulled a napkin from a white and red Veniero's bag and wiped icing from his pudgy face. Ryan could empathize. Veniero's made the best napoleons in New York. He had been there many times. It was a short walk, and a lunchtime ritual for HYA employees working in the Terrace building, but a little far for a Maryland lobbyist's casual snack. Also out of place, come to think of it, was the similarly fashion-challenged fellow down at the curb, reading a newspaper as he leaned up against a metallic blue Nissan with New York plates, its engine idling as it sat parked in a no-stopping zone. If Ryan wasn't mistaken, the paper was two days old—he could see Wednesday's front-page photo from here.

In the few seconds it took him to register these things, Ryan lost his appetite. He sprinted back up the stairs, two at a time, and powered through the revolving door, scanning faces as he went. He saw no one else he recognized. Nothing seemed out of place.

"I've lost someone," he said to the clerk manning the information desk. "Where are the stairs?"

"First corridor to the left, and it'll be on your right" she replied, pointing across the rotunda. "If it's a child, we can—"

"No, no need," Ryan called over his shoulder. "Unforgettable lunch date. Thanks."

He took off diagonally across the crypt. HYA screwing with him from afar, he got, but in for a visit? It could be coincidental—something strictly related to Hector's case—but his grinding gut didn't think so. The simplest explanation was usually the correct one: too many coincidences. And legal people wouldn't stand out like those doofs. They were muscle—schmucks who went wherever you told them to go, even if it meant standing in the pouring rain or ninety-degree heat in a suit for hours on end.

He found the empty stairwell tucked around the corner—wide marble stairs with an ornate turn-of-the-century cast-iron bannister—and bounded down to the lower level. It was ground floor, and there had to be a loading dock somewhere. At the bottom of the stairs, he pulled on the door and nearly ripped his arm off. The door was a fire exit, but it was stuck or locked. He jiggled and yanked again, but it was a no-go. *Calm . . . Breathe . . . Think.* They couldn't *all* be locked. He peeked up between the staircases. Lots of other choices. He sprinted back up, avoided Flanagan's office on the third floor, and exited on the fourth. The stairs on the other side were where he expected, and he pounded down them to the door at ground level. Thankfully, it was unlocked.

Right or left? There were no signs, and the corridor was empty. He chose left, and as he walked, he could see the floor ahead covered with cardboard, protecting the tile beneath. The walls were dented and streaked with dark skid marks from laden utility carts, and the air was growing steadily warmer and more humid. In the distance, he could hear the dull hum of air-conditioning. He passed another elevator bay. Freight only. *Bingo.* Dead ahead, through a set of open double doors, he could see the loading dock beyond. He stopped short of the doors and fought the urge to sprint through them. *Clear?* He couldn't tell. He put his coat back on, crept to the doors, and peered out. A delivery truck was unloading pallets of copier paper, but there was little else. The dock was protected from curious eyes by the ivy-covered walls of the surrounding colonial buildings, and a short, narrow cobbled alleyway in between them dumped him right into the parking garage, near the toll booth. He scooted off the deck and found his car without seeing another living soul.

To make sure no one followed, he used a few more back roads than usual on the way home and parked in a municipal lot near the boardwalk. A stiff gust of wind coming in off the water smelled saltier than normal, the breeze drawing moisture from the lower bay, where it mixed with the ocean. He was tempted to get back in the car, roll the windows down, and hide out a while. It was as safe here as anywhere. This sudden development was much more than he had planned on, but deep down, if he were to be completely honest, he had always known that HYA would come back. Hector had brought it on with his foolish vindictiveness, and he himself had all but ensured it with his rash phone calling. Meekae Skalski wasn't to blame; he had merely accelerated the situation. It was inevitable, but the timing was especially lousy.

He could dodge them today, but eventually, there would be a showdown. It was going to get him in trouble with Hamelin—consorting with the wrong people. He would have to stoop to HYA's level to beat them, and that was exactly the behavior Hamelin had warned him against. No matter what he did, it was a lose-lose—unless, in Hamelin's little black book, these were somehow the *right* people. Hamelin had said there were things in motion that he had no control over. Did that include HYA? Dear God, what ripples had this antiangel set in motion?

Ryan got out of the car and headed for the Phoenix. He needed aspirin and a beer . . . or two.

CHAPTER ELEVEN

Blued, Screwed, and Tattooed

The blue Nissan that had rolled past moments earlier was coming back now. Lost, perhaps? Ryan felt the hackles on his neck rise. He veered through a yard, skirted a hedge, jumped a low fence, cut across the next lawn, and jogged up Fourth Street through an alleyway.

No car. He had to stop winding himself up so, or he would be crazy by the time he got rid of Hamelin. He was a block from the Phoenix, and not even a pint of amber was going to do it. He needed a *real* drink: Van Winkle from Bennie's private stock.

Half a block later, the Nissan was waiting for him. As he passed, it glided out from an alley onto Fourth and rolled along quietly behind him. This wasn't someone needing directions. *Make a run for it, or call him out?* He couldn't fight the inevitable. He took a deep breath and maintained his pace as the hum of the tires on the brick pavement grew louder. The front passenger window rolled down as the Nissan glided alongside.

"Get in the car, Mr. Thomas," a gravelly voice said from within the car. "We all have better things to do today."

Ryan didn't recognize the face, but he did understand the business end of a blued large-caliber semiautomatic. He got in the car.

Within minutes, he was several miles outside Nevis, headed south, destination unknown. From the backseat, Ryan could see the driver's eyes flicking back and forth between his rearview mirror and the road. No one he recognized. Neither was the one riding shotgun, though he could guess their affiliation. Ryan turned his attention to the other backseat occupant: surprisingly, a woman. She was well-dressed, conservative—a hard, no-nonsense type.

He fastened his seat belt and concentrated on where they were headed. South. An isolated area so they could do him in? Not likely. They wouldn't have grabbed him in daylight—too many potential witnesses. A talking-to? It had been months since his dissociation from HYA, and until the narrowly missed encounter at the courthouse, not a call, letter, or so much as wish-you-were-here card. He'd been hoping they had their hands full with the inevitable internal power struggle following the elder Hector's death. Possibly, someone had gained the upper hand. Bishop—it had to be. "So I hear Bishop's getting the feel for things," he said. "Be sure and send him my best. Would you . . ."

The woman cut him off with a steely gaze. Small talk would have to wait.

Ryan knew these surroundings well enough. They were skirting the bald-cypress swamp. An easy place to lose something. The driver took a sharp left onto a winding gravel road and headed into the gloom of lofty trees standing in dark water and swamp grass. It was like traveling back to a primeval time. He had never ventured this far in—only around the edges. All he knew of the place were the stories that Van and others had terrorized the youngsters with at a beach bonfire late one night. With a shudder, he thought of Goat Man, the half-man, half-goat beast that roamed deserted country lanes, carving up unwary lovers and stranded motorists; and the ghostly calls of the murdered infant at Crybaby Bridge. Both legends originated here, and the people in the stories never seemed to make it out alive. The stories had scared the bejeezus out of him, too.

Under other circumstances, it was probably a majestic, awe-inspiring place. But even without the spooky stories, the stillness and the inky swamp water unnerved him. He was fairly sure the Patuxent River ran not too far off to the left. That would be west. He tried to keep oriented, the dense canopy gave him only peeks and hints of the sun's location. The car made a number of turns onto various, branching gravel maintenance roads and traveled another mile or so before it pulled off into a small clearing. By this point, he had no sense of direction.

The driver turned the engine off and the tall, burly man who had been riding shotgun got out and opened the back door. The woman exited from the other side and walked around the rear of the vehicle. "Get out," she said.

Ryan remained seated, looking at the dark water. "Talk in the car," he muttered. "I don't think any of us wants a scene."

"Get out," she repeated and the burly man took a step around the door toward him.

"Calm, okay? I'm cooperating. It was just a thought." Ryan got out and she gave him a shove into a landscape so deep and isolated that if they should leave him there, he would be old and gray before he found his way out again. His chest tightened as he looked at his reflection in the nearest pool. He couldn't back up with the woman directly behind him. He winced with every labored breath. He might die now, and he had no idea where they could even look for his dental records. It didn't matter. No one would ever find him here—only the birds. They'd get his eyes first. He tried to focus on the tweeting little yellow-headed warblers ghosting through the trees, and the little brown-backed water thrush as it bounced and flitted about on the duff and leaf mold. To his chagrin, the birds ignored him.

Moments later, he heard an approaching car, and soon a brown Acura rolled up alongside them. Ryan was being ordered into yet another backseat. The Acura reeked of cigarettes and sweat. The man waiting there had a receding hairline and wire-rimmed glasses sitting on a beaklike nose. It was a face he knew. He glanced at the two men in the front seat—no one he knew.

"Owens. It's been a while," he said. He glanced at the man's empty hands resting casually in his lap. He couldn't tell if he had a weapon underneath the brown Houndstooth sport coat.

"Nevis is a nice little town, well maintained."

"What do you want?" Ryan asked. He watched nervously as Owens reached into his coat, but relaxed a bit when he merely scratched a rib or two.

Owens smiled cordially. "Bishop wants the files back."

"So Bishop's in charge now. Tell him best of luck. I don't have anything from HYA. I walked away and left it all behind. Go check my desk. There's probably still a moldy organic whole-grain peanut-butter-and-pickle sandwich in the top right drawer."

Owens shrugged and looked out the window. "He's also concerned about your games and erratic calls of late."

"Like I said, I don't work for HYA anymore." Owen's nonchalance was making him nervous. Ryan shifted his body so he could watch Owen's hands better. "That was all worked out with Mr. Young before he passed."

"Mr. Young was in declining health for months. The board has had to review—and, unfortunately, rescind—some questionable decisions he made shortly before his passing . . . to protect company assets."

"I'm not a company asset," Ryan shot back.

Owens didn't respond immediately, but instead rolled down his window and whistled softly at the chirping birds a moment. Then he turned and fixed Ryan with a look that suggested his polite facade had begun to crack. "Mr. Bishop doesn't have patience for messes, especially one of the sort you and Hector have created here. He's given me carte blanche to resolve things. Your finding and returning his files would make him a very happy man."

"Exactly what files are we talking about?" Ryan asked, playing along as he tried to keep Owens calm. The cool breeze coming in the window helped clear his head, but the chirping outside, and the low rumbling call of a bullfrog reminded him of the dark pools waiting for him outside. His anxiety ratcheted up another level.

"*All* of them," Owens said shaking his head. "You were the last one to access the files before they disappeared. You gave the nerds a run for their money, but they eventually found your electronic fingerprints all over Mr. Young's files."

"I could have told them that," Ryan said, rolling his eyes. He cracked his knuckles and shifted back in the car seat. "I did a lot of personal work for Hector, including purging files for him—*routine* maintenance. If you could be more specific, I might know or I could point you in the right direction. But having files? Sorry, no files. Still, I can understand the concern. I know those files inside and out, and anyone who has *any* of Hector's files is dangerous. There are so many ways and places they could cause trouble—not only for Bishop but for all the partners. Now, there's a ripple effect."

Owens looked at Ryan with an expression someone might have while cleaning something repugnant off his shoes. "I've seen a lot of people go up through the ranks. The ones who rise quickly burn out fast. And the people they betray on the way up just love dragging them back down again. Not you, though. You were the only one that made it to the top and stayed there. We admired you. And yet, we all secretly hoped for a spectacular flameout of the great Hector Young protégé—proof that in the end, you were no better than the rest of us. You're one slimy bastard, Thomas. Don't assume anyone at HYA is coming to bat for you. The ranks are celebrating Icarus taking a nosedive—me most of all. I'm going to pluck your wings, one feather at a time, until there's nothing left and you come plummeting back to earth."

He pulled a cell phone out of his coat pocket and shoved it against Ryan's chest.

"Forty-eight hours. Prepaid. Use it, and quit playing phone tag. Second piece of business: we can't stalemate any longer. The State's Attorney's Office is getting ready to set a date for Hector Jr.'s attempted murder case. You need to convince them otherwise—that the shooting was accidental."

Ryan laughed. "No chance. If Hector walks, I spend the rest of my days looking over my shoulder. I'm not going to do that, and I'm not going to perjure myself. Hector will have to take his chances."

"Not acceptable."

"I don't give a steaming heap of shit what's *acceptable.* If Bishop's smart, he'll leave me alone and cut his losses with Hector. Why should he care if that slimeball rots in prison? He hated the Youngs. You're putting screws to the wrong person. Hector's the screw-up. Send a lawyer in there and make him keep his mouth shut. Plea deal. One of your in-house bright boys should have no problem handling this case."

"That might have been true with a lower-profile victim," Owens said. "The problem is *you.* Your stature in the community has made this a prominent case. The partners don't give a tinker's damn about Hector—just what HYA information may come out in the wash."

"It's not coming from me," Ryan said, waving the phone at Owens. "I run a respectable business. The last thing I want is to be tied to illicit activities. Lean on Hector. Slap some sense into him. I'm done with Bishop and all of you. Stay away from me and mine. Tell Bishop I don't know anything about any files, but if he keeps pushing, I'll do whatever's necessary."

"If that's the way you want it. But if I were in your shoes," Owens said, pointing his index finger at Ryan, "I'd think twice about this game of chicken." Owens gestured to the phone. "Forty-eight hours. Now, get out."

Ryan started counting. *One . . two . . . three . . . four . . .* Getting out of the car was an excellent idea, but a nagging, angry whisper bubbled and boiled within him. *Five . . . six . . . seven . . .* Insight washed over him like a tidal wave. He let go, and it swept him away. Ryan yanked the nine-millimeter semiautomatic from inside Owens's coat and pressed it into the soft gut beneath the polo shirt. "I have no problem trying out Mr. Owens's gun here," he said to the two men in the front seat. "I might also start waving it around to prove my point, so keep your hands where they are and don't turn around. Take this message back to Mr. Bishop or whoever it is you report to. I have a handful of files in my possession that would be quite damaging should they be released. Screw with me again, and I'll make sure they go public. If anything happens to me, they'll go public. Now, hike your asses back to New York and leave me alone." He glared at Owens. "Understand?" Owens nodded. Ryan popped the magazine out of the gun, then racked the slide, ejecting the chambered round out the window, and dropped the weapon to the floor. "Now, tell your friends over there to play nice and take me back to Nevis before I start entertaining ways to leak your files all over the internet."

Owens got out of the car and pointed at the Nissan driver. "We're through here. Put him back where you found him." He ducked back in the Acura and slammed the door.

Without a flinch or backward glance, Ryan walked past the woman and the burly meathead still standing by the Nissan rear door and climbed back into the car. As the Nissan eased past the Acura, he rolled the rear window down and spoke again. "The reason I never tumbled back down like the rest of them? Because I'm *that* good. Don't cross me." He rolled the window back up. "We're done here," he said to the driver. "Take me back to town."

Ryan's hands began to shake uncontrollably as his machismo collapsed like a deflated balloon. He took a deep centering breath, and self-loathing and disgust rushed in to replace the urge to dominate. He needed to pull himself together. What had happened back there? One moment he was exiting the car, then everything faded to black. The next thing he knew, he was waving a gun around and making threats. What had possessed him to act like that? It was as if he had lost control of his body. He closed his eyes and put his head against the cool window glass. He was screwed. Why had he told them he had files? Admitting he had anything from HYA was the one thing he had never wanted to do. He already regretted his impulsiveness in taking them in the first place.

Hector Senior's last request had been quite specific. He had wanted sensitive files destroyed before he died, and thought he could trust Ryan to do it. But Ryan had failed to see the wisdom in destroying what was essentially a ticket to freedom. So, of course, he had saved a few, but only as an insurance policy. HYA had created its own problems when it came calling for them. Bishop was a mover and shaker, but he couldn't possibly know everything they contained, and it was making him crazy. But Bishop's instincts told him, rightly, that the files conveyed tremendous power to the holder. And anyone who knew the significance of the information in them would *never* destroy them.

His little outburst had got him out of the swamp, and he and HYA were done with each other, at least for the moment. The no-nonsense woman was busy on her phone, and the driver had stopped checking on him in his rearview mirror. Owens would stay off his back for a while. Clearly, this car was headed back to town, and they didn't intend to rough him up—their personal style was a little more polished than Hector Jr.'s. On the other hand, they were quite capable of arranging for a few inmates to beat some sense into Hector—the same ones who were protecting his backside right now—and convince him that a plea deal and jail time would be an opportunity for some much-needed personal growth.

He could go home and change out of his fancy suit, but there was still a big red bull's-eye on him, pulsating like a neon sign. It was bad, but he had brought it on himself.

Ryan tapped his forehead against the glass and watched beads of sweat from his forehead trickle down the car window. What if he had pulled the trigger back there? Everything he had worked for in the past months—Van's trust, respectability, his business—gone in an instant. And who would benefit the most? He could picture the aurascope gushing bright-red sand. Ryan watched the freshly planted corn fields and smattering of farm buildings and houses as they whizzed by. He couldn't shake the feeling that Hamelin was hiding out there somewhere with his little notebook, keeping cosmic score. If he had killed Owens, all the good citizenry in the world wouldn't have saved him from the express train to hell that Hamelin would have thrown him on. No, of the two evils facing him, it was Hamelin he had most to fear. Indeed, everything else was just chess pieces within Hamelin's little game. *God, keep me safe from that demon,* he prayed.

The Nissan stopped short of the entrance to the Phoenix. Ryan slipped out of the backseat and watched until the car disappeared from view. He was a little surprised not to find Hamelin waiting for him. He tossed the cell phone into the trash can. When he got to his office, he closed and locked the door and set his phone alarm. The past was catching up with him, and an immortal lunatic was hovering God knows where, waiting to snatch his future away. He glanced over at the aurascope. The sand still looked magenta, but it was streaming faster, no doubt about it. He threw a tablecloth over it and settled onto his couch for a quick nap.

CHAPTER TWELVE

Nothing

Ryan stabbed an index finger at the alarm icon and rolled off the couch. He felt as if he had just nodded off, but if he shielded his eyes from the bright light of the phone, he could make out the time: midnight. It was dark and quiet out front, and the lot out back was deserted.

He had hours—at most, a day or two. HYA got it right that he had files, but they were foolish to think he would hand them over. He envisioned a quick powwow between Owens and Bishop, to gauge how serious they thought he was about going public. If they thought about it long enough, they would figure out that he couldn't release it all without incriminating himself. They would also conclude that no one but a fool would let the hot information out of his sight. And they would be right on both counts. Keeping the information close had been smart at the time. Now it was a liability, and the Phoenix was the first place they would look. He needed a new hiding place until he figured out how to sanitize the documents. He couldn't imagine that Skalski had missed anything of Mr. Young's that needed destroying. Young had been very specific. Skalski's info had to be something different but equally damning. He'd leave it alone and deal with the information he was sure of.

Right now his security revolved around a small silver key hiding in plain sight in the kitchen, dangling from a brass rack hook nailed into the side of the end storage cabinet. He grabbed it, a flashlight, a tube of wood glue, and some tools from Bennie's stash, then took a pry bar to the oak floorboards underneath his desk. When he had pried up a few, he got on his hands and knees and reached into the space, up to his armpit. His fingers patted and felt along the underside of the remaining planks, searching for the cardboard sleeve he had taped there months earlier. Nothing. He felt about some more. Still nothing. He sat up, peeled his shirt off, and wiped away the sweat that ran into his watering, stinging eyes. It had to be here. His fingers went over every inch of wood yet again. Nothing. He stood up and stepped back, fighting the panicky urge to do something—*anything* except stand there like a stone, studying the remaining floorboards. He pried up two more boards. Nothing. Flipped them all over. Nothing.

Visions of Owens's leering, laughing face flooded his brain. He swung the pry bar at his side chair, breaking the back out of it, then threw the bar back at the hole in the floor. He slumped down on the edge of his desk and studied the mess. All the planks, from one side of the room to the other, looked uniform and undisturbed.

He fumbled around for the flashlight, found it, and threw himself down on his belly once more. He swept the light to the left. Nothing. *No, wait.* He swept it back again. Straight ahead, he could see something . . . not taped, but flat, on the dirt floor of the crawl space, just out of reach. He poked the crowbar in and tried to drag it closer. Even with his arm fully stretched out, it was still just beyond his reach. He ripped up two more boards, and finally, the CD—still in one beautiful piece despite the gnawed edges and mouse droppings covering the dirty paper sleeve. He said a silent prayer of thanks, locked his office door behind him, and returned to the pantry.

It was 12:45 a.m. He should have been done by now. Skalski was wisely keeping his promise to stay out of sight no matter what, and there was still no movement in the rear lot.. He cracked the door enough to squeeze through and darted to the Leyland cypress tree behind the trash cans. From there, he crept along to the end of the privet hedges and then crossed to the deep shadows of the sycamores across the street.

He didn't hear or see anyone else except Mouse. Ryan slunk behind a boxy old station wagon, the last bit of cover before the parking lot on the land side and the bay on the other. Van's museum, shrouded in darkness, was surrounded by a gravel parking lot, with no cover between it and the station wagon he now hid behind. *Go now or go home.* He hotfooted it to the metal storage shed, popped the lock with his magic silver key, and disappeared inside.

Deeper darkness. He clicked on the flashlight and almost dropped it—spooked by a dozen pairs of gleaming eyes watching him from the shadows. Carousel ponies and menagerie animals, wedged side by side, ready to gallop, gambol, and trample over him in a last bid for freedom before their permanent attachment to the rebuilt Nevis carousel.

He scanned the line of hand-carved, painted creatures, looking for the white one with a garland of flowers around its neck—the leader of the pack, the king horse. It was on the end, majestic even in this dim light. In the last few weeks of his recovery, out of boredom, he had taken to watching the master restorer. And in the process, he had learned every hoof and hock of the proud beast. Heading straight to the end of the row, he flicked open his pocket knife and picked along the back of the saddle, beneath the cantle, cutting through the smooth line of adhesive. He pulled the top of the saddle free, then duct-taped the CD to the underside of the lid and glued it back in place. Let Hamelin and HYA figure *this* one out.

Ryan checked his watch again: 1:20—later than he had planned, but if he could get out of here unseen, the advantage was still his. He worked his way back around the carousel figures to the entrance, killed the light, and put his ear up against the door. He cracked it and peeked outside. Nothing but the chirr of crickets and the mating calls of Fowler toads hidden off in the swampy bottom to the south—all the normal sounds for a Nevis night.

He slipped out but didn't retrace his steps, instead cutting across town toward the beachfront. At best, he would run into no one; at worst, Officer McCall would threaten to arrest him for violating vagrancy laws by sleeping on the beach. The risk was acceptable. Sleeping or not, the rest of the night would be uneasy. The next move was HYA's, and that could be anytime. Once he had Skalski on a plane to Houston, he could sit tight until they decided to call his bluff. He felt in control for the first time.

CHAPTER THIRTEEN

Boundaries and Socks

Livia threw her apron into her locker, switched out her food-stained work shoes for some red cross-trainers, and put her charm bracelet back on. Unlike on other days, when she lit out as soon as the shift was over, she puttered about while Ryan talked to one of the local cyclists. When he was done, she grabbed him.

"I'm going down to Benedict Point today—want to come? I've heard it's nice. You've been dragging around here lately like you can't put one foot in front of another. You need a break." She tugged on his arm. "Come kick back with me for a couple of hours. We're prepped for the rest of the night," she said, pointing toward the filled garnish trays. "Nothing left to do. Unless the four horsemen suddenly pull up out front, Bennie can handle it."

It might have been an innocent question, and if he repeated it long enough, Ryan might have begun to believe it. But if Hamelin was responsible for Livia's mysterious arrival in Nevis, how capable was he of stoking friendship into courtship? Ryan wasn't sure he could trust her—or himself, for that matter. All week long, consciously or not, Livia had played the coquette: smiling, teasing, invading his personal space. And Ryan was ashamed to admit he had enjoyed it. Not that any of their behavior crossed the line. Harmless flirting was one thing; acting on it was something entirely different. If pushed, he would deny he had flirted at all. But even if it was an innocent question, going off alone with her would surely invite whispers and innuendo. Van didn't deserve that.

He looked up and saw Jean within earshot at the end of the bar as she waited for Bennie. She looked back with a laser-sharp glare. He let her burn holes in him, then returned the favor. He had never given anyone reason to doubt his faithfulness. He didn't understand where the attitude was coming from, and anyway, he didn't need a nanny in his own pub. That cinched it.

"Yeah," he said to Livia. "Why not? I need a break. But I drive."

Jean was wrong. If Livia crossed the line, he would warn her off—gently, of course. If he crossed the line, well, they all were in trouble.

They walked out to his black Porsche, and Livia waited as he put the top down.

"Hat?" he asked.

She shook her head. "No, I don't mind. I love the rush. Last guy I dated had a Jeep. We used to joke about him getting a fancy convertible one day. I didn't see you as the convertible type."

"Meaning?"

"Stuffy. But you've redeemed yourself with the car."

"Thanks. That does wonders for my ego. I have few toys, but I do like a nice car."

There was a serious side beneath her smiling and teasing. She wasn't priggish, but like someone who had grown up around older people. But maybe it was the work thing, because by the time they hit the main highway, they were loose, laughing and swapping car stories like old friends.

"So your last guy—he liked cars?"

"Oh, yeah, the faster the better. I probably know more about cars than your average dude. This is a great car—his kind of car. In fact, you remind me a lot of him," she said, turning toward Ryan and smiling.

"Ah, flattery," he said. "I like it." Flirting felt good. There was something sexy about the way stray locks of her hair framed her face, and a charm in her exuberance. Nothing like his initial impression of her. That made him chuckle. "You remind me of someone I once knew."

"A friend?"

"Sure, from what I can remember."

"Oh, that's cold."

"Sorry, I didn't mean it to sound like that. It was just so long ago. Circumstances change. You know how it goes."

"Yep, sure do," she said. "This is going to sound bold, but you're a walking contradiction, Mr. Thomas. At times, you seem happy, and at others, you seem miserable. If it's real, it should be effortless. Are you really that complicated, or just confused?"

The smiled slid off Ryan's face. "You're right. That was cheeky. Let's talk about something else."

"Sore spot? Sorry. I tend to say what I think." She stopped talking and watched the scenery flitting by: rolling farmland dotted with graying outbuildings and three-chimneyed white clapboard houses. "Why do these barns have boards missing on the side?"

"Tobacco barns. Boards are stripped out for air drying. Some of the finest tobacco you could buy came out of this area—not that I ever smoked any of it. They used to hold auctions in Upper Marlboro. Buyers from all over the world.

"Not much of a tobacco crop anymore, what with health concerns, land developers, and how labor intensive it is—mostly soybeans now. This area is a favorite of mine. Between the yellow soy in the fields and the black-eyed Susans along the roadside, the country's ablaze with color in the summer. Lots of nice old barns still around—empty and creaking there for years until a freak stiff wind gets hold of a weak one and flattens it. Real shame. I'll show you sometime, if you like. Lovely craftsmanship for something that's brutalized by the elements and houses stinky tobacco and horse manure."

Livia laughed. "I'd like that. How about showing me *that* one?"

"But not today—on a day when I'm happy," he said, with a side glance.

"Okay, it's a date," she said with a cagey smile.

Not the pushover he had thought when they first met. She was a survivor. The more he saw it in her, the more he connected with her. She reminded him a lot of Van. He could see them bonding. And he could use more friends like Livia: a good, nonromantic friend, nothing more.

Conversation came easily. They laughed at each other's jokes and listened out of genuine interest, not just manners. But there was an ever-present push and pull between them that Ryan couldn't rationalize or handle. As much fun as Livia was, she had a knack for getting under his skin.

He breathed a quiet sigh of relief when Benedict Point came into view. He parked near the boat ramp at the end of the bridge and jumped out to put distance between them. He watched Livia get out of the car in her short skirt. He liked it . . . a lot . . . and wondered how many of his other friends had such nice legs. *Damn it all.* He wasn't sure.

The place was quiet: a boat putting in, a few already out sailing—an average crowd for the beginning of the work week, early season.

"Ever been here before?" she asked.

"Several times, with Van. Never boating, thank God. We came to putter around, have a little alone time away from a town that sees pretty much everything." He wasn't one to kiss and tell, but he thought he'd lay it on a little thick to shut her up for a while.

"Of course. Nevis is pretty insular. Part of its charm, I suppose. You don't like boats?"

"Boats are fine—as long as they're on dry land."

"Okay, no boats. Bridges?" She nodded toward the long span behind him.

"Yeah, I'm good there."

They ambled down the bridge pedestrian lane and stopped halfway across to watch one of the early boaters maneuver his johnboat back onto its trailer for the long, sunburned ride home.

Livia called out to the young sandy-haired fisherman. "Catch anything?"

"Morning wasn't bad. Medium-sized carp and perch. Had a monster carp, but it got away."

His friend hopped out of the cab laughing. "He's lying. The big 'un always gets away. We didn't catch nothing. Only fish we're gonna eat tonight is canned tuna from Nick's grocery."

Livia gave him a thumbs-up but lost all interested as she noticed the sporty white Boston Whaler approaching the bridge from the north, sun top up and trolling as it headed downriver. Mesmerized, she watched it approach and disappear under the bridge. "Vantage Two-thirty. That's my idea of heaven. I don't ever want to go back to the boring concrete city. Someday, I want to buy a boat like that one: twenty-three feet of Paradise, only blue, and troll the little inlets. I want to live at the water's edge so I can look out and see forever, nothing in my way."

"That's noble enough," Ryan said, surprised at her passion and apparent seriousness. "But good luck on a blue one."

"Whattya mean?"

"Bad luck on the bay. Nobody's gonna sell you a blue one."

She studied him, eyes big and serious. "No blue? You're pulling my leg, right?"

"Serious. No blue on the bay."

"Who told you that?"

"Ms. Hardy."

She looked as if she wanted to argue, but turned away instead. "Well, it can be green, then. Close enough."

"Good luck with that, too."

"No, you're fibbing now. I've *seen* green boats."

"Ever hear of 'b-o-a-t'?"

"Tell me," she said, glaring now.

"'Bust out another thousand.' Forget the color. You'd need both of our jobs to afford the upkeep."

"Okay, well, maybe not now, but someday. Mark my words. I'm not really totally buying the blue thing, either, and you don't strike me as the superstitious type."

"If you mean making a connection between things that can't be seen or totally understood, then yeah, maybe I am. I'm not sure we have a grip on what life is really all about. But boats that are blue? I have enough trouble keeping up with the blues in my own life to worry about a blue *boat.* And I'm not one for the water." Ryan pointed to the yellow parasail gliding behind a speedboat as it skipped along. "Now, that's something I could keep up with, except without the water. I don't suppose you've ever been skydiving."

She threw him an indignant look. "What, I don't *look* the type?" She laughed. "Oh, I can see the wheels turning in your head. But you're wrong about me. Actually, I *have* been skydiving. After my boyfriend passed away, I went, to prove to him I could do it. Sounds crazy, I know," she said, blushing. "But I really think he saw and was proud of me. Depression can make you powerless, but it's amazing what you're capable of doing when you don't fear consequences. He told me he felt like a bird up there. I wanted to feel what he felt: free. I wanted to float away and feel free."

"Guilty as charged," Ryan replied. "I *am* impressed. A rush, huh, to fly like a bird?"

"Um, actually, no. Overwhelming nausea. I couldn't get out of the harness fast enough and went behind my car, heaving a dry stomach. Never again."

"I would have liked to see that."

"Not really. *I* can laugh, but you don't have permission to. You're supposed to feel sorry for me."

"Oh, and I do." Seeing her small hand tighten into a fist, he chuckled and darted farther down the walkway. "I'll bet you were a sorry sight."

"I hate you," she said, but she followed him across the bridge. "I'm starving. Nowhere to eat around here?"

"Nah, doesn't seem to be. On the weekends and later in the summer, there's a smoker that sits over by the shed. Great barbecue, and grilled kielbasa subs thick as your arm, piled high with green peppers and onions. We should open a pub, huh? We could build a place with a pier, like Pope's Creek. Patrons hop right out of the dinghy for grub and drinks."

"Pope's Creek? I guess that's another place you can take me—after we visit a barn. But we've got to think bigger than that. How about we start twenty-first-century curb service? They radio in their orders, and we deliver in our spiffy Boston Whaler."

"You're gonna get that boat one way or another, aren't you? Even got someone else to pay for it now."

"Yes, sir. When opportunity knocks, I answer. Besides, from the looks of that convertible, I think you're good for it. Am I wrong?"

"Maybe. Or just a little nosey," he said, miffed. He abruptly changed direction and started walking back the way they had come, leaving her to scurry after him. "Come on. Let's go see if there's anything to eat in the boathouse."

"Hey, look, I'm sorry," she called after him. "I was only playing with you. Your personal means are none of my business. I'll go wait in the car. When you're done looking around, we can leave."

Ryan couldn't tell whether she was sincere or manipulating him. She seemed to switch between being perfectly transparent and impossible to read. He couldn't dismiss her comments—she was pretty astute—and it annoyed him no end that he cared so much about what she said.

"Boathouse," he repeated, pointing to the blue metal portable building on the edge of the parking lot. She would probably be a lot less ornery if he fed her.

"Okay," she said. "Although I would have been perfectly happy to sit in that shiny black convertible and wait for you." She flashed a perky, smart-assed smile, and Ryan threw in the towel. She was miles ahead of him, and they both knew it. He walked into the boathouse.

"Vending machines." He fished around in his pockets for money. "Got any change? I have a couple of ones and some pennies. "Aw, crap, forget it," he said upon taking a second look. "Everything's empty except for a pack of peanut-butter crackers."

Livia took a peek, fished around in the bottom of her purse, and scavenged a handful of change. They watched as the coil turned, slowly pushing the crackers forward. The crackers came to the end of the coil, wobbled for a second, and then stopped without tumbling into the bin below.

"No!" Livia shrieked. "Those were all the quarters I had." She banged on the glass with both hands and kicked the bottom panel of the machine.

"God, woman, stop!" Ryan grabbed her by the waist and pulled her away. You're gonna get us arrested," he said, laughing. "We'll stop up the street. If I let you go, will you behave? Otherwise, I'm leaving you here."

"I'm good" she said, and pulled his hands away. "I can control myself if you promise to buy me something down the street."

"Cheaper than bail," he quipped. "Come on." He took her by the arm and directed her out the door.

They stopped at a convenience mart a few miles down the road. Two Cokes and a couple of hot dogs later, all was forgiven and they were back on good terms.

"We'll have to do this again," Ryan said as he pulled back into the Phoenix parking lot.

He walked around to Livia's side of the car and opened her door, never stopping to consider that she seemed to expect it. The Phoenix appeared moderately busy—good for the coffers, but after the trip to Benedict Point, business seemed like work instead of passion.

"Thanks," he said. "I didn't realize how much I needed that."

"I could tell. No problem. You look a whole lot better now," Livia said, and she leaned in and kissed him on the lips. She lingered just long enough to gaze into his startled eyes. It was something Marla might have done, but with Livia there was an authenticity that Marla never had. "See you tomorrow."

"Thanks?" Ryan squeaked as he watched her walk to her car. "Hey, you have no respect for other people's boundaries, you know that?"

Livia turned and smiled as she ran her fingers down the length of her hair to sweep it out of her face. "Sure, I do. It's mixed messages I have a problem with. Later, gator." She turned and was gone before he could find a suitable retort.

Flummoxed, he opened the door to the Phoenix and again found himself eye to eye with Jean, sitting at a window table. She immediately hightailed it to the kitchen area. "This day will never end," he muttered. Jean would never believe they had never touched each other before, let alone kissed, or that he was as surprised by the kiss as she was. She would go straight to Van for sure. He knew he had many faults, but even on his darkest day, disloyalty wasn't one of them. He was not so stupid as to casually throw away his relationship with Van. Still, that kiss had knocked his socks off. But was it because he hadn't expected it or just because it was so wrong? One more step and he would be walking open eyed into a relationship that could go somewhere, and at the rate they were going, it was bound to end up hurting someone unless one of them put on the brakes. Who was he trying to fool? He didn't have a healthy respect for relationships, and some of Hector's animosity toward him was probably justified.

He nodded to the wait staff and retreated to the sanctuary of his office, where he slammed the door and collapsed in a heap at his desk. The aurascope was quietly streaming rose-colored sand at an alarming rate. He ran his fingers lightly across his lips and groaned at the memory. His common sense had deserted him, and he was heading so fast toward red, he could almost hear Hamelin's taunting voice, dripping with *I told you so.*

CHAPTER FOURTEEN

Connections

Jean was so often a no-show for their girls' nights out, Van swore that her broad backside was glued to her Adirondack chair. At first, she had seemed busy with something she was excited about. Now she just seemed to be dodging phone calls. Van's patience was at an end. Good friends made time for each other, and if she had insulted Jean somehow, she needed to know.

After three straight days of no communication, Van walked right over to Jean's deck, tossed her sunglasses and keys on the redwood picnic table, and collapsed onto the yellow and green floral chaise longue. Jean was lost in the moment, head down as she pulled her fingers through her short ginger hair. An Old Country Roses china teacup sat nearby, the remnants of a pink-sprinkled sugar cookie balanced on the saucer's edge.

"What's up? Froufrou Royal Doulton tea party, and I've never seen you so deep in thought." She plucked a wilted petal from the potted red geranium sitting nearby.

"Gee, thanks." Jean scowled over the rims of leopard-print glasses pushed down on the bridge of her nose. "Froufrou, *hmph*! I've decided to be a china-cup person and not a Styrofoam one. Savor the moment. It's killing you, isn't it? My life is suddenly interesting, and you don't know what's going on. If I didn't think you'd pick my flower bare, I'd let you dangle for a while."

Van rolled out of the chair and moved away from the plant. "Je-e-ean-n-n-n, I always include you. If you don't tell me, I'm going home and then there'll be no one here for you to hold out on." She moved toward the steps. "See? One, two, three, four, five steps toward my house. Six, seven, eight down your stairs. Nine—"

"Okay, okay, but you're taking the fun out of it. I took your advice and got inspired. Put a bug in Ryan's ear and convinced him it wasn't in his best financial interests to pay me to do absolutely nothing. So, he gave me a new job. You're looking at the new entertainment director for the Phoenix." She punctuated the announcement with a little shimmy of the shoulders.

"*Whew.* I thought you were mad at me. My, haven't we moved up in the world! I'm sure you were putting a real dent in his wallet. What are you supposed to do?"

"Oh, I've been busy. If Ryan can't get some new liquor sources, they're gonna have to go all restaurant for a while. Neither Ryan nor Bennie is excited about that prospect, even short term. Naty Boh alone isn't gonna please everybody. Legworked it with some of the smaller breweries to showcase their beers: Flying Dog, Heavy Seas, Brewer's Art, Stillwater. Who can argue with a little Loose Cannon or Cellar Door? He wants to stay in Maryland—Delaware beer over his dead body, he said. They'll send someone with a pick-em-up truck, if they have to. And, drum roll, please . . . they're adding live entertainment, with me finding and booking the talent. I can run with this, baby." She swayed in her seat to a silent beat.

Van snatched the paper. "Ooh, I can help. I'm really good at this."

"Me, too." Jean snatched it back. "Pete, my ex, used to play gigs when we first met. He was a so-so drummer, and I was his biggest groupie."

"You, a groupie? Somehow, I can't picture you shaking your *little* bootie in a mosh pit."

"Still true," Jean huffed. "I booked all his gigs after we got married, and still had time to beat the groupies off with a stick. Airheads."

"Except you."

"Well, I don't know about that. If I'd been smarter, I might not have married him. But I was pregnant with—"

"Oh," Van said, grimacing. She looked away and studied her flip-flops.

"Oops. Yeah, he knocked me up. Making an honest woman out of me compounded the problem—two immature kids with no money, and him too irresponsible to provide for a family. Getting a divorce was the best decision we ever made for each other. I don't regret having Marla—just the ass who's her dad."

Van snickered. "I have such an awful picture of Pete in my head. I'd like to meet him someday to see how accurate it is."

"You'd be underwhelmed. Trust me. I think he's still a worthless schmo trying to get his break in show business. At forty, he should have a clue the dream is over and it's time to get a real job. No different from probably half the musicians on this list here."

"How are you deciding who to book?"

"The *boss* was very specific." Jean pulled out notes handwritten on a white paper napkin.

"Looks official, all right."

"Quit. Ryan's a hard man to pin down when he's busy. 'One: Blues. Guitar, harmonica, sax; separately, together." What the hell does that *mean*?" She frowned, and her lips continued moving as she read silently to herself. "Damn, I can't read my own script . . ."

"Eh," Van said, shaking her head. "That doesn't sound like Ryan. It's so vague. Are you sure that's what he said?"

"I don't know. He was talking so dadgum fast. I think it says 'This order. Two: Shag / North Carolina beach music." He gave me a couple of phone numbers with that one. 'Three: Country. More later. . . "Yeah, he's all hands-on and stuff. Had this blues guitarist . . ." She shuffled through her pile of papers. "Somebody Johnson. I don't know. I can't find him now. But anyway, I have to get back to work. If I don't get this Johnson guy booked, there's going to be the devil to pay. Go play with your boyfriend."

"I doubt the devil much cares what we do in Nevis. Put another bug in his ear about music on the beach. And maybe we can convince the blues guy to stick around a while. You can never go wrong with blues. Have you booked anybody yet?"

"The blues guy, a guitarist . . . Hamelin Russell . . . starts on Friday. I'm strictly a rock 'n' roll girl, but Ryan listened to his demo early on and declared him a keeper. Here, mug shot."

"Head shot, not mug shot, unless you're pulling them from HYA, in which case they all may be felons." Van gave the picture the once-over. "Blues, huh?"

"Head shot, mug shot—I don't care as long as they can carry a tune. This one's kinda cute. Should I tell him you'll show him around town?"

"Um, no. Don't go starting trouble." She smiled. "He's a doll. What woman couldn't get lost in those green eyes? You're booking all these people at the Bayside while they're in town, right?"

"No. Actually, Ryan said he'd take care of it. I didn't argue with the man. He was very dismissive and hurt my feelings. I decided, *Okay, Mr. Man, have it your way. If this gets screwed up, don't blame me.* Here's the one after him." She handed Van another picture, took her glasses off, and spun them around by one of the stems. "Speaking of the Phoenix, Ryan hasn't said any more about the new girl, has he?"

"Livia? No, nothing. Why?"

"How come Ryan takes away the bookkeeping from me and then turns around and gives it to her? He's all protective and stuff, and now suddenly he's trusting a stranger?"

"Don't complain, Jean. He's given you a nice new job. It's his business, and for whatever reason, his gut's telling him he can trust her. She's a smart, attractive girl. I would imagine she's even a little lonely and probably needs some friends."

"I don't think she's lonely," Jean said.

"I don't know about that. It doesn't look like she has ties to anyone. Everybody craves connection, Jean. It's why I'm a genealogist. You came in by yourself to eat at the Phoenix, and people comb their hair before they go buy a gallon of milk. Puppies snuggle, fish school, and birds flock. We need it, like air. Without it, we shrivel and die. And then no one cares. That's what people really fear. Maybe we should find her a guy."

"Like Ryan?"

"Yes, like Ryan."

"No, I mean *Ryan*."

"Are you trying to go somewhere with this?"

"I saw them kissing," Jean blurted out. "In the parking lot on Wednesday. It was *on the lips*."

"On the lips . . . kissing Ryan? *Phew.* No, there's an explanation."

"Yeah, she's a man-eating bitch. You have every right to hate her."

"I don't . . . hate her."

"Yes, you do. Admit it."

"Okay." Van threw down the picture. "I *loathe* this woman . . . from the moment I met her. She has no respect for what Ryan and I have. I'm tired of people asking me about the new girl, like I should be aware of *something* going on at the Phoenix. She's a taker, not a giver."

"Well, she sure was giving on Wednesday. Did you ever stop to consider that Ryan might be egging her on? He certainly wasn't putting up a fight."

"Pshaw. It's her. He'd never do that. We have too much of a connection. Details, Jean. Did he know you saw them?"

"They took a trip down to Benedict Point together. Don't know what they did down there. Just know they were gone a couple hours and when they came back and parked in the lot, they kissed. I was sitting at one of the windows—front-row seat. When Ryan turned away from her, he looked straight at me and kept walking."

"Once? Lots? How many kisses, Jean?"

"No tongue, for sure. I was so shocked I didn't count. Who needs to count? He's a man, for God's sake. What else would you expect? I didn't say anything, because I thought he would fess up. He hasn't said anything? If it was all her, don't you think he would have said something to you by now? Guilt zips lips. I swear he had to know I was going to tattle to you. You're gonna take a stand on this, right? She's declared war on your womanhood."

"I'm not going to call her out on the playground and beat her up, if that's what you're asking. I'll ask her to lunch, feel her out . . ."

"*Feel her out?* Christ. You'll be feeling her out while your boyfriend's feeling her *up*. Wise up, dummy. You need to call this biatch out on her shit."

Van swept her things off the table. "Enough. Look, I gotta go."

"Just make sure you've stood up for yourself. If you need help before then, like messing her up a little, call me. Same goes for Ryan," she yelled as Van disappeared from view.

Van took a left out of Jean's house and headed away from town. Where were they now? Together? Being inappropriately close? She tried to shake the images out of her head. Ryan wouldn't do that to her. He wouldn't sneak. He'd be up front, and if that was the way he felt, she could deal with it. After all they had been through, he would be honest.

Jean, in her straight-up way, was right. She should come out swinging—hunt them down and confront them both. Even though she and Livia were bonded in their common loss, she didn't trust the girl. Call it woman's intuition, but something wasn't right, and it almost felt as if fate had stacked the deck from the minute she showed up. It was inevitable that Ryan and Livia would connect. She had known it—and feared it—from day one. And boy, did they ever connect! The two were so engrossed, they couldn't see how obvious their attraction was. She was hearing it from everywhere. But kissing in public? That crossed the line. No respect. She was going to rip somebody's guts out and hang them on the boathouse pilings. When she decided which of them was the most at fault, this Hamelin what's-his-face wouldn't be the only one singing the blues.

CHAPTER FIFTEEN

Diversion

Mac's Pharmacy, with its heartwood plank floors and carved mahogany counter running the length of the back wall, was a wonder—a wonder that it had survived into the twenty-first century. Van waxed nostalgic every time they even walked past the place. Long gone were the pink and blue dyed chicks that had once filled the storefront windows at Easter, and the baby red-eared turtles, sold for fifty cents from a giant glass fishbowl in the back, casualties of political correctness and the County Health Department. But the building itself hadn't changed a whit in the forty years Van had known it. Behind its turn-of-the-century facade on Seventh Street, it was the perfect place to escape to if you didn't want to contemplate the future.

Ryan walked in, pulled a wad of paper out of his pocket, and smoothed it out. *Deodorant.* He scanned the overhead signs in the back until he found it, right next to the diaper aisle. He spent the next few minutes picking up and reading the back of every variety on the shelf, and when he had found the right combination of antiperspirant and scent, he selected the checkout with the longest line. As he waited for his turn at the register, he studied the shelves lined with eyewash, eardrops, and corn remover. At the end of each row sat an eye-catching glass amphora filled with colored liquid— red, white, blue—for the July Fourth celebration, he supposed. But the color display at the register was far more interesting: a lighted sign that read "*Pharmacy,*" its color changing continuously through the spectrum. He liked the blue, but before he could really appreciate it, it had morphed into violet and then to a taunting ugly shade of aurascope red. He wondered if there was a pause button one could hit to keep it blue. The sight of Hamelin, leafing through *Sports Illustrated* at one of the magazine spinners at the rear of the store, drove the thought right out of his head.

Ryan walked over and pulled a magazine from the rack. "So glad you decided to make an appearance," he said. "Decided to take a break from *testing* me?"

Hamelin didn't look up. "First, the girlfriend," he said, flipping to the baseball scores. "The *second* girlfriend, just to clarify. Kissed her. What the hell were you thinking? *Not,* I suppose. Just going with the feeling?" He closed the magazine. "The problem, Ryan, is that you can't just do what feels good, and expect things to turn out right. It's as if you hadn't heard a word I said. None of this bodes well for a good-citizen image. Admit it: you're struggling with temptation right now. The old ways are beginning to look good again. The hand itching to feel that comfortable grip of the gun, hot little number working at the bar who takes up more of your free thoughts than your actual girlfriend. Seriously, dude, two-timing your *mother*?"

"Shut up. That's why I'm here whiling away time, embracing the mundane, avoiding complications. Out of sight, out of mind—no temptation. Wrestling with this isn't bad. *Actions* are where the trouble is. The more you meddle, the more screwed up it gets. You're screwing with things that are way above your station. Stop tempting me. You know I can't handle this woman. For whatever reason, I can't. But that doesn't make me a bad person."

Hamelin closed the magazine and stepped forward until he and Ryan were toe to toe. Ryan backed up out of arm's reach and looked away from the immortal's withering gaze.

Hamelin whipped out his notebook. "Pushing for conviction of H. Young—plus. Helping Mr. Skalski—also a plus. Lusting after own employee—minus. Associating with known criminals—minus. Possessing illicit material for personal gain—minus. Lying to best friend—oh, there's a doozy: double minus. Misleading significant other—double minus." He snapped the book shut. "You are headed down a perilous path, my friend. I've placed some faith in you, and you are blowing it. Good head on your shoulders—plenty of common sense. But right now you're such a screw-up. Don't mistake what I'm saying. Ms. Williams is a lovely young woman. You could do worse than spend time with her. In fact, it might give you a little distance and perspective on Ms. Hardy. But you needn't handle the situation so poorly. And moving in with Van—thought you'd pull a fast one? How is that going to work for you? I'd have thought you wouldn't want her involved."

"She's *not* involved."

"Now she is."

Ryan snatched the magazine out of his hands. "Leave Van out of this. I didn't tell her anything. Honest."

"Keep it that way—better for everyone." Six minuses and two pluses," Hamelin said, shaking his head as he gently but firmly retrieved his magazine. "So, what color is the sand in the glass?"

"Shh! Not so loud!" Ryan hissed. He glanced around to see who might be listening. "No idea. I do have a life. I'm having a hard enough time keeping up with all this nonsense you're throwing at me . . . Besides," he muttered, "it creeps me out."

"Not for long. When that sand becomes red, your fate will be out of your control and the issue will become a black-and-white one: saved or damned. Are you ready for that? Humans can be so deluded with false hope. When their hourglass is slow and blue and life's path is clear, they blow it with indifference, pride, and pettiness. I had an inkling you could handle this. Most people never get a second chance. On a professional level, I'd hate to see you blow redemption. To be candid, it reflects badly on my judgment."

"Professional? *Pfft.* When did on-the-clock betting become professional? Everybody makes choices. I don't have control over these people. And don't think for a moment that I don't know what you're up to. Throwing Livia Williams at me. You're crazy if you think I'm going to totally blow it and fool around with this girl. Van is too important to me. I was being very careful, and I didn't invite her to kiss me. You know that. I still haven't done anything inappropriate, illegal, or in any way wrong. And guess what? The sand still isn't blue."

"So what you're telling me is that if you gave in to your true nature, it would be a lot redder. That's not exactly what we call good self-control."

That's not what I'm saying, damn it. This *is* my true nature."

"Ryan, Ryan, Ryan. There is a darkness in you that's clamoring to take control, and when it does, that sand will quickly change. Let *that* creep you out. You're running out of time, and I'm running out of patience. Get with the program. There's no guarantee you'll get another pass at blue."

"Aha. So you do know what's going on with me: the blackouts, the calls to HYA. And speaking of HYA, don't you understand? I *don't want them here.* They're going to destroy everything I've worked for. Tell me you didn't bring them here."

Hamelin shook his head. "I didn't bring them here. Your bad behavior did. I don't have time to keep tabs on everything you do. That's why I gave you the aurascope: so you could."

"Time for baseball stats, but no time for me. You have to know how hard I've tried to separate myself from all this crap. You're purposely making this more difficult than it needs to be. Clue me in. I have no earthly idea what choices I'm supposed to make. A little direction would save us both some time. Can't you hang around for a while and help me?"

Hamelin shook his head. "I'll see what I can do, but I'm not going to cheat. Soon we're going to need to make amends. It might all come down to plan B." He turned to go, then whipped right back around. "One more thing. There's a great little bistro on the West Side that has divine Franco-American takeout. I think the young man in the cellar is getting a little tired of leftover meatloaf." He gave the magazine rack a spin and walked away. As he passed a toy boat display near the front register, he swiped something off the top shelf and shoved it into his pants pocket, leaving the magazine in its place.

"Wait. What amends? Tell me about plan B." Ryan dodged magazines flying off the spinner in every direction like errant fireworks. It was no use. Hamelin was gone, as if vaporized into thin air.

CHAPTER SIXTEEN

Kiss and Tell

Didn't I see you driving that snazzy Charger out there?" The flirtatious man in the red-and-blue checked shirt seemed mesmerized by the flashy brunette behind the bar. He took another leisurely swig of his Southampton Imperial Russian stout—the last of Bennie's New York stash—without taking his eyes off her face.

Marla nodded.

"Let me guess: sugar daddy?"

Marla burst into laughter. "Daddy, without the sugar." With a crook of her finger, she brought the man closer, almost close enough to brush her lips against his ear. "Mike doesn't have any money, and he's in Houston now." She pulled back and waited as Ryan passed through—never giving her his direct attention, but enough of a threat to give her pause. She might not have spoken at all if she had seen him coming. When she heard his office door click shut, she turned back to the patron, but the man in the checked shirt had already crossed the room and climbed into the passenger side of a car at the curb. He was cute, in a way. She stuck her lower lip out and watched as the blue Nissan took off so fast, its tires chirped.

She pulled the lip back in again as soon as she noticed a young construction worker at a side table checking her out. Maybe he would ask her out. She sent him a cold Naty Boh on the house.

The bag with the stick of deodorant hit the office wall with a *whump,* and the floor with a clatter. Ryan sank down amid the detritus strewn about his office, and covered his head with his arms. Where the hell was the aurascope? Dear God, he was devil's toast now!

The door squeaked open, and Marla poked her head in. "Am I in trouble again? Everything okay in here?"

Ryan didn't bother looking up. "Peachy."

"Looking for something? Maybe I can help."

Marla, helpful? He gave it a shot. "Yeah, sure. Let me know when you see a big thing that looks like an hourglass with magenta sand."

"Haven't seen it. I put the one with the red sand on the shelf above the main bar. It looked festive, like the big jars in Mac's Pharmacy. Seen those? We still need to find a white and a blue one."

What I wouldn't give for a blue one, Ryan thought. He pulled his arms off his head. "*Magenta* sand?"

"No, it's red like Pretty Pearly Very Berry, my Cover Girl lipstick. I'll let you know if I see the magenta one." She closed the door.

"Marla, wait!" Ryan yelled as he scrambled to get up. "Where . . . where's the red one?" He chased her back into the main room. Sure enough, there sat the aurascope, on the top shelf behind the bar, its sand racing from the upper chamber to the lower. Not as red as he feared or as magenta as he remembered—more of a rose tint and definitely pouring faster. Ryan pulled it down and took it back to his office.

The only way Hamelin would leave town and life could be salvaged was if Hamelin won the game. Ryan didn't understand why Hamelin left him to fend for himself. Maybe it was against the rules to help him, but then, the guy didn't seem above bending the rules if it worked in his favor. Hamelin was a drama instigator, and if lying kept his shallow cosmic game going, he was not above it. He could deny it until the Second Coming, but he was actively playing the game. And by the color of the sand, it would soon be over.

The immortal made him feel like a chastised student. He wasn't ready to talk with Livia about her unsolicited kiss, but with Hamelin breathing down his neck about it . . . Maybe that was Hamelin's subtle way of helping, and Ryan wasn't getting it. In that case, he didn't have much choice, but he would have to do it without alienating Van. He would be blunt but gentle and put Livia in her place.

There was no way they would get any privacy at the Phoenix. Fred's deli seemed innocuous enough.

To keep everything on the up-and-up, Ryan picked a table near the door, within view of the blue and gold macaw caged in the alcove between a double set of doors, methodically shelling peanuts. Livia walked in right behind him. Ryan checked his watch. Six o'clock exactly—she was either punctual or anxious to see him.

She looked the bird over before sitting down. "Is he legal to be in here where they serve food?"

"Junior? He's always been here. Nobody complains, and I think maybe they turn a blind eye because he's a town institution. Either that or they hide him whenever the inspectors come in. They say he speaks German, but I've never heard a peep out of him. We can move if you want."

She stared a moment, half twisted in her chair, thoughtfully biting her lower lip. "Pretty." She turned back around and gave Ryan her full attention. "No, I'm okay here. Why are we meeting here instead of the Phoenix?"

"It's not what you may think. We need to talk about your kiss."

"What about *our* kiss?"

"Don't do it again. First of all, Van and I have a relationship, and you completely disregarded—"

"Ah," she said, nodding. "So that's what this is about. I had no idea you and Ms. Hardy were an item. I haven't seen much of her since we first met. I'm sorry, I would never disrespect someone else's relationship, and I could accept what you're saying if you hadn't kissed me back. When you did, you put a whole new set of rules into play—house rules. No man in a truly committed relationship kisses back. When I looked you in the eyes, your eyes said *yes*."

Ryan shook his head. "No, they didn't. That's the oldest excuse in the book for forcing yourself on someone. You took me by surprise. You know you did. Second, it's not appropriate for a work relationship. It's a harassment suit waiting to happen. Don't let it happen again. Nothing personal—it's just not appropriate for the workplace."

"You think I'd file a sexual harassment suit against you?" she asked.

"No. I might have to let you go because of *your* harassment. The law is blind that way."

She didn't lash out at him as he had expected—just stared and blinked several times. He could almost see the gears cranking in her head.

"Look," she said, putting both hands flat on the table. "I was once in love—*totally* in love. If he hadn't been taken from this earth too soon, I would be married now to the most wonderful man that ever walked this earth. You wouldn't exist in my world. The last time I talked to him, I was in the middle of something and said I'd call him the next day. But there was no tomorrow. Losing him taught me to live every day like it's my last, and never fail to let people know I care about them. You're so conflicted and *so-o-o* full of it. It's galling, is what it is. I enjoy being around you, Ryan. I know we have a connection. You feel it. You can't run away from feelings. Maybe the thing you have with Van is real and she's the right person for you to be with, but to deny you have feelings for someone else is wrong. You should explore all the possibilities and make the best choice, not the first choice."

Ryan brought his hand down a little too hard next to hers and then snatched it back. For the second time this week, he checked around to see if he was making a spectacle of himself. The place was empty. "God, you're blunt. You're asking me to cheat and not even batting an eye."

"I'm not," she insisted. "I'm planting seeds of doubt in your mind that Van is the *only* one who can make you happy. Open your eyes, man. There are other women in the world who would love to be with you."

Did you have an open relationship with your old boyfriend?"

"That's cruel, and so unworthy of you. No, we didn't."

"What happened to him?"

"He died in an accident here in the States while I was off on an internship overseas. We were going to announce our engagement when I got back. It was a good relationship," she said matter-of-factly.

"Never cheated on him?"

"Never."

"But you want me to cheat on Van."

"No. I want you to be more honest than you're being right now. How can you be with Vanessa if you have feelings for me? Don't look so shocked. You're either playing games or in denial. She deserves to know . . . if she hasn't already figured it out. Women know these things. I like you, *really* like you—something I never thought I'd say again to *any* man. There are times when we really click. That's when you're not thinking too hard, just going with your feelings. Then, *bam,* you start to think it through. You act like you've crossed some imaginary line, and retreat back into this emotional shell. It's frustrating. I want to grab you and tell you it's okay to go with the flow. You sitting here having this conversation tells me I'm right. Otherwise, you'd have already sent me packing."

"Christ . . ." He ran his fingers nervously through his hair. "This isn't some wild forbidden romance. I'm in a committed relationship, and no, I *didn't* kiss you back. The only rules at play here are common courtesy and mutual respect. And equally importantly, it's inappropriate for our professional relationship. I don't date my employees. Your help at the Phoenix has been golden. I'd hate to fire you. Got it?"

She played with her nails. "Well, then, if I misread the situation, I apologize. Since I make you that uncomfortable, I should probably leave. If it's not working out, it's not working out. You have Bennie back, and it would be a good time for me to go anyway. Yes, that's probably what I should do," she murmured to herself. "It's good we had this conversation. Makes me realize why I was here in the first place. The job was short term, remember? I've loved being here in Nevis, and I appreciate you taking me on, Ryan. This little town takes me back to happier times in my life, and I can't remember the last time I felt this good. But there's some awkwardness here that, apparently, neither of us wants to deal with. If I go now, we can part friends. Life is obviously somewhere else waiting for me. I need to find it. Otherwise, I'm going to make the mistake of hiding out here pretending everything's cool and it's where I should be." She slid her chair back and got up.

"No. He reached for her but didn't rise. "We can deal with this. Sit, please. I'm not suggesting any of that. You don't have to leave. I'm sitting here having this discussion because we *do* get along well and I've had a lot of fun these last few weeks. But maybe we've gotten off on the wrong foot. Bennie and I would like you to stay on. You feel like part of the team. We just need to be clear about the ground rules. If there is a song and dance going on here—and I'm not saying there is—can't we change the tune and be friends instead? I could really use a good friend like you. Good friends are hard to come by."

"Friends?" She mulled the word over as if trying out the taste of some exotic fruit. "So the rule would be no kissing, touching, or becoming intimate with other employees." She sounded serious, but the look in her eyes seemed to say something else.

Ryan threw his hands up in the air. "You're the most aggravating person I've ever met in my life. Either I'm not making myself clear or you're too stubborn to hear it. I can't believe you would be so brazen that you'd play me like this on purpose. It'd be better if you leave. You don't need to come in anymore. Pick up your things. I'll give you a month's severance pay."

"If that's what you want," she said, staring him straight in the eyes. "I'll be in later today to collect my things. Thanks for the severance. If I had a job to go back to, I'd tell you to keep it, but I'll need it. Thanks for the opportunity, Ryan."

"Now, wait a minute. What happened to your job?" he asked. His eyes narrowed. "You said this job wouldn't be a problem."

The longer it took her to answer, the darker his countenance grew.

"Well?"

"Long story. They didn't like me being away for the couple of weeks, so they fired me."

Ryan cocked an eyebrow. "God, thanks for the guilt trip. Now I feel like a bastard. I can't fire you if you gave up—"

"I don't need your sentimental bull crap." She gave her chair an extra shove as she slid it under the table. "Spend some quality time with that guilt. And I hope your answer to every problem isn't to fire your friends. What'll you do when you're left with nothing but a roomful of enemies?"

"Oh, I have lots of enemies, believe me." He ran his fingers through his hair again and dug his fingernails into his scalp. "Listen. We're both so hotheaded we're burning down the house out of spite. Can't we compromise here? Sit down and let's start over. We really do need you at the Phoenix. Please, don't go."

"*Voila!* You've proved my point. I've spent the last fifteen minutes dragging you over hot coals and back, and you still can't let me go, can you? The answer is, *no way*, Ryan—not until you can decide whether it's the Phoenix or *you* that really need me. You have my number, *sir*."

CHAPTER SEVENTEEN

Control

What do you mean, you don't know where she is?"

Jean looked up from a pile of overflowing manila folders. "Exactly what I said, Ryan. Do I look like her mother?"

"Any other day, you two are joined at the hip. You told her, didn't you?"

"Did you really think I was going to keep your dirty little secret for you? Damn straight I told her. If you were any kind of stand-up guy, it would have been you who brought it up. And I'll bet you haven't told her about Pickett's house, either, have you? Didn't think she'd find out? She's full of doubt now and you've confirmed every suspicion I ever had about you. She deserves better. She should find someone better. Like . . . well, like *him*." She fished Hamelin Russell's picture out of the stack and waved it under Ryan's nose.

Ryan snatched the picture and wadded it up into a ball. "Christ. You have no idea. Why do you have *his* picture?"

"You told me to hire entertainment. You're looking at it."

"He's no musician. Where did you get this?"

"He was referred by the talent agency. You picked him out in the stack of demos I gave you. This one."

Ryan snatched the CD out of her hand. "No way. I don't want him."

"I've already arranged it. Plans are made."

"Unmake them. This is some sort of sick joke, trust me. Find someone else. Oh, and thanks for all your help finding Van."

"Anytime," she sneered.

"I am so close to firing you."

Jean scooped the folders into a heap and offered them to him, one eyebrow cocked.

Ryan seethed. "Fired. Send it all back to the Phoenix."

As soon as he was out of sight, Jean picked up the phone. "He's looking for you."

At the far end of the boardwalk, away from the shoppers and strollers, Van watched the osprey hit the water feetfirst, then carom off it and wheel away again toward its nest on top of a utility pole, its catch wriggling in its talons. If Ryan knew her all that well, he would know where to find her. The longer she sat on the boardwalk, the darker her mood grew, yet the more clearly she could see. She had been wrong and foolish. She could claim Ryan as her own forever, but deep in her heart, she knew that the claim could be only as her son. Anything else would rob them both of what was cut short the first time around. Ryan's blossoming relationship with Livia was a natural progression of what James's life might have been. She couldn't be both lover and mother. She was going to have to choose—that is, if Ryan hadn't already chosen for her.

He was nowhere to be seen, and she found herself sitting alone at the end of the boardwalk. She hated to admit that she had given him more credit than he deserved. Reluctantly she got to her feet, and as she did, she caught sight of him strolling down the boardwalk toward her. He was carrying something in his hand.

"Ice cream?" he asked when he got close. "It's in a Dixie cup. There's a wooden spoon in there, too." He offered her the brown paper bag.

"Well, at least you learned *something* from me," she said. She took the bag and peeked inside.

"Everything that means anything, I learned from you." He pointed to the bench, and as she nodded, he sat down beside her.

"How did you know I was here?" she said.

"I think I know you well enough to guess where you'd go if you were upset. I'm thinking good old Jean told you about Livia kissing me in the parking lot. I wish she hadn't done that. You should have heard it from me, and you would have if she hadn't run off to tattle. But honestly, why would you think I'd cheat on you—in the middle of town, in the Phoenix parking lot in broad daylight? Cut me a little slack. I would have at least checked into the Sleazy Time Motel, don't you think?"

"If you were so intent on telling me, why didn't you? Jean said you saw her sitting right there. I'd much rather have heard it from you and avoided the embarrassment of hearing it from someone else."

"I'm sorry. But Livia blindsided me, and I felt I had to nip it in the bud. We had a frank discussion down at Fred's today. I didn't want her to think that was acceptable. I made it clear how I felt about you."

"She kissed *you* and you *never* saw it coming?"

"Exactly."

"If you wanted to maintain a business relationship with this girl, why did you go down to Benedict Point with her? Isn't that asking for trouble?"

"No. Well, yes, I suppose—in hindsight," he said, backtracking. "I already knew before we left that everything would be on the up-and-up."

"And you got that idea across, so you were both singing off the same sheet of music, so she didn't get the wrong idea?" She shook her head. "Why is it everyone can see the attraction between you two, except for *you*? And when you talked today, she made it clear she had no ulterior motives where you're concerned?"

Ryan looked away.

"I see." She shivered and shifted her focus to the whitecaps being driven shoreward by the evening breeze. "I've noticed the way you look at her, Ryan. There's an intensity and focus that lights up your whole face. Can you even *look* at her without smiling?"

"There's been nothing but innocent banter going on between us. It doesn't mean *anything*. If you see so much, then I hope you can also see what I'm dealing with. She's up in my personal space all the time. I find myself reacting to—"

"Stop. I don't need an apology—or an excuse. The attraction is obvious." Her voice softened. "If anything, it's me who should be apologizing. I tried to keep you apart when I first met her. I knew you would fall for her."

"What are you *talking* about?"

"You've met Livia before."

"Not that I know of."

"That wasn't a question. Trust me, you have. She told me when she came—the first day I met her. She was James's girlfriend, the one he was dating when he died—*your* girlfriend. According to Livia, you two were ready to announce your engagement when you . . . passed."

Ryan shot to his feet and took several steps away from her. "No. No, no, no. She's a manipulator, playing games or something." He turned back around. "Or is it you? You're not happy with our relationship. I'm not attentive enough . . . honest enough. You want me out of your life, and you're trying to push me away." He shook his head. "*This* is how you're going to do it? You think I'd really buy this nuttiness? One of you is not being truthful here."

Van set the bag of ice cream aside, stood up and closed the space between them. "I know it's hard to hear," Van said, "but it *is* true. I didn't even know you had a girlfriend. She said she was in Europe when you died, saw my picture in the paper for the Phoenix opening, and came looking for me. She's heartbroken over your death and still trying to put her life back together. I feel for her."

"You feel for *her*. What about *me*? She's been here three and a half months, and you're just getting around to telling *me,* the person most affected by this? What kind of person . . . ?"

She grimaced. "I thought I deserved you not knowing. Please forgive me." She reached for his hand, but he stepped farther away. "Ryan, I'm sorry. I was so wrong."

Ryan stood slack jawed. "'Wrong' doesn't begin to capture it. How could you possibly be so cruel? All these emotions I've been wrestling with. You watched me struggle with temptation and guilt and did *nothing*? Not because you wanted me to figure it out, but because your selfish interests got in the way."

"I wasn't trying to be cruel. I wasn't thinking about you at all. I wasn't thinking . . ." She closed her eyes against the intensity blazing from his. It didn't help. "Because I didn't want to lose you, that's why!" she shouted. "I got stars in my eyes, okay? I let myself become something I'm not, something I shouldn't be. Because I knew that if you two met, you'd love again. You can't fight true love. It's fate—you're supposed to be together. But, damn it, don't think for a minute I like either one of you very much right now."

She smiled feebly at a strolling couple who had stopped to stare, and eased back down onto the bench, shoulders sagging. "We can set things right here," she whispered. "You two have an obligation to see where this could go. Maybe I need to learn to be a mother again. I could try to love her like a daughter-in-law. Maybe if I could focus on you being James—*James* being happy—I could free myself from the pain and longing of losing him. Because . . . because it never really goes away. Even though I love you, the loss never goes away. But all this, this makes everything the way it was, before it all got taken away. This could make it all right. How did we get to this point of having it all right again?"

She burst into tears and buried her face in her hands.

"Shit. You're actually running with this nonsense." He let her cry. "You're out of your mind. What makes you think you can live my life for me?"

"I'm not—"

"Oh, yeah, you are. This is more about you feeling guilty. You've spent all your free time these last few years daydreaming about a little boy, someone you've had total control over. Maybe you should let your little fantasy boy grow up, because the real one sure did. I'm an adult, and I'm going to make my own decisions about who I date and who I fall in love with. Did I let you interfere the first time around? You didn't even know there *was* a Livia. You couldn't name half the people I went out with. It wasn't your responsibility then, and it damn sure isn't now. You're so willing to dismiss my feelings and define our relationship without considering what I feel. I made a terrible mistake. I never should have gone to Benedict Point with her. Like you, I thought I could control things, make it clear I was off limits. Now, thinking back, I can see where I was sending her mixed signals. If you'd just told me . . ."

"We both made a mistake, but we can talk our way through this and do the right thing."

"*The right thing?* You have no idea. My life right now is hell. HYA is harassing me, Ham . . . oh, forget it."

She darkened. "What does HYA want?"

"They grabbed me off the street and they're issuing ultimatums—ones I can't meet. I can't afford to have Hector Young running free, and I can't give the information back."

"What information?"

"The favor I did for Hector Senior. His last request . . . He wanted files destroyed. HYA thinks I took information from his files instead of destroying it. They want it back."

"Did you?"

He hesitated a moment before answering. "Yes."

She rolled her eyes and shook her head. "I thought you washed your hands of all this when you threw the account information away. For God's sake," she said as her eyes teared up, "give it back. It's not worth it."

He shook his head. "I had a change of heart. I can't give it back. It's the only insurance I have against them swallowing me whole."

"And yet, they're still harassing you. Give it back. This is all salvageable."

"Salvageable? Hardly. I never would have thought you could hurt me like this. What's there to talk about?"

"Us," she said.

"I don't think you know the first thing about what '*us*' means. He looked at his watch. "I can't be around you right now. I'm outta here."

He left her alone, still crying.

Betrayal. He had never seen it coming. All this time, all this guilt. And Van, the person he trusted most, held the key to all of it. She and the twisted angelic instigator who was intent on making life *right* again.

He tried to visualize Livia somewhere besides Nevis—those liquid blue eyes that watched him as if they could read his thoughts, that stirred something he couldn't quite put into words. Warm blue eyes the color of calm, tropical ocean. He couldn't place them, but he couldn't shake them, either. The push and pull of a karmic connection . . . Now he had an explanation. He had known her, loved her, and she had loved him enough to still be telling people about it.

Livia was a puzzling combination: fragile darkness that begged to be healed, and spunky ferocity that refused to be tamed. She was good for him, and God knows he was drawn to her youthful, sunny vitality. He wanted to get lost in her and feel young and free—free to make choices he had been robbed of. Choices that shaped who he was and the direction his life took. But he was just as drawn to Van. Calm, intelligent—she challenged him mentally and made him feel secure in every way. But for every thought of her, there was one of Livia to counter it.

How had he and Van ended up where they were? It had started in a whirl of activities and revelations. Maybe they were too quick in their assumptions. What did he want from her, really? It had seemed simple enough: a relationship. But had he ever really considered what was the best kind? They both had accepted a romantic one, mostly by default. It was the easiest, the most organic, and, if Livia hadn't come along, a reasonable choice. But now there were other choices. Maybe the easy choice was the wrong one. Maybe he needed to shove the blue box farther back in the drawer until he thought this all through.

He lay down on the first empty bench on the other side of the green. "How could life be so mixed up?" he asked the tree limb overhanging the bench as he pulled out his phone and dialed. The call went to voice mail. "I'm sorry. We need to talk. Please call me back."

The helplessness and confusion—he couldn't handle much more. He closed his eyes and gave in to the numbing, cold black fog that crept over him, submerging him. He blacked out to the buzzing of his phone as it slipped from his hand and thumped softly onto the grass.

CHAPTER EIGHTEEN

Scheduled but No Agenda

Ryan's wallet was forty bucks lighter, a quarter tank of gas was gone, and nine hours had elapsed that he couldn't account for. No receipts in his pocket, calls on his phone, or memories in his head. This was far and away the longest blackout yet. He yanked the stainless metal tray out from under the bowls of lemons and other cut-up garnishes and flung it like a Frisbee into the kitchen area. He couldn't see what it hit, but its flight ended in the clang of metal against metal, and shattering glass. It didn't solve anything, but it felt good.

"I surrender," Livia's quivering voice called from the kitchen. "I'm sorry. I'll come in the front way."

"Livia! God, are you all right?" Ryan rushed into the back area, broken glass crackling under his shoes. Livia was cowering against the door. He grabbed her by the shoulder and then recoiled. "Good Lord, what happened? You look like you went half a round with Manny Pacquiao."

Livia brushed her hand across her cheek. "It looks worse than it feels. I hopped out of bed and forgot my laptop was on the floor—did a face plant into the armchair. It was either me or the laptop. I'll heal, but I couldn't afford another computer. S'all right."

"Jeez, Livia, all up your arm, too! Are you sure you're okay?"

"I'm fine." She stepped away, obliging him to release her. "You did a really lousy job of making lemonade out there," she said, pointing back over her shoulder.

"And a hell of a mess in here."

"It's too early. Why did you call me and then not answer your phone? What is it you think is left to talk about?"

"Why didn't you tell me you were in a relationship with Van's son, James?"

"You brought me all the way in here to quiz me on my dating history? I was going to work two weeks at your bar. Why should I discuss my private life?"

"You didn't feel peculiar hitting on the boyfriend of your dead fiancé's mother?"

"Not really. You gave me every indication you felt the chemistry between us. You and I . . . it seems to outweigh any relationship I might have had with her." She looked around. "Don't you want to talk in your office?"

"No, I'm fine here. Bennie won't be in for a couple more hours. I need to know why you *really* came to Nevis. Nobody comes here, gives up a whole other life, and stays."

"Van did." She lobbed the remark to him, but he didn't field it. "I specifically came here to meet James's mother," she continued. "Couldn't have been more up front. I told Vanessa the first day I met her. She didn't tell you? Evidently, she didn't think it was your business, either."

She sighed and surveyed the room once more before walking past him into the empty bar area where she tossed her Coach bag on the closest table. "If you don't mind, I feel more comfortable seeing who's coming and going." She sat down and waited until he joined her. "Look, I've never made it a secret that James and I were involved. I can't help it if her son and I loved each other. Agenda? I don't have one. What's wrong with you people and your fascination with my private life? I've stayed here because I like Nevis and its quaintness, the peacefulness of the bay. I like the Phoenix; I like you. What do you want, my soul?"

"No, never. And you're right. Normally, I wouldn't ask such a personal question, but we both know this isn't *normal*. It's too fast." He stopped and struggled for the right words. "You told me you'd come back only if I said you were important to me. You *are* important to me." He threw up his hands. "There, I admitted it. There is something between us, and we need to figure out how to handle it so nobody gets hurt."

"Including Vanessa?"

"You have to accept that I still have a relationship with her. We've talked about *things*. That's my personal shit that I don't want to go into. You've totally disregarded our relationship so far, anyway. Just know that I care deeply for her and she knows it. I have no secrets from her."

"None?"

He hesitated a beat. "None."

She smiled at him. "What I've been saying all along. Let's see where it takes us."

He nodded and shoved his hands in his pockets. "Well, I, uh, guess we should, um, discuss you working here . . . if you want to come back, that is. I can put you back on the schedule tonight . . . if you want."

"Hm-m. Yes. That's a definite yes, but I need to make some arrangements."

"This afternoon easier?"

"Definitely. Let me go home and I can be back for the afternoon shift. That work?"

"Perfectly. I have a foot-deep box of invoices you can take care of.

"Then I'll come in at eleven. And thanks. I know we're on a good footing if you trust me enough to let me help you with that."

"What's not to trust?"

CHAPTER NINETEEN

Blue Raspberry

At midafternoon, the waterside was dotted with small groups, mostly families, spread across small sections of beach. Their colorful striped umbrellas claimed the few prime patches where the coarse yellow sand was not yet eroded to bedrock by nature's relentless drive to reshape the landscape. Van scanned faces and tried to match one with the picture. She could do this. Jean insisted that Ryan had fired her, and someone had to take the guitarist to the Phoenix and introduce him around. That was the last place Van wanted to be. After her fight with Ryan, things were awkward enough right now. So here she was, wandering on the beach, head shot in hand, searching for Mr. Russell. He had insisted on the meeting place—she chalked it up to a diva's sense of entitlement. She could put up with it for half an hour, and then she would take a few photographs.

Sage-hued Parkers, sailboats, and whitewashed deadrise work boats prowled from horizon to shore, following wind or whim. Close in, a Boston Whaler bobbed along, engine sputtering at a crawl as it trolled the nearest pier for crabs attached to the pilings, just below the surface. Squeals of excitement echoed over the water, and a long-poled net emerged from the depths with a blue crab entwined in its mesh. Van watched as panicked shrieks replaced squeals when the crab landed in the bottom of the boat instead of the catch basket, no doubt putting up its dukes, ready to fight for its life. She preferred the history and character of the old workhorse wooden boats, but Whalers were okay if you were into speed and style.

It didn't take her long to zero in on what always captured her heart: children. They darted back and forth, shooing cormorants into the water, unable to resist the urge to try to touch them despite their parents' warnings. Van laughed at their endless buckets of water, scooped half full in haste, and half of that sloshing out in transit, carried to finish sand castles that were hours in the building and took seconds to destroy. Such was youth: always dashing off in a hurry to the next great adventure. She used to be like that, but now she turned and tried to etch those images into her brain, even if it meant looking at people's backs as they moved on.

"Excuse me, Ms. Hardy?"

She turned around, and there he was, the photo made flesh: tall and lanky, with solicitous emerald eyes that exuded kindness. She dangled the picture in front of him. "Mr. Russell?"

"That's me. Is everything all right?"

She nodded. "Just people watching."

"One of my favorite pastimes. You can learn all kinds of things by watching people." He pointed at a mother and child hiding from the sun under a baby-blue umbrella. "That's what I'm talking about. There's a tale to tell there, don't you think?"

Dressed in a floppy white hat and oversize blue and yellow swim trunks, the little boy looked to be about three. They watched as the two played in the sand, laughing and chatting as they sifted sand through a blue plastic fish into a red bucket.

In an instant, it was the boy, his mother, and Van on the beach as all else receded into the background, like so much white noise. The scene brought back joyous memories for Van, but they were fleeting. The purity of the experience was quickly tainted by the past as pangs of loss squeezed her from inside. She longed for a little hand to hold, but she would never be a grandmother. A lover of lineage, surnames, and family trees, and her line would end with her. The meticulous records she had kept for those to come would, at best, be filed away in some dark corner, to be thrown away one day as worthless junk, no better than the useless assortment of papers saved by Mrs. Morgan, her hoarding neighbor.

She reached into her pocket and pulled out the card that had been like a thorn in her side all day. Baby animals in varying shades of blue. It was from Jay, one of James's friends, announcing the birth of his first child.

"Joyous news?" Hamelin asked.

Yes. A friend of my son's." And it was indeed wonderful news, but it hurt all the same, in a way that she could never expect others to understand. She wished him the best from the bottom of her heart, but that same heart also ached for what she would never have. Guilt piled onto her sense of loss, making it hurt like new again. She had meant to tell Ryan about the news, though she definitely wouldn't broach it now. Not that he would get emotionally caught up in it the way she was. He couldn't identify with anything related to his past life. Keeping him informed was more for Van's own benefit than for his. She had struggled alone with it all . . . until now. Then she remembered she wasn't alone. The guitarist was not quite as "diva" as she had expected, and she felt the sudden urge to explain it all.

Hamelin cocked an eyebrow. "Some things go without saying," he said with a nod. "I suppose we could stand here forever, but we should probably get on with the pressing business of the day." He cocked his head toward the men's restroom. "If you don't mind, I need to visit over here before we leave."

"I'll be right here." Van shoved the card back into its envelope and noticed with regret that the mother and child were packing up to leave. She wondered where they were off to and whether she would ever see them again. They didn't look like locals. The woman took the blue Popsicle out of the boy's sticky little hands and threw it away. She pulled a moist towelette out of a packet in her beach bag and wiped off his face and hands. Van half expected him to put up a fight—3-year-olds were good at that—but he surprised her by happily following his mother, pointing and asking question after question as she gathered up the bucket and other beach toys, and stowed the umbrella on their little plastic wagon. They headed back to the boardwalk, the woman patiently matching her child's little steps. And when they got there, he darted ahead, squealing as he ran, straight into the outstretched arms of a second woman coming down the walk. She stooped and scooped him up, showering kisses on his upturned face and sandy-blond hair. Livia Williams.

Livia hardly broke stride as she tossed her water bottle into the trash and toted the child back to the blue Ford Volt, its tires rubbing the curb as if it had been parked in a hurry. The boy clung to her, his arms wrapped around her neck, as she buckled him into a car seat and removed his hat.

He turned toward the bay one last time, and for the briefest instant, his eyes locked with Van's. Every nerve in her body fired in that one electrifying moment. He was James in perfect miniature. Her Nikon camera dangled, forgotten, from her neck as she stood burning, afraid to breathe or blink lest the vision disappear, a cruel trick played by her damaged psyche. The boy looked away, releasing her from his thrall, the spell broken. Livia was hardly in the passenger seat before the car began to pull away from the curb. Van started after them, but the loose sand under her feet slowed her. She watched, helpless, as they stopped at the end of the street, turned right, and headed out of town.

Van glanced over at the restrooms, but Hamelin was nowhere in sight. No picture and no witness. Still, she had seen what she had seen. She retraced the little boy's steps back to the trash can. As she suspected, the Popsicle stick was right on top. She fished it out, and the plastic bottle, too.

"I hate to interrupt a good thing. Ready to go now?"

Van banged her knee into the metal can. "Whoa, Mr. Russell. You sneaked up on me." She slid the stick and bottle into her camera bag and wished she could bury her hot, blushing face in the sand.

"No sneaking. You were otherwise engaged with the garbage. I believe we're both done here. Shall we go?"

Oh, God, just half an hour more. The transient guitar player was insignificant in the scheme of things. But Livia had a son—*James's* son—and if she intended to keep it a secret, she had just made a whopper of a mistake.

CHAPTER TWENTY

Bluesman

Van dumped the musician on the first reliable person she saw.

"Bennie, this is Hamelin Russell, the guitarist playing on Friday. Hamelin, meet Bennie Bertolini, bartender extraordinaire. Mr. Russell wanted to look the place over and have a chat with Mr. Thomas, if he's here. And I need a moment of your time, Bennie."

Bennie waved the glasses he was holding. "Mr. Russell. Stage and a mike set up over there. Marla was serenading us earlier. You'll be a nice change of pace. I'll let Mr. Thomas know you're looking for him. Van, hon, it's gonna be a moment."

"Text me first chance you get," she said. "Otherwise, I'll have to follow you around. It's *that* important." She pointed toward the front door. "Hamelin, I'll be right outside, waiting for you."

Ducking Hamelin's winning smile and invitation to stay, she slipped out the door without having to talk to anyone else.

Hamelin found Marla's beater acoustic on the chair, played a few chords, and had it tuned in seconds. Right there in the corner, he launched into a quiet rendition of "Cross Road Blues"—a virtuoso performance that only those closest to him could hear. Then, apparently satisfied, he acknowledged the smattering of applause, put the guitar back, and strode toward the prep area. Several steps into the kitchen, he met Ryan, bringing empties back to the bar.

Ryan backed away. "What are you doing here?"

"This is Hamelin Russell," Bennie yelled across the bar. "He'll be playing guitar in the Phoenix next week."

"Great bar here," Hamelin said, giving Ryan a nod and a scintillating smile.

"Pub, not a bar," said Ryan, looking peeved. "Mr. Russell, I wasn't expecting you."

"I thought you called and wanted me to come round," he said with a wink. "Something about papers in your office for me to sign. I must have misunderstood you. No problem, there's a baseball game I can still catch on channel four. I'll be out of your hair—I can see you're busy."

"No, wait." Ryan scrambled to put the steins down on the nearest empty table. "I *do* need you . . . to sign something." He motioned Hamelin into the back room and closed the door, positioning himself on the opposite side of his desk.

"It doesn't matter if the door is open or closed," Hamelin said.

"It's about *time* you showed some interest. Why didn't you tell me I knew Livia before? She was my fiancée?"

Hamelin nodded. "Informally so. The intentions were there."

"For God's sake, why didn't you tell me? You've been pushing us together ever since you got here."

"No, I haven't. You *should* be together, but I haven't pushed anything. You two have done it all on your own, as it should be. If I had told you, you would have felt a sense of obligation. Obligation has no place in this."

"But it would have explained so much."

"You have a bad habit of wanting all the answers from me. Stop trying to think it all through. If you love this woman, follow your heart. It's simple enough."

"It's never simple when you love two women."

"No experience in the love game—can't help you there. Ms. Hardy seems to have a good grasp of the situation. Maybe you should follow her lead, but then, you don't trust her anymore, do you? Seems as though nobody can trust anyone nowadays. As I've told you all along, I'm just an observer. I don't get involved. You said I wasn't paying you enough attention, so here I am. You're a very hard man to please, Mr. Thomas."

"An observer masquerading as a guitarist. What did you do with the real one?"

"You're looking at him. I'm not bad at all."

"An angelic guitarist. If I didn't know you better, I'd be intrigued."

"Not an angel—they don't like to get their hands dirty."

"Nonangel, then. And how did you become this nonangel, anyway?"

"So now you feel like bonding? Excellent. We can spend as long as you'd like." Hamelin pulled the broken side chair up to the desk. "As I said, I'm not an angel but not a mortal, either. Something . . . in between."

The desk phone buzzed and Ryan answered it, keeping one eye trained on the *nonangel*. "I'll be out in a minute," he said and hung up. "So, how do you earn your wings?" Ryan asked.

"Stop thinking silver screen and little bells. It's not like that. I am what I am. Not evil, not good. I just am. You're terrified of me, but I form deep personal bonds with the people I transport. They appreciate what I do for them. They don't fight me. In the moment between life and death, I'm right there, holding their hand."

"You are alarmingly omniscient and you treat human life like a business asset to be collected and deposited into some netherworld bank. You are shallow, calculating, coldly detached, and utterly lacking the sadness and melancholy to play the blues. What's not to be terrified of?"

"Not at all. Playing the blues is a religious experience for me. Don't you know your Bible? The blue note is a prayer to God in three persons and all his works, the five loaves at the Bethsaida, and seven—divine perfection? I could go on and on; the connections are endless. When played right, there is deep meaning and soulful experience—like the rosary, counting beads, or any other form of devotion. While I may be above, and indifferent to, the human plight, I can experience both humanity and the divine through the sorrows of others."

"Then you feed off the emotions of people."

Hamelin shook his head. When I collect someone, I share their sadness, fear and emotional pain . . . to make it easier. They are more than willing to leave everything behind and follow me into the next life. The emotions . . . well, they just sit there not being used until I want to play."

"So you're stealing the emotions of the dead?" Ryan shuddered. "Charming."

"I'm not *stealing.* It's recycling. They have no need of it when they've passed on. Existence becomes something entirely different."

"I pulled your demo, Ryan said, studying Hamelin closely. "Blues. I inherited a sizable collection from my namesake—David "Honeyboy" Edwards, Charley Patton, Pinetop Perkins—and I've studied the remarkable career of Robert Johnson. If I'd closed my eyes, I would have sworn that was Johnson himself playing your demo. How is it you play like a man who's been dead for almost eighty years?"

Hamelin seemed to warm to the conversation. He locked his hands behind his head and stretched his long legs out in front of him. "I met him once, summer of 'thirty-eight, when I came for him. We had a handshake deal. I gave him a few extra hours in exchange for teaching me how to play—not perfectly, mind you. Unlike the great Johnson, I wasn't willing to trade *my* soul for perfection, but I can play close enough. Perfection died a few hours later, with the acquisition of Mr. Johnson's bartered soul."

Ryan shuddered again. "You're lying again. That never happened."

Hamelin shrugged. "I also pipe and fiddle."

The desk phone buzzed again. Ryan ignored it. "How *old* are you?"

"Old," Hamelin said, with a gleam in his eyes.

"This is appalling. You *do* terrify me. With you, death is so cut and dried, matter-of-fact. You don't seem to sense any of the repercussions. Death guts the people left behind—just levels them. Sometimes, it completely destroys them. How can you be so cavalier? And everyone else acts like you're the most charming guy they ever met." Ryan shook his head. "I don't get it."

"Because I probably am. You'd see that if you didn't feel compelled to fight me. I tried to establish a rapport with you the first night we met. You refused. My existence is dedicated to providing a bridge between this world and the next. You see me as something I'm not, and fail to see me as I am: a benevolent creature dedicated to preserving world order. As in any other form of commerce, I can't afford to become personally involved, but I do synchronize my personality with my charges and their significant others. Thankfully, I am a merciful service provider." He smiled broadly.

"You're a bullshit provider. I'll wager you pulled wings off flies when you were alive. You were the corner bully. How'd you ever get into heaven?"

Hamelin scooted his chair back and got up. "No more info. Girlfriend number one is waiting out on the curb for me. She showed me the boardwalk earlier, and I promised to walk her home—lots of evil lurking out there, don't you know."

"I don't want her involved with you. I'll walk her." He made a move for the door.

"Not necessary," Hamlin said, fixing him with his stare. "She has nothing to fear from me. Besides, she's avoiding you." He cocked an eyebrow. "You understand all about awkwardness with girlfriends, right? Besides, you've already involved her. It might have been smarter to leave her out of all this and not move into the pickle boat house. If you could let go of her and live life the way it was supposed to be, we could perhaps part ways."

Ryan walked back to the desk and jabbed an index finger at Hamelin. "That's unfair. I didn't ask to be here living *this* life. 'Supposed to be' doesn't count anymore. If it did, I would never have died. I would have lived out my years as James Hardy. There's a reason for all this."

"Face it. *You*," Hamelin said, pointing at Ryan in turn, "are a person of little significance, squandering the gift."

"Squandering the . . ." Ryan scowled. "Where are you getting this?"

"I know what I need to know."

"Not saying you're right, but playing along, what would I be doing if I wasn't *squandering the gift*?"

"Life is all about searching for your own answers. Good ones for oneself, one's fellow man. And they're often the simplest, most direct answers—ones that come quietly if you open your heart and allow them in. What good would it do you if I gave away all the answers? You're going to take to heart only what you work out for yourself. Suppose I gave you the wrong answer and you spent all your time trying to conform to *that*? What a waste. Redemption day would come, and how much better off would you be?" Hamelin asked, raising his hands, palms up. "*S.O.L.* better is how, right?"

Ryan paced toward the door and then back again to the desk, clenching and unclenching his fists as he sorted out what Hamelin said. "Of course, you would never give me misleading info, would you, Hamelin?"

"Of course not."

Ryan scoffed. "Because you don't know, do you?"

"I know what I need to know," he repeated. "If you haven't made your life purposeful by now, perhaps you should just chalk it up to failure. Don't expect others to bail you out. Keep your eye on the prize."

"I'm not sure what the prize is anymore."

The office door creaked open, and Livia poked her head inside. "What prizes? Pardon me for interrupting, Ryan. Just wanted to let you know I'm here."

"Okay, thanks for coming in on short notice. I'll be out in a minute. Mr. Russell and I are almost done, I think." He looked to Hamelin. "Aren't we?"

"Yes, it's all progressing as it should," Hamelin said while gazing at Livia.

She smiled and offered her hand. "I don't believe we've met. I'm Livia Williams."

Hamelin shoved his hands down in his pockets. "Yes, I know. Sorry, I never shake on the first date, Ms. Williams, but it is nice to finally meet you. Ryan has said nice things about you. I feel I know you."

"Oh?" Livia flushed and looked at Ryan. I'll just be out here," she murmured, and closed the door. Seconds later, it opened again. "Oh, and, Ryan, thanks." She waved a little blue toy boat at him. "Someday, it'll be full size." She closed the door again.

Ryan took his confusion out on Hamelin. "Would it have killed you to shake hands with her?"

Hamelin rolled his eyes. "Haven't you had enough coddling for a while? I see by the aurascope, you're running rosy. Work a little harder, my friend. The stakes haven't changed."

Ryan watched Hamelin join Van on the sidewalk. He had never seen her face more drawn and haggard. Hamelin grazed her elbow, and to Ryan's surprise, she didn't flinch or recoil from his touch. She might now be involved, but with luck, only peripherally so.

CHAPTER TWENTY-ONE

Designs and Motivation

Van relaxed a little as Bennie parked along the dirt pathway. He didn't seem eager to get out of his car in the middle of the woods on the sketchy side of town, but he had agreed to meet her and solemnly promised to do it discreetly. So here they were.

"What's so wrong that we couldn't talk at the Phoenix?" he said. "We discussing Ryan?"

Van patted the empty space next to her on the felled tree trunk she was sitting on. Her gaze returned to the acorns at her feet. She tossed one toward a squirrel clinging to the trunk of a nearby oak. "Whatever would make you think that?"

Bennie put his handkerchief down across the trunk and gingerly sat down next to her. "Lots of changes since I went on vacation. New staff in, old staff out, live entertainment . . . Hey, one of 'em upsetting you?"

"Old staff, fine. Live entertainment, fine. New staff, *problem.* The problem has a name: Livia. And before you start assuming anything, it's not what you think. When she first came to town, she told me she had dated my son, James, and wanted to meet me. I believed her. She sounded sincere. But I'm beginning to wonder if she had other motives in coming here. She's latched right on to Ryan. I don't get her—don't trust her, either. I think she's a problem for him, only he doesn't see it yet."

"Van, hon, the first thing I learned as a bartender was, don't get involved. Second thing I learned was, don't even *think* about whatever it is you're not getting involved in. Sure, I'm a good listener. Everybody's got a story, but I don't take it all home with me. Ryan's an adult, and he's also my boss. I don't keep track of him, and I don't make judgments about how he lives his life."

She shifted her eyes to him. "And how would you feel if he cheated on me?"

"Has he?"

"Well, no." She dissected one of the acorns in her hand and threw a piece at the squirrel.

"Then what are we really talking about here?" Bennie's eyes darted toward the squirrel. Bolder now, it crept closer across the leaf-strewn ground. "Please don't encourage that thing," Bennie said, standing up. "Can't they carry rabies?"

Van shooed the squirrel away with a wave of her arms, and thrust her handful of acorns at Bennie. She wiped away a tear that threatened to roll down her cheek. "I saw her on the beach today. Bennie, this woman has a kid, and I'm telling you, the resemblance to my son, James, is uncanny. If he's not James's son, I'm the queen of Sheba. She must have been pregnant when he died. I'll bet she never even bothered to tell him. And now she's brought him here, and not one word about him. I'm his *grandmother,* for God's sake! What kind of person does that? She has designs on Ryan, I'm telling you. He's perfect husband material if you're a single young woman with a child to look after. How did she think she was going to get away with this? One look at that kid, and I see James all over him. I'll take her to court. And I'll get custody, too. She doesn't have the right to do that. How can—"

Bennie dropped the acorns and brushed his hand off on his pant leg. He sat back down, wrapped his arm around her and pulled her close. "Van, if this is her son, sadly enough, she *does* have the right. But slow down for a second. Take a breath. Let's talk this through because you're jumping to all kinds of conclusions. *If* he's James's son, that's probably why she didn't mention him to you. Put yourself in her shoes. As a mother, wouldn't that be your biggest fear: that the grandmother or some other relative might want custody or badger you for visitation rights? Would you have exposed your son to risks like that with a woman you didn't know? Not a chance. On the other hand, single women do adopt and become single parents. It's possible, right?"

She squeezed her eyes closed and massaged her temples with her fingertips, trying not to cry. "No," she said in a trembling voice, "I'm telling you, the kid is a dead ringer. There's no doubt in my mind. I'm going to fight her, but I need help. Please, Bennie." She fixed her tear-filled eyes on him.

Bennie grimaced. "First off, consider not doing *that*," he said, shaking his head. "I think it's the wrong approach. Reach out peacefully to her. Befriend her. She deserves that much if she's the mother of your grandchild. And don't spook her. If what you say is true, and you scare her, she could take off and you'll *never* find her. The two women James loved should be able to find some common ground and get along." He cocked his head and gave her a gentle squeeze. "He wouldn't have wanted it any other way, would he?"

"Oh, Bennie, logic doesn't cut it here. Emotions aren't logical, and you know it."

"No, they're not. That's why you asked me here, right? Cooler heads, and all that?"

Van nodded and went back to studying acorns. "Will you help me figure this woman out—if not for my sake, for Ryan's? We have no idea what personal agenda is driving her."

Bennie sighed and gave her another squeeze. "Van, you know the answer to that. All I'm gonna say is, be absolutely sure what you're doing."

"Like DNA?"

"And all the consequences, intended and otherwise. Every action makes ripples, and you can't know where they all go. What turns out okay for you could be devastating for somebody else. Anticipate the ripples and act accordingly. Proof is one thing; action's something else."

"You and Ryan have been close for a while. You know all about HYA and what—"

"Whoa!" Bennie pulled his arm away. "I never get involved in Ryan's business. I run his pub, period."

"Wait," she said, grabbing his hand. "Don't get angsty and leave. I understand where you're coming from, and I'm not asking you to violate any kind of 'bro code,' but I need you to do something for me. If I can get this child's DNA and get a sample of my son's, could you . . . *would* you pass it on to someone who can tell me if they're a match? No specifics. I don't have to know anything else—just that. I swear Ryan will never find out you helped me. It'll be between you and me. I'll take it to my grave. Please, Bennie. I have a right to know if I have a grandson. If it matches, I'll slow down and think this all through before I do anything. I don't want anybody to be unhappy or feel threatened."

"I . . . don't know. It goes against pretty much everything I stand for."

"This baby needs to know there are other people here for him."

"You need to make sure your motives are pure, or somebody's gonna get hurt here—maybe you, Van. Take a hard look at what you really want. You want this cute, duplicitous young woman away from Ryan, or do you want a relationship with your grandson *if it can be proved* that's who he is? If the child is not your son's, where's the problem?"

"You haven't been back long enough to see that those motives go hand in hand, Bennie. Watch her. You'll see."

He stood up and picked his handkerchief up and shook it out before stuffing it in his pants pocket. "No promises. When you get the stuff, you get back to me. *Then* I'll make the decision. Till then, no promises, okay?"

Van threw her arms around him. "Okay, thanks, Bennie. Does she work this week?"

"She's not on the schedule, but she did come in today. Ryan told me to take her off. Didn't say why or what schedule she'll be working. Seeing as how he only hired her temporarily, I can't really say what's on his mind. He was gonna ask her to stick around a while longer. Maybe that's up in the air. Don't know."

"Oh, God, she can't up and leave now! If you hear anything, will you let me know? I don't want to hurt anybody, but the idea of James's son being out there and me not being a part of his life . . . that would tear me up inside. And this woman, she's despicable."

Bennie put his hands up. "We're gonna stay focused, right? Right. Don't make up new problems before we've solved the old ones." He glanced around them. "Okay, I'm leaving before that furry beast comes back. Call me when you have something and we can meet again. Make it someplace *indoors* next time."

Bennie wasted no time in returning to his car. As Van watched him drive away, she realized it was a cosmic event when Bennie gave advice. Even though he hadn't promised to run the tests, he was one of the most principled men Van had ever met, and he would do the right thing in the end. The DNA on the Popsicle stick would be proof enough the little boy was a Hardy, and once Ryan found out the child was his, he would never forgive the deceit. She pulled out her phone and did the one thing she would have sworn she would never do in a million years.

"Hello, Richard, it's Vanessa . . ."

CHAPTER TWENTY-TWO

Demon Unleashed

If Ryan James was going to get depressed about the first girlfriend and obsess about the second, he could do it on his own time. Ryan Llwellyn fought through the murk toward the light, struggling to raise his own consciousness. He bobbed to the surface and seized alertness and control from Ryan James. *Too bad about the betrayal, James. Never put your trust in anyone else, especially a woman.* He didn't mind knocking boots with them, but he never stayed long enough to become entwined in their little melodramas. They were invariably clingy time wasters.

He had no inkling why he was fighting for control of his own body. Maybe he had gone crackers. He had seen it before. Simmons—a stable guy on Monday, blowing his brains out Tuesday because he couldn't take it anymore. Or Mortie, a childhood friend, locked away at Saint Mark's because he couldn't distinguish between what he lived and what he dreamed—talking to himself all day long as he tried to make sense of it all. Ryan Llewellyn had been thinking—God, he had nothing but time for that—about how best to cope with it all. Owens was right. Those who went up fast burned out fast. The key to maintaining alertness and control of his own body was pacing. When he had exploded all over Owens, he had used up too much energy and lost control. By contrast, James Hardy's control seemed insurmountable when his adrenaline kicked in. So if he took things slower, more methodically, he might be able to maintain dominance over Hardy longer—*permanently,* if things went according to plan. The previous Thursday night's nine hours of unbridled freedom was just the beginning.

His path was clear: coax HYA back out of its cautious wait-and-see attitude and tie up a few loose ends. With Ryan James mooning about, today was the perfect day to execute plans. He rummaged through the Phoenix's office, and the heap of papers on the desk eventually yielded the address and telephone number he needed: Michael Flanagan, Senior Assistant State's Attorney, Calvert County, Maryland. He stuffed the buff-colored five-thousand-for-fifteen-bucks business card in his shirt pocket and took off for Frederickton.

Ryan Llewellyn ignored the "Open" button on the control panel and let the elevator slam in the face of the old man on crutches hobbling to board. There were other elevators, and anyway, maybe the old geezer would be inspired to move a little livelier next time. He rode up to the third floor and entered the state's attorney's office, bypassed the reception desk, and headed straight down the hallway toward the private offices.

"Sir? Sir, I have to check you in." The slight auburn-haired woman at the desk scrambled to cut him off. "I have to buzz them before you can—"

Ryan Llewellyn kept walking. "Mr. Danielson is expecting me."

He was intercepted by a well-dressed man coming from the other direction. "Mr. Thomas? I'm Shelton Danielson." He offered his hand.

Ryan Llewellyn ignored it. "I won't take up your time, Mr. Danielson. I'm on a tight schedule today."

"I understand completely," Danielson said, withdrawing his hand. "Sometimes, things can't wait. As I told you on the phone, Mr. Flanagan's Monday schedule is tight, and he's tied up in meetings, but he said to make sure you get taken care of. I'm in the loop. Unfortunately, the IT technician has chased me out of my office to set up a new computer, but we can find another place." Danielson escorted him past several doorways before ducking into an unoccupied room at the end of the hall. "We can talk in here. Have a seat," he said, flipping on the light switch, although the conference room was already bright with natural light streaming in from the windows flanking the left side of the room. A series of framed inspirational prints promoting teamwork and innovation hung on the walls to the right, and the center of the room was dominated by an oak conference table and coordinating maroon upholstered chairs. "Beautiful weather, huh?" he asked, glancing out the window.

Ryan Llewellyn shook his head and sat down. "No chitchat. Things are heating up with the Hector Young case. That's what I'm hearing, but I haven't heard anything from *you* lately."

Danielson pulled out a chair and sat down next to him. "Well, that's true. There *has* been sudden movement in the case. Overworked, underpaid," he said, fanning through the stack of folders in his hand. "Somebody's giving you some good intel. If they're on our staff, I'm gonna be all over them."

"Not from your office. What's the story?"

"There's been nothing but legal stalling and pussyfooting around until the last few days. Hector Young is spending some serious dough on lawyers. They're good—at gumming up the legal process. Sometimes, I feel like they have deep . . . you-know-what on somebody. Anyways, we've finally managed to shake things free, and we're expecting a date for trial anytime now. Now you know everything we know." Danielson smiled and leaned back in his chair, crossing his legs at the ankles.

"I don't want this to proceed to trial, and I don't want to testify."

"Come again?" Danielson said, uncrossing his legs and giving him a blank stare. "I'm not following you. You've been *driving* us. You've been a very motivated witness in this case. Young's a nutcase. We can nail him on any number of charges: arson, felonious assault, attempted murder . . ." Danielson pinched the top of his nose and took a breath. He sat up straight, both feet on the floor, and continued in a softer, more measured voice. "Listen, this is nerve-racking, hard on witnesses. You're the victim here. It's traumatic. We understand. But we're going to be there with you every step of the way to put this bastard away—if not for good, then long enough that he'll be pissing in a bedpan and shuffling out the front door of prison with a walker. Cold feet? No problem. We can handle it."

"Listen carefully one more time. *Not* testifying."

Danielson cleared his throat as he twisted the folders in his hands into a tight roll, and he studied the carpet a moment before he spoke again. "Without a cooperating witness, it's going to be difficult, if not impossible, to present enough evidence to convict him. We don't have a case without you, and Hector Young deserves what's coming—"

"No, and if you subpoena me, I'll plead the Fifth."

"Privilege against self-incrimination? But *why*? What could you possibly be afraid of? Unless you haven't been forthright with us." He stood up, sighed, and tossed the curled folders onto the table. "Have you discussed any of this with Mr. Flanagan? No? Maybe you don't understand the extent of this, Mr. Thomas." He loosened his navy tie and unbuttoned the top button of his shirt before settling his hands on his hips. "This case has been hanging for weeks, and you'll pardon my French, but you're gonna pull this shit now? Do you realize the man-hours we've put into this? This is open and shut with you testifying. Important people are going to explode all over us if we don't nail Young. You need to speak with Mr. Flanagan directly. We're not going to drop prosecution because you're having second thoughts. Hector Young tried to kill you, and the state of Maryland is going to hold him responsible for his actions."

"Answer one question for me," Ryan Llewellyn asked as his gaze moved from the necktie to Danielson's hand sweeping nervously through the prosecutor's hair. "Maybe I've gotten a little confused."

Danielson brightened hopefully. "Yes, of course! What's got you confused?"

Do I have the right, in this case, to plead the Fifth?"

"Yes, but—"

"Shh, as I thought. Simple question, simple answer. The honest tax-paying citizens of Maryland are paying you to do more important things."

"Quite frankly, it's not enough if you're going to pull this." Danielson yanked his tie off and tossed it on the table.

Ryan Llewellyn pulled out his wallet. "How much?"

"Oh, for Christ's sake, were it that simple!" Danielson said, shaking his head as he dropped back down in his chair. He took a deep breath and studied his client a moment. Then he pulled his chair closer. "What's really going on here?" Tell me. It never leaves this office. Attorney-client privilege. I . . . we can't represent you if we don't know what's going on in your head."

Ryan Llewellyn put his wallet back. "You don't need to be inside my head. I have nothing else to tell you. I want this over with. It's gone too long. I don't want it hanging over my head anymore."

"It's not going away if we let him walk," Danielson said quietly. "You think he's not going to come after you or some other innocent person or, God forbid, someone close to you? Have you thought of that? We need to ensure that the good citizens of Maryland are safe from people like Hector Young."

"I've known Hector a long time. Things . . . emotions got a little out of hand." Ryan shrugged. "I believe we can come to a common understanding about what happened. I wouldn't even be surprised to see us resume our working relationship. This is a personal issue, and the legal system is now getting in the way." He stood up, grabbed Danielson's limp hand, and pumped it once. "Make it happen."

Danielson got to his feet, wiping his forehead with the back of his hand. "I'm obviously not explaining things well. I'll go pull Flanagan out of his meeting. Quite frankly, he'll have a piece of my backside if I don't. You sit right here."

"I have to go. Just let him know what I've decided, and we're all done here."

Ryan Llewellyn left Danielson standing in the corridor, thunderstruck, ready to sprint to his boss's office the moment Ryan was out of view. *Let him run.* Time was short. As soon as he had Hector Young back in the fold, he could get down to business. Getting Hector to do what he needed done would be the easy part.

All the elevators were traveling up. Ryan Llewellyn stabbed the down button again. If he opted for the stairs, the bell would ding and he would have to hotfoot it back. To hell with the elevator. He opened the door to the stairwell.

"Mr. Thomas! Wait, Mr. Thomas." It was Flanagan, flying out the office door with his suit coat half on, Danielson following closely in his wake. "A word, Mr. Thomas," he said breathlessly.

Ryan Llewellyn cocked an eyebrow and waited.

"Mr. Danielson told me about your decision," he said, smoothing out his hair and straightening his tie. Please, come back inside. We need to discuss this. There are complexities here that I'm sure you'll want to consider. Won't you come back inside for a moment?" He swept his hand toward his office.

The elevator bell dinged, and the door opened. Ryan let go of the staircase door, sidled past the two men, and hopped into the elevator. He hit the button and calmly watched the door close in Flanagan's face. But Flanagan was as quick. He stuck his foot in the gap and bounced the moving doors back open again. Shooting Danielson a glare that froze him where he stood, he joined Thomas in the elevator.

Neither spoke as the doors closed and they began their descent. Then abruptly, Flanagan leaned forward and pulled the stop button.

"I hope you'll pardon the extreme measure to get your attention. Obviously, whatever is said here is only for your ears and mine. What the fuck do you think you're doing? The *Fifth*? Really?"

Ryan Llewellyn leaned back against the wall of the elevator and checked his watch. "I've explained it all already. I don't want—"

"Oh, we're way beyond what *you want,* Mr. Thomas. It's all about the big, hungry legal system now. Justice needs to be served its big, meaty portion. I need a conviction. That would make a lot of people happy—the *right* people happy. If not, I'm going to look foolish, and I've worked much too hard for you to put me in that position in the public eye."

"This has gone on too long. I'm not testifying. I'll sign whatever you need me to sign to invoke my rights. Draw it up; send it to me. Now, if you don't mind," Ryan said, nodding to the control panel, "tempus fugit."

"Young is guilty as hell. I don't know what you're smoking, but if it's got you thinking either of you is walking away from this scot-free and leaving my people to clean up the mess, you probably should think about cutting back. I am not dropping this prosecution."

"Mr. Flanagan," Ryan Llewellyn said, drawing himself up to his full height but avoiding eye contact, "you have a brother-in-law, Miles Booker?"

Flanagan's eyes narrowed. "Why?"

"New money, runs an international shipping company out of Baltimore Harbor—isn't that him? Does a lot of business with a New York company called United Trans-World Commerce. That would be the old money—*HYA* old money. Tell me, Mr. Flanagan, will the voters be sympathetic when they discover that your family is rolling in all that *old* money?"

Flanagan punched the button, and the elevator resumed its descent. "Don't threaten me, you goddamn punk. You know all about old money. You're a crook like Young, and it shouldn't be hard to find something about you that isn't kosher. I would imagine a smart inquiry would be to the state liquor board." How, exactly, did you set up business so fast?"

The elevator doors opened to the lobby, and Ryan Llewellyn got off. "See you on election day," he murmured as he walked away. Flanagan could threaten all he wanted. Only desperate men threatened. And Ryan Llewellyn didn't give a shit about liquor licenses; he had no long-term plans to hang around Nevis.

"Sooner." Flanagan pounded his fist into the elevator side panel as the door closed.

CHAPTER TWENTY-THREE

Bully and the Bastard

Ryan Llewelyn moved on to item two on his list. He put the extra-large soda down on the convenience-store counter, then pushed the hot dog under the condiment dispenser. Chili and nacho cheese slopped out, filling the bottom of the cardboard container. He dropped a five on the counter and walked out without waiting for change.

Item number three had him off to the Phoenix, where he found the aurascope in a corner of the office beneath a couple of days' dirty laundry. Pinkish-red sand was flowing at an alarming rate. Ryan Llewellyn centered it in the middle of the desk blotter and sat down in the chair behind the desk. "Son of a bitch!" he growled. He cursed God, the devil, and Hamelin Russell with every colorful blasphemy he could think of.

Hamelin spoke quietly behind him. "I have never heard such language in all my years, and I would never have expected to hear the likes from you, Ryan James."

Ryan Llewellyn grinned. "I knew you couldn't ignore that." He pushed back in his chair and propped his feet up on the desk. "What's up?"

Hamelin stopped in mid stride.

"No, don't stop. Come on in. So we're clear and don't waste each other's time, I have you figured out. You're a bully with no authority. You're not allowed to make decisions on your own, and as I see it, you have no job here."

Hamelin's face lit up in one big glowing smile, and the air around him shimmered. "Ryan *Llewellyn* Thomas! Well met! I've been waiting for you." He approached and offered his hand.

Ryan Llewelyn shrank away from the offering. "Not a chance."

Hamelin laughed. "Worth a try. I was beginning to think that no amount of baiting would coax you out." He looked skyward. "Thank you, Jesus. "I think we've both had enough of the cat and mouse—all that lurking and hiding. Where's Ryan James? And Hoffa?" he asked, checking under the desk.

Ryan Llewellyn picked up a pencil and doodled several connected circles along the border of the blotter. "Dark and deep. Momentarily called away, trying to cope with some heavy emotional issues," he said, laughing at his own wit. "Not one of his finer moments, but it allows me some roaming time. The dog had to pee, so I let him out," he said, nodding toward the pub's back door.

"Without a leash?"

"He's a biter. Now, let's skip the small talk," he said, pointing the pencil at Hamelin. "My time is precious. We both know you can't collect me without taking James Hardy along, too, and you're not authorized to do that. He's under the ludicrous impression there's a higher authority that has given him a second chance to achieve something special. Crazy, for sure, but who are you to mess with that? Surely, you knew *I* wasn't going to make it easy for you, that you couldn't do your little song and dance and I would just follow after you like some spellbound child. What's a screw-up like you to do, Hamelin? Quite the quandary."

Hamelin walked over and closed the office door. When he turned around, his eyes were bright and shining. "I'm going to love the shocked look on your face when I yank you right out of that body—when you're guard is down and you're riding high, thinking you have us all beaten. It'll be fun. *Soon,*" he said with a smirk.

"Don't think so. We both know you're powerless right now."

"I would have had you the very first day if you hadn't walked Vanessa back to the pickle boat house. I could feel your fear and confusion. Do you think you're the first person to put up a fuss and try to beat fate? Here's *your* news flash: there's no gaming this system. I have never failed to collect a soul I've been sent for, and I've dealt with far craftier than you. Time is not really a factor when it comes to eternal damnation. I can wait. Your appointment to burn is sealed."

Ryan Llewellyn took his foot and shoved a side chair in Hamelin's direction. "Take a load off, then, because there's no such thing as *never.* Admit it: as long as James Hardy and I coexist in here, you're stuck."

Hamelin walked over and sat down. "And so are you, my friend. You're *dying* to get rid of him, aren't you? With him in there, you're not free to do anything you want. Oh, a few calls here and there, appointments made and broken. HYA is wondering what your problem is. Give up and save us both a fight. I know you better than you know yourself: all your insecurities, bad decisions, indecisions. Don't be so brash. Your voice may be full of bluster, but your weary face reflects the true state of affairs. You can't fight a war on two fronts. Ryan James is giving you a run for your money. Fool that you are, you underestimate him. Big mistake. What happens when he gains control again, as he inevitably will? In the long run, good always bests evil. You'll outwit yourself in the end, as arrogant asses always do."

"Nice try, Hamelin, but I'm not going anywhere. The longer I keep you tied up here, the more off schedule you get, and the more pissed off your superiors will be. Sooner or later, they'll pull you out of here, and I'll be free to do what I want. But hey, no hard feelings here. It's tough for me to admit, but I actually owe you one. If you hadn't come here stirring things up, I'd never have resurfaced. *Ripples,* I think you called them.

"And *this* thing . . ." Ryan Llewellyn picked up the aurascope, its pinkish-red contents almost entirely spilled into the bottom half. "This is no friend of *mine.* Its helping you sort me out so you can pluck my soul out of this body and complete your assignment. But you're clueless about what is Ryan James and what is Ryan Llewellyn. And it apparently escapes you that there *is* good in me." Ryan Llewellyn tossed the scope gently back and forth between his hands, testing its weight, eyeing Hamelin's reaction. "What a silly, silly toy." He drilled it like a football across the room, where it hit the wall with a surprisingly loud boom, exploding into thousands of slivers of blue, red, and magenta shrapnel.

Hamelin stiffened, eyes flashing with an unearthly fire, and the room lights flickered. Decanters on the side table bubbled and boiled and fired their stoppers at the ceiling. Chestnut, copper, and amber liquid spewed upward and burst into savage, hungry flames that licked along the ceiling, and the desk jittered as the floor quivered and shook. Ryan Llewellyn sat wide-eyed and rigid until the shaking ceased and the flames snuffed themselves out, leaving a trail of scorch marks on the drywall.

Hamelin's eyes dimmed, and calm returned. "That changes nothing. It's all in motion now. You can't change the playing field."

"Tell me about this field," Ryan Llewellyn taunted. "Like the pickle boat house. I'm intrigued with all the fuss over this squalid little beach house."

"The bonds of family and love run strong there. That house has a serenity that even I don't dare disrupt. Ryan James is at his strongest when he's inside—deep associations and connections. After all, isn't that what mortal life is all about? And you're partially correct: there is no way I can separate your and Ryan James's spirits inside there. But as you've also noticed, you have no place there, either. As long as he lives there, you lose. Your existence will be reduced to erratic, disconnected moments stolen in his moments of weakness—weakness that, by the way, will ebb and fade as he finds his destined place in this second life. And it's not only *places* that will help defeat you—it's people, too, and the bonds they feel and create with each other, because you have no concept of them or of how powerful they can be."

"And so you're throwing all these people at me why—so that I can exemplify good citizenship?" He snickered. "Ryan James will never walk away from Van or take off with that hot little number behind the bar. If he was going to, why would he still be living in her house? And as long as I'm meddling, he'll never get away from HYA." He tapped his head. "I know these things—inside track, remember? I'm going to destroy anything and anyone that gets in my way. That will be on your shoulders. This Williams woman—you want her and James together? I can help that along. And I could kill her with my bare hands . . . during sex . . . on our honeymoon." His dark eyes danced.

"Oh, stuff it. I'm not impressed with your silly tripe. Nothing you can say will shock me. Ryan James would never let you harm her. You said so yourself; you're in his head. You're terrified of their relationship, and *she* will be the one to bring you down."

"You're a betting man. How much?"

Hamelin shook his head. "No bet. Too easy, not to mention a conflict of interest—although the thought of humbling you is tempting. I also wouldn't bet on performance issues if Pasadena is any indication."

"I don't drink anymore."

Hamelin chuckled. "See what smugness will get you? Be very afraid. You know only what Ryan James knows. What's out there that he hasn't figured out yet? Huh, Mr. Know-it-all? Chew on that a while. But this is idle chitchat. Why are you letting Hector Young off the hook? If he comes after Ryan James, he comes after you. Surely, you recognize the problem here."

"The only person who hates David Bishop more than I do is Hector Young. I need him. Let's leave it at that."

Hamelin gave a weary sigh.

"Whatever. Hamelin, as long as we're dishing out advice, here's some for you. Stop getting personally involved. As you said at the beginning, this is just business, nothing personal. You don't need to get huffy and break up the joint, or take your marbles and go home. I'm enjoying our little whatever-this-is. Don't overextend yourself and spoil it. And to show there's no animosity on my part, how about a little bonding before I trade for something a little less ostentatious?" He pulled a set of Porsche 911 Carrera keys out of his pocket and dangled them in front of Hamelin.

Hamelin's eyes lit up like a Christmas tree. "Bonding? There's not a chance I'm leaving Ryan James to your devices, and it has never been more personal. Ryan James deserves a life without you lurking about, waiting to cast your evil shadow whenever you find him in a vulnerable moment."

"Don't worry about any tug-of-war between Ryan James and me. Once I figure out how to get rid of that dumb little shit, it's going to be just me."

"You don't understand the state of affairs here, do you?" Hamelin pulled out his trusty notepad. "Ryan Llewellyn Thomas, born in Delaware on July twenty-first, 1977. Mother Ellen Marie Seagle, Father Edward Michael Thomas." He flipped to a dog-eared tab in the back. "Hit by a bus on May seventeenth, 2010, resulting in injuries that proved fatal. Has it never occurred to you that you're *dead,* Mr. Thomas, your soul fragmented from here to hell? It's impossible for you to maintain control."

Ryan Llewellyn rolled his eyes. "Seriously?" He shook the key ring again.

"This changes nothing," Hamelin said, snatching the keys. "Gas?"

"More than enough."

CHAPTER TWENTY-FOUR

Whore's Shoes and Hand Grenades

It was like a nightmare, but he wasn't sleeping. Pressure like a great weight made breathing difficult as an unseen force held him down. He flailed upward, but the light-reflecting surface was still far above him. He pushed again, and with a jolt and a gasp, his face broke the surface. Ryan James awoke on the passenger side of the 911 Carrera, slumped up against a window smeared wet with saliva. He was in the far back corner of the Phoenix back lot, feet covered in empty potato-chip bags, heels kicking against empty Dr. Pepper bottles shoved under the seat. A scarlet satin stiletto heel jabbed against his back, and the keys still dangled from the ignition. His pride and joy looked as if it had been parked by a beginning student driver—backed in diagonally across two spaces. Ryan didn't know whether to cry or just kill the party responsible. The car was covered in mud, with half a red azalea bush poking out of the right rear wheel well. A black garbage bag was caught on the exhaust pipe and half shredded from miles dragging the pavement. Ryan slipped in the rear door of the pub and threw his keys down on the desk. What the hell was going on? God only knew what had gone down last night, but it had to be Hamelin. Having him around was like going to bed cradling a live grenade with the pin missing. He pulled out his phone.

"There a problem, Ryan?" Bennie stood at his office door, his forehead etched with deep creases.

"With *me*? What could possibly be wrong?"

"I've been talking to you since you walked in the door—three questions in a row, and you haven't heard a word I've said."

Ryan sighed. "Sorry, Bennie. No, I wasn't listening. Life's a little complicated right now. What did you need?"

"I think the bigger question is, what do *you* need? You look exhausted."

"I feel like I pulled an all-nighter. Couldn't sleep . . . finally ended up dozing on the couch," he lied. "I might have imbibed a little too much. I wasn't . . . in here last night, doing anything crazy, was I?"

"Stop the drinking, bud. You weren't ever in here that I saw."

Ryan nodded. "Apparently why I don't remember. So, enough about me. What's up?"

"Watch the front? Marla's late again and I can't be two places at once. Flying Dog is due any minute, and I've got to go kiss their patootie just right. Still can't get anywhere with Butch and Lee, so I thought I'd butter up one of the few friends we have left."

"Of course. Go do whatever. I'll keep tabs."

"Ryan? I don't want to know any details, but there's a . . . a woman out front asking for you. She's . . . well, she's . . . Ah, hell, there's a hooker out front asking for you, and I don't want any more information than that."

"A *what*!" Ryan sneaked a peek through the doorway. The Phoenix was open to drawing in new customers from all walks of life, but a blue-eye-shadowed, ruby-lipped floozy with a skin-tight skirt and a barely concealed pair of double Ds didn't really fit the profile. Mickey, the delivery guy from Trout's Produce, pushed back the brim of his Baltimore Ravens cap and stood drooling while Tim Parker, the town letch, had already relocated from his usual window seat to the closest empty bar stool.

"Morning," the shapely redhead called. She waved a scarlet stiletto heel at him. "Where's my other Louboutin? Had fun last night, but I got places to go, hon."

Ryan shuddered, and his eyes darted around to see who else was in the pub. "Last night?" He grabbed her hand and pulled her through the kitchen to the back door. She didn't appear to be a big talker and didn't protest. Pointing to the mud-spattered Carrera, he said, "I think your shoe is still in the car. "I won't keep you, *hon. I'll* call *you,* okay?" He patted her on the back, eased her out the door, locked it, and fled back inside. He didn't look the delivery guy in the eye, but he could practically hear the chuckle as he signed the invoice and sent him around back to find Bennie.

No one else was in the bar to witness his humiliation—not that it mattered. In a small town like Nevis, gossip spread like wildfire, mutating faster than a virus as it spread. By lunchtime, the whole block would be discussing his kinky secret life. And after supper, the wives would handle it from there.

He poured a cup of black coffee, sat down at the bar, and poked his way through the history on his phone. A missed call from Flanagan, but no voice mail—hopefully a breakthrough in the case. There was one missed call from an unlisted number, but no voice mail. That was possibly New York. No one at HYA would be dumb enough to leave a phone message. Most troubling were three outgoing calls to HYA. Worse yet, you couldn't get any higher up the food chain than the private lines of Bishop, Shector, and Treadwell. There was no way he had made these calls or trashed his car. That wasn't him. Now, the hooker—that was where it got a little complicated. His track record wasn't squeaky clean there, but not because of any bad behavior by him. Ryan Llewellyn Thomas evidently had no problem paying for a good time. After the bus accident and soul transfer, it had been a delicate problem telling several lovely ladies of the evening that their services, while perfectly satisfactory, were no longer needed.

His eyes flitted away from the phone log long enough to see Marla slinking past him.

"Shoot," Marla mumbled under her breath. "Ryan, I have a good reason. I forgot to set my alarm. I'm sorry."

"Uh-huh," Ryan mumbled, his attention already back on his phone.

Marla turned and looked at him. "No lecture? *Sweet.* Nice new Audi S-six. Get sick of the Porsche?"

His head jerked up. "Say what about the car?"

"Your new car. I saw them hauling off the old one. Audis are nice, but I hope you paid a lot less than that sticker price. *'Spensive.* Coulda' gotten a Charger or something."

"Oh, God. He *traded my car*?" Ryan launched off the stool and into the parking lot, where he found a sleek black Audi, neatly parked in one of the two spaces occupied only minutes earlier by his cherished Porsche. "Son of a bitch!" he snarled at the elegantly understated car. He turned on Marla, hanging back at a safe distance. "Who was . . . Did the dealership take my car?"

"The old one? I guess so. There was a Bay Motors car out here."

"Hamelin," Ryan muttered, swearing under his breath. He punched up the dealership and dialed the phone number, kicking the metal garbage can on his way back inside.

CHAPTER TWENTY-FIVE

Limes and Bitters

An exasperated look from St. Bennie stopped the finger drumming. Ryan stuck the end of his pen in his mouth and chewed. That coward Hamelin was a no-show, hiding out somewhere in the hereafter, afraid to show his face. But thankfully, after pleading inebriation as an excuse, an offer of a year's free beer during Friday happy hours had convinced Bay Motors to void the bill of sale on the Audi. The tow truck was due back anytime now. His head flew up every time someone strolled down the sidewalk past the Phoenix's front windows. This time, it was a well-dressed man. He ventured inside.

"Can I help you?" Ryan asked.

"Please." The man removed his eggshell-white fedora. It was Richard Hardy.

"You've got to be kidding. What do you want? There's a soda machine down the block."

Bennie discreetly disappeared into the kitchen.

Richard set the fedora on the bar and slid onto a stool. "I'm here to talk to you if I can have a moment of your time. Then, if you want, you can throw me out."

"So talk."

"I'm here to apologize for my bad behavior the night we met. I don't harbor any ill feelings toward you. Vanessa's and my relationship is over. She's probably already told you all this," he said, swiveling left and right on the barstool. Right?"

Ryan remained stone-faced, though he was seething inside. Was Hamelin responsible for Richard's sudden appearance? And if so, how did one go about annihilating an immortal?

"So . . . that's all I really came to say. You look like you already have a set of opinions. That's all right; you can believe what you want about me. This is something I've needed to do: tidy up a few things. I don't know or care what Vanessa's relationships are, but I do care about *her*. As long as you treat her right, I'm good with you.

"Well, okay." Richard picked up his hat as Ryan continued to glare. "I wasn't expecting the key to the city and a welcome-home parade. I came to make what amends I could. Good-bye, Mr. Thomas." He offered his hand.

Ryan nodded but ignored the hand. His expression remained remote as Richard put his hat back on and headed for the door. "What'd you do with the money HYA paid you to sell the deed to the town?" he blurted as Richard pushed the door open.

"Excuse me?"

"You heard me the first time."

Richard returned to his seat and tossed the hat down on the seat next to him. "Soda water with a splash of lime. What do you know about the money, son?"

"Son?"

"Sorry, no offense meant. What do you know about the money, Mr. Thomas?"

"Louis Vuitton shoes, nice tan line under your watchband, prissy hat. You blew through the whole million, didn't you? That's why you're back. But she'll never take you back, no matter how much you've cleaned up."

"Six months ago I would have decked you for that. But today . . ." He shook his head. "Well, not today. You may *think* you know me, Mr. Thomas, but you couldn't be more wrong. And apparently, you don't know Vanessa as well as you'd like to believe. She called and asked to see me. But let's assume for argument's sake that you know just enough to try and get under my skin. You know about the money because maybe your little establishment here isn't as squeaky clean as you'd like people to believe, or because maybe it's just *you* that's dirty. Whichever. I'll never have to worry about money again, but money doesn't run my life. I got lucky in the strangest of ways, but money doesn't solve every problem. As you can see, I don't drink anymore. One major problem solved. Whatever time left that God plans to give me, I can work on the rest."

"You *wanted* to spend it all."

"Why do you care? I'm no threat to you. Vanessa has a life of her own now. If her choices make her happy, I'm happy for her, although I'm not sure what she sees in you. You sound like an insufferable prick. Instead of carrying all that anger around, you should enjoy life. There are no guarantees, you know."

"I know all about guarantees, trust me. If you were truly respectable, you'd donate the money to a good cause instead of living off your ill-gotten gains. You know where the money's from, but you can't give up the luxury it provides. So who's calling who dirty?"

"Spoken like someone who knows. Good-bye, Mr. Thomas." Richard scooped up his hat, slid off the chair, and nearly bowled Vanessa over in his haste.

"Van! I didn't know you were behind me."

"Richard."

"Great to see you," Richard said, his face softening. He leaned forward and kissed her cheek. She didn't back away.

"You're . . . you're *here,*" she said. "I thought you were going to meet me at the house." Her eyes flitted to Ryan.

"That was my next stop. "Can I buy you a drink before we go?"

"Uh, I don't know if that would be a good idea."

"Coffee . . . tea for you, if you like. I don't drink anymore. It doesn't have to be here. It's nice out. We could walk down to Betty's and get sweet tea and a macadamia cookie, like we used to. Better yet, Cap'n Mike's. What do you say? No strings or ulterior motives."

"Okay. I need to talk to Ryan, but I guess we can do that later. Can we talk later?" she asked.

"If you can find the time. I'm here all day . . . with Livia."

"See? No problem." Richard offered his arm.

Van winced. "How about I meet you out on the street in a moment, okay, Richard? I won't be long." She watched him leave before addressing Ryan again. "Ouch. Guess I deserved that."

"You made your opinion pretty clear the other day. You're not one to mince words. I don't expect you're here to retract anything, are you?"

She shook her head.

"Didn't think so. So why are you here, then?"

"I can't take the silent treatment anymore. We need to talk."

"I believe we said it all on the beach the other day. You made *our* position very clear." He rubbed his hand across his eyes. "I'm sorry; this isn't coming out the way I've practiced it. I'm not this angry; I'm not." He gestured in Richard's direction. "It's him. Don't get messed up with Richard again. You know you can't count on him in the long term. He'll hurt you, and if he does, I'm going after him."

"Hon, he isn't, and you won't. I'm not going back to him. He and I have something to discuss. We're always going to have a connection. It's one of those things. You, on the other hand, need to be more generous and forgiving. Richard was a wonderful father, and you need to accept that. If he knew . . ."

"Oh, no. For God's sake, he can't ever know. Promise me you won't tell him."

"I can't, but if I ever did, the circumstances would be compelling. Right now, I can't begin to imagine what that would be." She glanced out the window. "Listen, I've got to go. I can't leave him waiting out there on the curb. We'll talk again."

"Sure. We'll make it a foursome. It'll be cozy."

CHAPTER TWENTY-SIX

Spitting Image

Van and Richard sat down in a corner booth at Cap'n Mike's and ordered a couple of iced teas. She studied her ex-husband over the rim of her glass. *Thinner.* They hadn't seen each other since their divorce; the split had been that contentious. She worked her way across his face: etched with a few lines now, the eyebrows sporting a smidge of gray. *No deceit there.* He seemed up front, and his eyes sparkled with a familiar gentleness.

"Thanks for coming," she said. "To be honest, I wouldn't have been surprised if you had hung up on me. How did you end up in the Phoenix? That was a surprise."

"Killing two birds with one stone. I needed to apologize to Mr. Thomas. For my bad behavior . . . Well, you know. You were there. Not one of my better performances."

"Apologize?" she repeated.

"Don't be polite. How I acted at the end of our marriage was unforgivable."

Van laughed. "Yes, it was, but I never expected you to admit it."

He laughed, too, flushing a little in the cheeks. "To progress," he said, raising his cup.

"To progress," she agreed. "And you're not drinking anymore? That's wonderful! Such a waste of a good man. It broke my heart even more, if that's possible."

"I know. I spent four months in a California rehab. It saved me, but a little too late for us. If only I'd hit rock bottom sooner. Maybe . . ."

Van shifted in her seat and began rubbing her thumbnail. She had been hoping to avoid rehashing their relationship.

"Sorry. But for what it's worth, if I could take it all back, I would."

"What did you do with the money, Richard?"

"What money? Everyone keeps asking me about money. Why does everyone think it's polite to ask people about their money?"

Van arched her eyebrows at her ex. He still had an obnoxious streak.

"Contrary to prevailing thought, I didn't spend it all. Give me a little credit. I'm not the ass I used to be. I was smart enough to use it to get healthy." He motioned her closer with a crook of his finger. "I put the rest in an offshore account."

"Betty Ford is expensive. There was enough left over to bother leaving it offshore?"

"Van, I might have hit rock bottom, but it's awfully hard to blow three mil that fast."

"*Three* million?"

"I don't know how you got all your info, but I'm assuming not much goes on at the Phoenix that the owner doesn't know about. Was he thinking more, or less?"

"A million."

Richard nodded. "Initially. I was able to transfer two mil more to a new account before the first account dried up. There is no honor among thieves. The deal I made was for six."

"To sell out Nevis and its residents to HYA."

"Yes. The cocky son of a bitch in me enjoyed sticking it to his estranged wife. It was despicable—vintage *me.*"

"Why'd you keep it?"

He shrugged. "Why not? Give it back to the likes of the man who made the deal so he could use it for some other noxious enterprise? Didn't make sense to me; supporting deserving charitable causes does. Is that something else you can hate me for?"

"I don't hate you. It's a relief to see you've changed. It helps me forgive you." She studied Richard's expression. He didn't appear to understand the dissolution of his deal with Hector, or that Ryan had paid Hector back to save Richard's neck. But *how much* had Ryan repaid Hector? Ryan had led her to believe that it was only a million dollars. Somebody was shading the truth.

"Now if I could just get those bozos to stop following me around . . ."

Van stiffened. "Wh-what makes you think someone is following you around? You should call the police if someone's stalking you."

"Nobody's *stalking* me. I've just noticed a blue car—look, it's nothing. Let's talk about Ryan."

"No." She put the dinner menu down. "That's a topic we're not going to discuss. We'll both leave here with hard feelings, and I don't want that. Our conversation and the crab imperial are going to be pleasant memories when we leave here tonight."

"No, no evil intentions. You're sure he's—"

"Good enough for me? Don't try to be my mother. He's a good guy."

"I want to make sure he doesn't hornswoggle you. I still care about you."

Van narrowed her eyes at him.

"Ah, the look." He put his elbows on the table and rested his chin on his clasped hands. "Please just listen for a second and don't assign dark motives. You do what you want with your life, but I have some concerns about that guy. Who's the waitress at the Phoenix with the long blond hair?"

"Livia?" she asked, pausing a moment as an elderly gentleman passed close by on his way to the cashier. "How do you know about Livia?"

"So there *is* something between those two."

"Nothing's going on between *those two*." She chased the lemon wedge around in her drink with her index finger. "Like what?"

"I noticed he couldn't take his eyes off her, and the *way* he looked at her . . . I used to look at you that way: need and passion. Guys do notice *some* things. He's smitten."

"*Hmph.* She's the help."

"Sometimes, it's fun to screw the help."

"Is that what it was with you?" she spat, and drew back away from him.

Richard took his elbows off the table, putting even more distance between them. "Touché. Sorry, but I'd be lying if I denied that it added to the excitement. I feel like I'm going to be saying 'I'm sorry' for ever. Don't *you* have any regrets?"

"Many. But the crazy thing about life is, it doesn't care what you regret—it just keeps rolling along. It's all I can do to keep up."

"We should probably drop this. I can see you're getting all worked up. Keep an eye on him; that's all I'm saying. Or if you think he's a good guy, watch *her*. It's not always the guy." He grabbed her hand and squeezed. "Come on. Let's order the crab imperial or at least an appetizer before you're not talking to me again." He caught the waitress' eye and waved.

"We're getting close." She wasn't sure whether Richard was trying to push every button she had, or whether it was just dumb luck. She felt her carefully planned agenda dissolving in rancor. "Let's take a breath and change the subject. I wanted to ask you something while you're here."

"Agreed. Fire away."

"This is embarrassing . . ." She wriggled her hand loose from him. "But I need a favor."

"Hon, we both know where we stand, but you should never be afraid to come to me if you need help. I'll always be here for you. All ya gotta do is ask."

"I need your DNA. She grabbed her purse, upending it and spilling lipstick, her wallet, and other sundries all over the booth seat. "Not blood—saliva. If you'd swab your cheek . . ." She pulled out a sealed vial and scooped everything else back into her purse.

"Slow down, sweetie. I'm not going to bite your head off. What are you gonna hang on me now—an illegitimate child?"

"Oh, no. Nothing like that. It's for genealogy. For James. You share the same DNA. It's time to put him on my—"

"Give me the vial and stop stressing. If it makes you feel better, it's the least I can do. Comes with one string, though."

She pulled the vial back. "What?"

"When the results come back, *whatever* comes back, can you share it with me?"

"Of course!" Van gushed. "I'll tell you exactly what the numbers are and what they mean."

"Thanks. Enough said. Give me the vial." He looked at her, and his eyes misted over. "You should know I'd do anything for you. It's great seeing you again. I didn't ever think it would happen, but I'd be lying if I said I hadn't hoped for it. Vanessa, I'm truly sorry for everything I put you—"

"It's in the past, Richard. Don't keep beating yourself up over it. We're both happier now, aren't we?"

The mist became a raindrop that flowed down his right cheek. "I had a checkup last week. Not good, hon, not good."

"Dear God, what is it?"

“Colon cancer. Even if you hadn’t called me, I would have called you, to let you know. Everything I have goes to you if I—”

“Stop. Just stop. What stage? They can treat it, right?”

“You need to know where things are.”

“I know you. The same place they’ve always been. Richard, what stage?”

“Stage two—not so bad. I’ll start radiation and chemo soon. Then they’ll go in and remove what they can. I thought you should know.”

“Oh, God.” She threw her arms around his neck and hugged him for a long time. He smelled crisp and fresh—Lauren Polo Blue—and it brought back memories of happier hugs and intimacies they had shared. Everyone who had ever been anyone to her was either gone or threatening to leave her. And there were so many things he didn’t know. It wouldn’t be fair to let him die without knowing. She would never forgive herself.

CHAPTER TWENTY-SEVEN

In the Bag

Van took a seat at the bar and set the brown paper bag down, keeping a protective hand on it. Business was steady, but she'd seen it busier. More booze had been available in town during Prohibition than was currently on tap at the Phoenix. As if to emphasize the fact, one of the taps gave a loud pop and sputter and sent foam spilling over the glass and onto the black-and-lime-green Air Jordans worn by Donald, the newest waiter.

"Bennie, the Bud's out."

"Jesus, Mary, and Joseph, not this second. Flying Dog 'em. Next time, give me a heads-up when it . . . Jenn, can you speed it up? Food's backing up, hon."

Van caught Bennie's eye and offered an encouraging smile. He ignored her. She picked up the bag and slid off the stool.

"Vanessa Hardy, what can I help you with?" Bennie asked, finally acknowledging her.

"Bennie." She hid the bag under her arm and squeezed tight. "You have your hands full. We can talk later."

"No. I thought you'd be stopping by. That what I think it is?"

Her eyes darted around the room.

"They'll be in later. Come closer so I can quit yelling."

"As long as you're not going to yell at *me*." She came back and sat down.

"Oh, my. Is that how I look?"

"It's what the entire place *feels* like, from the moment I walked in."

"This the project?" he asked. "Both parties?"

She nodded. "Listen. If this is what's bothering you, I'm sorry. I can't stand to see you like this. Maybe I'm asking too much. It was a bad idea, and selfish of me to burden you with it."

"No, just give it to me. As much as I'd like to agree, it needs to be done. I'm not going to say it's the right thing; just that it's the best thing. Ryan's walking around in a fog . . . doesn't know if he's coming or going. He spends most of his time locked in his office, eating enough food for two people. I don't think he's at the Bayside anymore, and he looks so tired, I don't think he's sleeping anywhere."

"He's staying with me. The Bayside is renovating.

"Bayside will renovate when that cheapskate Chesley sells it."

"Why would Ryan . . ."

"His office door is locked all the time now, and he's threatening to fire anyone he catches in there." He leaned in close until he was whispering in her ear. "Even with all his crazy dealings with HYA, I never saw him like this. Something's wrong."

"I told you. It's *her*. She comes to town; he falls apart. She's the only explanation. What do we really know about her?" Not bothering to wait for so obvious an answer, she said, "Only what she wants us to know."

Bennie studied her for a moment. "Haven't seen you here lately. You two on the outs?"

"Eh, maybe '*reassessing*' would be a better way to describe it. Right now I'm more worried about *him* than about *us*."

"Leave the bag."

"So you've found someone?"

"No more questions. They invite second thoughts. Don't know the time frame, but not long, I think. Now, beat it. Go do something that isn't thankless."

"Aw-w, Bennie, you're killing me. If you change your mind, call me. I'll get it done some other way."

For the rest of the evening, Bennie kept the paper bag secreted in the oversize pocket of his apron—weighing the consequences of doing something he couldn't take back. He must be getting old. It wasn't wise to get immersed in other people's lives. No good would come of it, but by the same token, nothing good would come of inaction, either. Van's voice kept ringing in his head. *"And how would you feel if he cheated on me?"* He guessed she wasn't too far off the mark. Over the years, he had seen a lot from behind the counter: flirtation, infatuation, lust—the gamut. Ryan and Livia were truly smitten. Ryan was fighting it, but it seemed halfhearted—a battle already lost. What puzzled Bennie most was why, after all the crazy things he'd seen, Ryan should self-destruct over this particular woman. Benny would bet his autographed Carl Yastrzemski home-run bat that the two of them hadn't reached the point of no return, but they were close.

He looked at his watch. It was a quarter to closing, and the place was dead. "My treat tonight. You people are free to go home if you can lock that front door. That okay with you, boss? We're dead here. You, Liv, Daniel, Mae, vamoose."

"Seriously," Ryan said. "Livia and I'll take the kitchen, and we'll call it a night."

"Nope. I've *already* called it a night. Scram. I need some alone time with my bar. I'll give you five minutes to clear out before I call the coppers." He pointed to the door.

When he had them all out on the sidewalk and Ryan had locked the door behind them, he walked over and bused the last of the glasses, including Livia's, which he picked up gingerly by the rim and slid out of view on the top shelf. He pushed it behind the Arizona shot glass with the skeleton in a festive sombrero, resting against a saguaro cactus, and the caption "If you can't stand the heat, get out of Arizona." He took a deep breath and picked up the phone.

"Jerry, Bennie Bertolini. I'm calling for Ryan . . . Yeah, down in Nevis . . . Not bad. We're making a run . . . Listen, Ryan needs you to run some tests . . . a rush job, end of the week would be fine . . . How can I get them to you? . . . Hey, let me give you my cell. Too many hands pick up this phone . . . Yeah, thanks. Ryan owes you one."

Bennie hung up the phone and looked around the empty pub. He'd had a good run here, but this wouldn't be the last bar he ever worked in. He'd deal with it. Sometimes, protecting the people you cared about outweighed what you had to sacrifice.

CHAPTER TWENTY-EIGHT

Even a Bastard Will Barter

Meekae Skalski was dead: tangled fishing nets, cinderblocks, and a body washed up in storm surf on Galveston Island. Ryan watched the detective's lips move up and down and tried to decipher it all. How did HYA find out where Mike was? And why go after the little fish when they were giving *him* free rein? Did they think he'd sent Skalski out of town with stolen info, or were they just testing the waters to find out how he would react to their snuffing the kid? He cupped his forehead in his hand and doodled a hanged man on the legal pad. Meekae had trusted him, but Ryan hadn't cared enough to sacrifice anything but a little surplus cash to protect the naive, hero-struck geek. He had conveniently pushed him along to Houston. Hamelin was right: he was a failure.

". . . traced back to your credit card, Mr. Thomas. When was the last time you saw—?"

"Mr. Thomas has already answered that question, *twice* now." Attorney and longtime friend Andrew Becker seemed to have things in hand. Ryan did as he had been told: kept his mouth shut and tried to take it all in. "Mr. Skalski was a former business acquaintance who contacted Mr. Thomas several weeks ago asking for financial assistance. Generous man that he is, Mr. Thomas lent money to the deceased in the form of a plane ticket to Houston. Mr. Thomas had no other recent personal contact with the individual in question and no subsequent contact after the ticket purchase."

". . . name or whereabouts of an attractive young woman traveling with him?"

"Mr. Thomas doesn't know anything else. As you might expect, this is a shock for anyone who knew Mr. Skalski. By all accounts, he was a fine, upstanding individual. Now, unless you have any *new* questions, this is a good place to stop. You know where to find my client should additional questions arise. Just contact my office, and I'll set . . ."

Blah, blah, blah. Becker needed to handle it. HYA was tired of sitting on its hands, and what they hadn't found in Houston they would soon be hunting for in Nevis.

Ryan slid the keys to the Porsche back into his pocket and walked back inside the Phoenix. All he really wanted to do was head off in any direction and drive until he and the car hit empty. Where the hell was Hamelin? Three days since trashing the car and destroying Ryan's reputation, and he still hadn't shown his face.

Stepping inside, he heard something rustling around in his office. Too big for a rat or even a raccoon. Bennie had too much pride ever to be caught in there, and he had chewed Marla out after she removed the aurascope. Either the biggest raccoon ever born was chewing its way through his things, or an unwelcome guest had taken up residence.

Ryan eased Bennie's Red Sox bat from behind the trash bin, inched his way along the wall, and peered between the door and the jamb. He never got a chance to swing the bat, much as he would have liked to. For there sat Hamelin Russell, feet propped up on the desk, chomping on a bag of Beer Nuts, with an unopened bottle of Bud Light on the blotter.

Ryan lowered the bat. "Where have you been, coward?"

Hamelin glanced up but continued picking through the stack of recent mail. "No need to shout. I always have a general idea of what's going on. Last one if you don't place an order," he said, holding up a Victoria's Secret flyer.

"Sorry to interrupt you there, you manipulative son of a bitch," Ryan said, locking the office door behind him.

"After your terribly busy schedule of late, I knew you'd want to talk. So talk."

Ryan's eyes narrowed. "An innocent friend is dead, there are calls to HYA on my phone, a hooker's shoe in my car, no beer suppliers, and I threatened to kill someone—and, apparently, I meant it. Only a few people have these HYA phone numbers. Nobody else could be using my phone. HYA has declared open season on me, and I need you to come clean. Why am I slipping back into the old Ryan Thomas? I'm hallucinating? You're screwing with my head? What?"

"Not exactly. Didn't I tell you that your only worry was the demon in your head? I merely unleashed what was already there."

"Ryan Llewellyn Thomas is back, and we're battling for space in the same body?"

Hamelin bobbed his head as he opened another envelope. "Of *course* Ryan Llewellyn is back. I've been expecting him since I got here. He had to come out sooner or later—God knows I've baited him enough."

Ryan reached back and grabbed the hair at the nape of his neck with enough force to hurt. "I think I'm losing my mind, and *you're* using me.

You've unleashed a criminal and you don't have the decency to give me warning? I was right. From the moment you arrived, I've sensed a black shadow weighing me down. It's growing stronger, and he's wearing me out. I'm paying the price here, man. He's sabotaging my life, and you seem okay with that. I just ran a whore out of my bar after, it seems, spending some time with her the night before. I have no control, and from the look of my car, I think you're enjoying this way too much. I suppose you also knew the bastard was getting rid of my car, and you didn't try to stop him?"

"Of course I didn't interfere. I'm interested in people, not *things*—though it is quite a fine vehicle," Hamelin said with a twinkle in his eye. "I don't care what kind of car you have. That's something the two of you will have to settle—maybe one of those drivers-ed cars that have the extra brake pedal for the instructor."

"Don't enjoy this. Get serious and help me get rid of him." Ryan balled up his fist but relaxed it as he caught the warning in Hamelin's eyes. "Yeah, I know, don't touch you." He grabbed a leg of Hamelin's chair and dumped him onto the floor. "I'm so glad we mortals can amuse you. Go fuck yourse—no, on second thought, you might procreate, and the world couldn't take more of you. Get out of my life, jump back in whatever little genie bottle you popped out of, and take your goddamn scope of Damocles with you."

Hamelin rolled over on his back and cradled his head on his arm. "You're the one that has to get serious, and it's about time. We both want him out and gone. But to succeed, you have to give this your all. What are you prepared to do?"

"Why are you *encouraging* him? All you've done is make things worse . . . *way* worse."

"Because I can't take him to hell if he isn't out where I can get at him. His soul is drawn to me and calling out, as it should, but he's a crafty one. Ryan Llewellyn and I have bonded quite nicely, unfortunately for him. Once I know all about a subject, they're at my mercy."

"Why is he calling HYA?"

"Simple enough: he has an insatiable need to be in charge."

"But how is that possible? He's *dead*. Hasn't that registered yet?"

"He's an egotistical bastard who refuses to accept the inevitable. Right now there is still enough of him remaining in his body to cause no end of trouble. He knows you have HYA documents, and he's going to barter his way back in."

"Oh, God, has he met with HYA while I've been . . . indisposed?"

"Not yet, but it's not for lack of trying. You keep getting in the way, and now they don't trust him anymore. He knows about the information, and he knows where you put it."

"Please tell me you didn't visit the storage locker last night—the carousel horses?"

"No, we didn't go there last night."

"Amen. Thank you, Lord."

"That's going to be our *next* outing. He promised I could drive again." Hamelin sat up, the air around him shimmering and humming softly.

Ryan closed his eyes, struggling to ignore the light and sound. "You are so naive. Don't you understand he's bribing you? You're never going to catch him by partying every night. He's playing you. That's what he does."

"I'm not allowed to interfere. If Ryan Llewellyn needs a wingman right now, I can oblige, but that doesn't mean I'm not doing my job. You do your part, and let me do mine."

"Thanks for sharing," Ryan said as he winked at him. "It won't be tonight, and you're never to drive my car again. Understand?"

"Yes, but—"

"No buts. Leave my *things* alone."

"Fine, but you're not making things any easier here. Ryan Llewellyn will never fully trust me. That's not what he's about. But when I seem accommodating, he assumes he has the best of me, and his mind turns to other, seemingly more important things. He's never been bested by anyone, and he's not willing to acknowledge that *I'm* the most important thing in the room. He'll eventually lower his guard, and if you keep your end up, we'll have him. Otherwise, he'll do whatever it takes, including destroying anything that gets in his way—you and anyone else associated."

"Van? Livia?"

"No doubt. Now, back to my original question: what are you prepared to do to clean up all this mess?"

"Any . . . *almost* anything," Ryan said. "What are you suggesting? And where's the aurascope?"

"Gone, I'm afraid. A lost opportunity." He sighed. "The bastard destroyed one of my favorite . . . tools. There'll be no more patience on my part."

"Hypocrite, say it. *Things*—one of your favorite *things.*"

"*Enough.* I've had enough of you, too, I might add." He got up off the floor, his hand clutched to his chest. "It's agonizing to feel a soul calling so loudly and not be able to embrace it. You've been no help up to now, and suddenly you're whining that *he* has to go? He and I could have been gone long ago if you had cooperated instead of fighting me."

Ryan threw his hands up in the air and sat down at his desk with a sigh of resignation. "All right, it's clear to me that this is all a game to you, Hamelin, and you're not going to leave me alone until you've won. So we're going to play according to your rules: no more good citizenship or frustrating colored sand. We fight dirty, and when we're done, you're going to get the hell out of my life—no more ripples. You understand me?"

"Clear as a mountain stream on the third day of creation. First off, you need to deal directly with Ryan Llewellyn. Your nemesis is much more aware of you, and what you're doing, than vice versa. He's fighting for survival while you have become complacent. You thought you'd beaten him, but he's still lurking inside. To get rid of him, you're going to have to take him by surprise. You need to get a jump on him. Give up the HYA information you stole. Then he doesn't have anything to barter."

Ryan shook his head. "That's the only insurance I have to keep them from coming after me."

Hamelin walked over and leaned across the desk, cocking an eyebrow at him. Ryan pushed back in his chair, but remained seated. "And what a marvelous deterrent it's been so far, hasn't it? No. You're not going to return it to HYA. You're going to deliver it to the district attorney's office, to prosecute Hector Young with. I'm right in assuming it implicates him?"

"Without a doubt. An accounting of offshore activities covering years—account numbers associated with paying all the partners and major HYA players. I have lists of all money in and all money out—where it came from and who it went to. It's enough information to bring them all to their knees. And that includes me, Hamelin, just in case you should happen to feel a little pang of concern. Hector Young was a shrewd businessman and a better player. He had something on everybody, for times just like this. Listen. I don't have a death wish, and I'm not willing to take on the whole organization. There are more people to consider than me. Anyone I know would be a walking target, and I'm not going to risk their lives."

"And you don't think they'll kill anyone right now that stands in their way? Mr. Skalski should serve as an object lesson on who you're dealing with, my friend. Don't be foolish."

"And how am I supposed to get the jump on Llewellyn when he's always in my head?"

"By going to the places he can't go—even in your head. Like the pickle boat house, for instance, where he has absolutely no control. He's told me so."

Ryan felt the air in the room rise several degrees. He got up and put more distance between himself and Hamelin. The guy might be well acquainted with death, but with issues of the heart, maybe not so much. "Now isn't a good time. We're not speaking."

"You're not *speaking*? That wasn't an invitation. Get over it. Either you trust me, or I go to plan B. I'm done coddling you."

"Plan B? We're just now getting to plan *B*? What has all this other craziness been?"

"*Not* plan B. I'm authorized to use plan B only as a last resort. It's an exception to the 'do no harm' credo. Think of it as fission, of a sort—something like a scientist splitting an atom. Your soul goes one way; Ryan Llewellyn's goes the other—"

"What are you waiting for? Just do it! Why haven't you already thrown him under the bus? Skip the foreplay, for God's sake!"

". . . way. It's risky for you. The two of you are too tightly bound. Ryan Llewellyn is expendable, but you . . ." He shook his head. "There is a chance you won't return to your body—not that you'd be lost out in the ethers somewhere. Your soul would go to purgatory to await further sorting—salvation or the other thing. Fission is the most powerful tool I have, but I can't guarantee your safety, Ryan James."

"But you've done it before, so you'd be practiced."

"It doesn't matter how practiced. It's a crapshoot, and it's frowned upon. Like deliberately crashing your computer—you do it only when there's no good way around it."

"Since when have you cared who's frowning?"

It was the first time Ryan had seen Hamelin fresh out of witty retorts. He stood mute, meeting Ryan's gaze with a blank stare. "Hamelin?"

"Lose the man, forfeit the game," he muttered.

"Say what? You heartless coward! How is it they ever let you back out of hell after you transport a soul there?"

"Judge not, that ye be not judged," Hamelin sniffed. "You have no idea. The eternal emptiness of dragging souls there . . . Everyone has their own personal hell. And if you want to help Ryan Llewellyn find his, stop lashing out and get on task. Here," he said. "Heads up." He pulled something out of his pocket and flipped it through the air to him. "You'll need this."

Ryan caught it one-handed. It looked like a silver coin with a guardian angel on one side and a cross on the other.

"Wing it," Hamelin said, answering the unspoken question on Ryan's face. "Oh, and one more thing. While I can't intervene directly, I can offer some helpful advice. If you haven't heard from your lawyer recently, call before you go over there. He's dealing with a lot right now." He picked up the remote control and flicked the TV on and off several times in quick succession.

"Stop." Ryan reached for the remote. "Give me that."

Hamelin waved it around, just out of reach, before handing it over with a chuckle.

"Why do you do things like that?"

"Isn't it obvious?"

Ryan sighed and shook his head.

"Because I *can*, and that's my point. Stop believing you're in control, because you're not. You may think you're playing the game, Ryan James, but there's a difference between *playing* the game and merely being caught up in it. As long as you refuse to compete, you're losing. Better to play to win. Hunker down, Mr. Thomas; your ordeal is almost over."

CHAPTER TWENTY-NINE

Devotion

Staring at the coffee grounds in the bottom of his cup, Ryan could make out a misshapen three-legged cat, or maybe a dog—nothing more insightful. Maybe one had to use tea leaves.

Getting the CD out of the warehouse on the sly would be iffy. Carrying it all the way to Frederickton would be all but impossible—the meatheads would be hanging out all over Nevis. He couldn't do this himself; someone else had to retrieve it. Given that it was her shed, Van would arouse no suspicions, but they weren't speaking. And the little blue box? It lay smashed and shredded in the bottom of a garbage can at the Phoenix—minus the ring, of course. He had tossed that into his Dopp kit and tossed it up onto the top shelf of his closet. As far as he was concerned, Richard's visit had put an end to their relationship. It hadn't taken Van long to call her sugar daddy. Hell, they probably never stopped talking. Ryan hated to see her back with him again. It wouldn't last, of course. Richard Hardy was a loser. For her sake, better that she get him out of her system now than later. Better for Ryan, too, that she find someone else. He couldn't live up to her expectations on top of Hamelin's. Going for broke meant there would be no time for niceties.

"Bennie, you've been awfully quiet this morning," he said. "You're avoiding me."

"Who, me? Nah, busy keeping up. Why would you say that?"

"Kidding, Bennie. Lighten up. Talk to Van recently?"

"Van? When was the last time she was in? Guess she's not speaking to me, either."

Ryan set down his cup. "Are you going to answer every one of my questions with one of your own? You're even less chatty than your normal laconic self. What's up with you?"

Bennie went back to polishing the overhead cabinet fronts. "Am I? I mean, sorry, but I'm doing double duty, if you haven't noticed. It's a bit short around here with Marla running off on us and Livia calling in sick. No, everything's normal. Nothing major other than Marla. Same old, same old."

"Marla's gone? I knew something was up. You can feel the tension in here. Where is she?"

"Houston. Left a note for Jean."

"Hou-Houston?" Ryan sputtered, choking on his Dr. Pepper. "What would be in Houston?"

"Not a *what,* a *who.* Said she was going to live with 'Mike,' who-ever that is."

"Mike *Skalski*? How . . . ?"

"Don't know nothing else. Jean's a basket case, and all I could get out of her that was fit to repeat in polite conversation was 'Mike.'"

The "attractive young woman" traveling with Skalski. How the hell did *that* happen? The girl had a built-in antenna. They'd had no trouble getting Mike out of Nevis and to Houston, and Ryan had gotten no SOS calls or smoke signals. Skalski would have cautioned her to keep his whereabouts a secret, but Marla, airhead that she was, must have blabbed to someone. And where was she now? The thought of that beautiful boneheaded girl, chained to a concrete block and swaying with the surge at the bottom of Galveston Bay, put a cold knot in his stomach.

"Phone number? Address?"

"Don't think so. That's why her mom's so upset. She hasn't contacted her since." Bennie worked his way out of the room and started on the stainless steel cabinets in the pantry area. "Now, we done with twenty questions? I got things to do."

"Yeah, no, I'm good, Bennie." Ryan wiped his mouth on his sleeve. "God bless you, Mike Skalski," Ryan said to no one.

"He'd better if Jean ever catches up with him," Bennie said.

Ryan ignored him. Mike was dead, but he was still a giving soul. The kid had given Ryan everything he needed to take to the DA, and he needn't go anywhere near the shed to do it. Mike's stolen files were still neatly tucked away in the bottom of Hoffa's dog food bag. It was good stuff—maybe not as complete as the files on the CD in the shed, but probably enough to do serious damage to key people at HYA. Where was that bag? He checked the kitchen to no avail, then the other obvious places: his office, the storeroom with its floor-to-ceiling cabinet space. The bag of kibble had been shoved aside, tripped over, and spilled, and now it was missing.

"Bennie, where'd the dog food go?"

"Aw-w, you found her?"

"No, she hasn't turned up. But where's her bag of food?"

"That poor baby—I keep hoping she'll turn up. Dunno about the food. Last time I saw it, it was on top of the boxes that had to be broken down for recycling."

"No boxes back there."

"Maybe somebody threw it out with the trash. Did you check out there? Pickup's not till tomorrow."

“Damn it, what’s wrong with everybody? The dog’s coming back.” Ryan yanked the back door open and pulled the lid off the first trash can. A swarm of flies boiled out and swarmed around his face, chasing him several feet back.

Undeterred, Ryan approached the can again, like a cat stalking a snake. He snatched out a piece of cardboard and flipped the top layer of trash out of the can, fending off flies with his other hand.

Flies inside the Phoenix were the last thing Bennie needed. He closed the door and went back out front to keep an eye on Donald, who was struggling with the Phoenix’s seat-of-the-pants management style.

“Bennie, you have a call.” Donald laid the phone down on the bar top. “Somebody named Jerry.”

“Sh-h!” Bennie said, grabbing the phone. “You don’t need to go shouting people’s business when you answer the phone. Go bus those two front tables.” Bennie took the cordless into the kitchen—as far as he could get from the back door and still get a signal. “Jerry, you work fast. I thought you were gonna call back on my cell . . . No, it’s okay . . . No, you just missed Ryan. In town? Uh, sure, you can drop it by, but I need a time. Don’t want it going to anyone but me, know what I mean? . . . Noon? Hold on.” He put the phone on mute and walked over to check on Ryan. He was up to his elbows in garbage. “Hey, you heading out before lunchtime?”

“Leaving soon. Why? You need me to stay a while?”

No, no worries.” He unmuted the phone. “Yeah, noon works fine. Thanks.” Bennie hung up the phone. He hadn’t expected results back this soon. Apparently, dropping Ryan Thomas’s name got one immediate attention.

CHAPTER THIRTY

Noonish

Ryan came back inside, holding aloft a sealable sandwich bag as if it were the Holy Grail. "Found it, halfway down between the cardboard and a half bushel of ripe crab shells. Thank God I sealed the bag."

"What is it?" Bennie asked.

"This flash drive, my friend, is my guarantee of a happy tomorrow. Send someone out later to clean up the dog food, would you? I'm covered in crab innards." He headed for the sink. "Who's not busy here that I can send on an errand?"

"Rita's here early."

Ryan sealed the drive in an envelope and scrawled on the front, then sealed it in a second envelope and addressed it to Van. "Rita," he called to the middle-aged local woman who cooked for the Phoenix on her days off, "would you mind delivering something for me? I'll put you on the clock right now. In fact, we'll make it double time if you can get back here before your shift starts."

"You know you don't have to do that, Mr. Thomas. I'da' gone even if you just asked me. But you have a deal—Mama needs a new pair of shoes."

"I knew I could count—"

"Would Ryan or Bennie be around?" The booming voice sounded familiar. Bennie checked his watch. It was only ten thirty, but that Bronx accent was hard to miss. He bolted from behind the bar so fast, the new waitress dropped the tray she was carrying, spilling hot crab soup down her apron. But he wasn't fast enough. Ryan had the angle and cut him off.

"Jerry Pernell! My God, long time. What brings you here? Not that I'm not delighted to see you." Ryan gave him a bear hug. "Wandering a little far from the city, aren't you?"

"You know I take customer service seriously. Didn't have anything pressing, so I thought I'd come early—personally bring what you wanted and get a mini vacation all at the same time. What could be better than getting out of the city, and a day at the shore? *Months* overdue."

"What I wanted," Ryan repeated, looking puzzled. "Yeah, what's up with that?"

"Bennie said you were pressed for time, so I gave you premium service—I'm early and throwing in personal free delivery. Your prints came back with a match."

"Really?" Ryan glanced over his shoulder at Bennie, who stood a few feet behind him, stopped short by the wariness in Ryan's eyes. Bennie backed up slowly until the bar was between him and his boss. "Bennie takes care of business. I never have to worry with good old Bennie around. What's the match?"

"Livia Williams, twenty-four, Nantucket. Studied law at the University of Maryland. Mother, Marie Anna Gasparella, from Manhattan . . . father, Dennis Williams from Nantucket. That's all I have right now. Got one other source checking, but I doubt it'll turn up anything different. Her background's ho-hum. That enough?"

Bennie's breath caught. Ryan's face froze in place for an instant before he regained his composure. His gaze shifted back to Bennie again. "*More* than enough. Thanks for getting back so fast. I'd hang with you for a while, but I have something urgent to take care of with Bennie here, and it won't wait." He pulled out his wallet.

"Wait. Don't you want the other test? The two Y DNAs came back a perfect match; no mutations. If they share a surname, they're definitely related. If you need more than that, I'll have to go back and get them to write it down—too much mumbo jumbo. I'll send the report. I thought that would suffice for now. I know you don't like hanging around waiting on people to get back to you."

"How well you know me, Jerry. Unlike some people, I'm a straight-shooting guy—no mumbo jumbo." Ryan pressed a wad of bills into Jerry's palm.

Jerry smiled a crooked-toothed grin and slid the bills into his shirt pocket. "Okay, I'm out of here, Ryan. Pleasure as always." He nodded at Bennie. "Nice workin' with ya. Let me know if you need anything else."

Bennie gave a half wave and a nod. "Talk to you again sometime." His hand hit the rim of a mug sitting on the bar top and tipped it over, sending a rivulet of lager racing down the bar top. Ignoring it, he watched Jerry Pernell's back disappear out the front door.

"A word," Ryan said, gesturing toward the kitchen.

Bennie threw his towel over the puddle and walked to the rear corner of the kitchen. When he turned around, Ryan was inches away.

"What were you thinking, Bennie? Did you really think he'd trust you enough to run the prints without talking to me? Only honest fools trust people in this business. The one person I thought I could rely on without fail, checking up on me behind my back—and pulling old New

York associates back into my personal business. Yours is the most unexpected of betrayals. What is it you've got against Livia? Why couldn't you have brought your concerns to me directly instead of . . . instead of this nonsense?"

Three inches shorter than Ryan, Bennie pulled himself up to his full height and returned Ryan's steely gaze. "We've tried, Ryan. Many times. You have a blind eye where she's concerned. I knew you'd never listen. She's not aboveboard."

"Who else did you run tests on?"

"Why don't we talk again when you've had a chance to absorb all this?"

"Bullshit. What's to absorb? She's who she says she is. Who else, Bennie?"

"I only asked for one test. He lost me with the rest."

"Bad liar. Who's related?"

"Now's not a good time, Ryan."

"Now's the perfect time," Ryan growled. He stepped forward, and Bennie backed up, banging against the metal storage cabinets.

Bennie sighed and raised his hands in submission. "Livia's son, Mattie, and Richard Hardy."

"Son?" What son?"

"Mattie . . . Matthew. He's three or four. Van—er, *people* have seen them down on the boardwalk together."

"Van started all this? And she thinks Richard Hardy is his father? That son of a bitch fathered a child while they were married? I'll kill 'im."

"No, Ryan, wait. Not exactly. Van used Richard Hardy's DNA to run the test because Richard's and James Hardy's DNA would be the same. Matthew is *James* Hardy's son."

Ryan blinked. "*James* Hardy? Not possible." He gave Bennie a shove. "You're lying. Van never mentioned a grandson. She would have mentioned a—"

Bennie shoved Ryan out of his face. "Enough, Ryan! She didn't know. The girl must have been pregnant when Hardy died. He probably never knew, either, rest his soul. Sad situation all around."

Ryan turned away. "You're fired. Be out of here as soon as you can collect your things."

"Fair enough," Bennie said, pulling his shirt back in place. "I expected as much. As a friend, I did what I had to do. I've already put out a few feelers in New York. But tell me, Ryan, who is she *really*?"

"Fuck off."

"I understand you're upset, but this isn't your fight. It's between Van and Livia now. She's a loose cannon, Ryan. You don't really think she visited here on a lark. Think about it."

Ryan turned away. "Beat it, *friend*."

Bennie slumped back against the wall, ignoring the cell phone ringing in his pocket.

"Aren't you going to answer it? Maybe Jerry has dirt on more tests."

Bennie answered it but avoided direct eye contact with Ryan's withering stare. "Jerry, you lost? More information from your other source? Yeah, I'm listening, go ahead . . . You're absolutely sure? No, I'll make sure he knows. Thanks for calling back. If it changes, keep us in the loop." Bennie finally looked at Ryan, standing in the center of the room, full of rage and thunder.

"Seems Livia Williams isn't as clean as Jerry thought. His second source dug something up. She's Earl Jackson's half-sister, out to avenge her brother's death. And according to word on the street, guess who's at the top of her list?"

"Earl Jackson didn't have a sister. That's all he had?"

Bennie shrugged. "Yup."

"Earl was one of my closest friends. No sister. What did he *really* say?"

"I'm telling you exactly what he said. You just don't want to hear it. Jerry's not pulling this stuff out of his ass. You know the scuttlebutt's out there. If I've heard it, you have, too. Hector may be cooling his jets in jail, but he hasn't been idle. His spin on what happened here has been getting a lot of play in Hector Young and Associates circles. Hector may have tricked the Diablos into killing Earl Jackson out on the boardwalk, but you're smart enough to know he wasn't gonna take the fall for setting up Earl. Nevis was *your* operation. Word is, he came in when your ineptness threatened to take it all down. Loads of people blame you for Earl's death. Did you think ignoring that would make it go away?"

"Those people can say what they want. It doesn't make it so. Earl didn't have a sister."

"Just like James Hardy didn't have a kid. How safe do you feel sleeping with the enemy?"

"I'm not *sleeping* with her. And who's to say she's the enemy?"

"Jerry Pernell. Come on. *Earl's sister?* She would have been honest with you if she had good intentions. Livia dumb-lucked it. She had James Hardy's baby and comes looking for Van and, lo and behold, finds Ryan Thomas, the one man she has a score to settle with—who just so happens to be romantically involved with James's mother. Coincidence? If you think so, I've got a piece of Nebraska beachfront property you are gonna love!"

Ryan glared at him and turned away. Bennie, shorter but stockier, grabbed his arm and spun him around. Ryan shoved him away but didn't swing. Neither seemed inclined to close the gap and tangle a second time.

"Don't be a fool, Ryan. As long as Hector Young Senior's son sits in a jail cell down the road, you're involved and in their crosshairs. *This girl* is fully involved. It's a family business, for Christ's sake. There are no coincidences where HYA is concerned. This should be a wake-up call for you. How many years have I known you? Yeah, that's right: plenty. And not once, *never,* have I gotten involved in what you do. God knows there were times when I wanted to. Out of respect for the friendship we had, listen to me. The facts speak for themselves. Warning bells are going off everywhere."

"I want you gone before I get back." Ryan headed out the front door, and Bennie went for the phone.

"Van, it's Bennie. No, I'm fine. Heads up. You know those prints we talked about running? They came back positive . . . doesn't matter. Richard and Mattie came back a perfect match; he's your grandson, for sure . . . Things are all screwed up here . . . Tried to keep your name out of it, but it slipped out. Ryan knows everything. He's on the warpath, and I think he's headed your way. He's cuckoo—asking me questions about what he did the night before, bringing hookers into the bar. Did you know he traded in his car? Up and trades his car, then acts like a madman for doing it. He's fired me, and there's no way I'm gonna be here when he comes back. I haven't seen him like this since the old days. Sweetie, you may want to think about making yourself scarce until he gets his head screwed back on straight."

Bennie hung up and went in search of a box for his things. There was nothing left to say. His instincts had been right, and he had achieved what he set out to do. Livia was bad news, and now Ryan knew it. Maybe one day he would come to his senses, but by the look on his face, it wouldn't be anytime soon. And as in a marriage gone sour, he would never fully trust Bennie again. And for that, Bennie was truly sorry.

CHAPTER THIRTY-ONE

Blue Flame

Ryan hit the fresh air and instantly felt the familiar surge of power as it tugged on him and tried to pull him under. But he burned with a blue flame. Alert and driven, he felt the adrenaline course through him like lifeblood. The force faltered, sputtered, and stopped like an engine out of fuel.

James Hardy had a son. *He* had a son. Van knew it. Livia knew it. Everyone but him had known it. It was HYA all over again: lots of smiling faces, but all acting in their own interests. His stomach tightened and heaved. He could forgive Livia. She had no idea who he really was. But Van had suspected he had a son, and never breathed a word, just as she had never mentioned Livia's backstory. What a reality check. Bennie was right about one thing: Ryan had let too many acquaintances into his inner circle. But then, Bennie was wrong, wrong, wrong about everything else. Ryan would have trusted him with his life. There was no circle anymore—only a point on a page, surrounded by emptiness.

One phone call had wiped it all away. He would begin anew, starting with his son—his one beacon of light and hope.

The lines on the road shimmered as if heat waves were rising off them on a midsummer day. But the distortion was less about a battle with Ryan Llewellyn than about his own general fucked-up-ness. He felt his ego splatter like a possum under a barreling eighteen-wheeler. He ran the red light at Mill Road and sped out of town. At Uncle Charlie's Spur, he breezed through on yellow. But as he approached Ice House Lane, the adrenaline began to ebb and he slowed down. Much as he wanted to see his son, he needed to keep a clear head. Otherwise, Livia would throw him out.

He felt a twinge of guilt as he pulled into the Sleepy Time Inn's parking lot. The place was the butt of a thousand Nevis jokes, but he hadn't realized till now quite how shabby it really was: flaking paint, an unpaved parking lot with more weeds than gravel, and a row of 1960s nylon-webbed aluminum lawn chairs looking out from the upper balcony. The kind of place people rented by the week or by the hour.

Ryan climbed the crumbling steps two at a time and found room 208 on the end. He hesitated a moment at the dented yellow door. Now that he knew they shared a history, he wondered if Livia would somehow look different. His mind went back among the pictures hung on Van's walls, trying to imagine his features reflected in Matthew Williams's face. He got nothing. He rapped three times on the door, but there was no response. He banged harder, like someone ready to put his fist through it.

The door opened a crack, but the security chain remained in place. "Ryan? How did you know . . . What's wrong?"

"Let me in. We need to talk. *Now.*"

"Now's not a good time. I'll call you later."

"*Now.*" Before she could close the door, he kicked it. The molding splintered as the chain broke free. He pushed his way past her and made for the bedroom, resisting an inner plea to approach slowly and cautiously.

"Ryan, stop!" Livia clawed at his arm, but he shook her off. "I'm calling the police."

Ignoring the threat, he went to the side of the bed and stopped, dumbstruck at the sight of the blond toddler sound asleep. The turn of the nose, the little puckered lips—the boy was a perfect little image of James Hardy. Still, it was a child that Ryan could readily identify as his own. With a paternal gentleness he hadn't know he possessed, he lifted the child from the bed and eased him up to his shoulder. The little eyes fluttered briefly, and he stirred before growing quiet again.

Ryan nuzzled against the youngster's soft cheek, enthralled by the gentleness of his quiet, warm breaths. Memories flooded his brain, overwhelming him as he held the little reflection of himself. A cascade of colorful images, conversations, and feelings rushed in, making soft explosions inside him. In a moment, he remembered. And he loved it. It was completeness. He closed his eyes, and there, without benefit of a picture or any visual cue, he *was* James Hardy.

He turned and looked at the mother of his child, and the raging anger that had blown him down the road and through the door dissipated with the breath that was now sucked out of him. He felt the surge and power of pure love—connection and understanding, and the ache to cherish, caress, and protect—electrifying every nerve in his being. Without a doubt, this had been the love of his life, the woman he had vowed to spend it with. In a moment, it all coalesced into the reason for his existence, and he no longer feared squandering his gift. And then he saw the gun.

"Put Mattie back where you found him," Livia said, motioning toward the bed, "or I'll start with your right kneecap."

"My God, what happened to you?" he asked, seeing for the first time the dark bruises running down the inside of her arm.

"Back. In. The. Bed. Now."

One look in her eyes told Ryan that she had it in her to shoot him. He snuggled Mattie back under the covers and stepped away from the bed while slowly raising his hands above his head. "I wasn't going to hurt him. Why didn't you tell me you had a son?"

"I work for you. Doesn't mean I have to tell you my life story."

"Who's his father?"

"Christ! Could you be a little more blunt? My son is none of your damn business." Her glare would have cut through anyone else like a hot knife through beeswax, but Ryan was having none of it.

"In the most peculiar of ways, it *is* my business."

"It's complicated, and no, not your business. Who sent you to break into my apartment?"

"Nobody sent me. Did they say they'd be back?" he asked, looking at her arm. "I feel terrible. I could have made it so much easier for you if I had known you weren't alone . . . and staying in a dump like this. How complicated could it all be?"

"Complicated."

"James Hardy—he's Mattie's father?" Ryan watched as she struggled to deny the relationship that continued to define her life years after his death. "I thought so." The knowledge converted to adrenaline, driving up his heartbeat and the pulsating rhythm in his temples.

"I'm going to give you till three to leave. *Please* leave. You need to leave."

Mattie stirred and rolled over. Livia's eyes darted to the baby and back to Ryan again.

"He's sick. I can call someone to make you leave."

"Who on earth would you call?"

"The manager."

"Just the manager? I'm not going to hurt anybody. Here, I'll move away from your son. I'm trying to understand what's up with you." He nodded toward the living room. "Can we go out there and talk?" You know me by now. You know you can trust me. I'm here out of concern." He was unable to resist the urge to take a final peek at his son. "Mattie looks exactly like his father."

"You . . . *knew* him?" She hesitated, then lowered the gun. A soft look reshaped her eyes, and Ryan thought he saw a glimmer of trust there. He gambled and took a step forward. "Uh-uh," she said, "you didn't know him. Stop right there." The steely-eyed resolve returned. She adjusted her grip and took aim again.

Ryan's eyes never left hers. Those eyes had haunted him from the day they met. They were wary and guarded, but even now, as she struggled to keep the upper hand, he could read her. She was desperate to trust him. Hopefully, it was because she could read him, too. Not because he was the lesser of her evils, but because she understood him in a way that no one else ever had.

"So Hardy *is* the father. I don't know much about him, just what Vanessa's told me."

"You won't tell her, will you?" I don't want her to know."

"Van? Of course I'll tell her. Life can be cruel, especially to those that care and love. The woman has practically wallpapered her living room with photos of her son. It's not like she doesn't already suspect. She's seen the two of you together. But, don't go after Van. You've definitely got the wrong impression. She's suffered, too, and yet, for someone with every right to be bitter, she isn't. I've never met a more caring person. Slow down and think logically, Livia. No court would give her custody over the biological mother. Now, want to put the gun down so we can talk? Where'd you get the bruises?"

She nodded, and the gun began to bob a little. "She'd fight me for him. I know it. I never would have come here if I had known how driven she is. People like her always get what they want. I'd lose him . . . and James—the last little piece of him. I can't." She looked toward the bed, and the tears came. "My little miracle. It couldn't bring James back, but he changed *everything.* No more frittering away life . . . He brought me purpose."

"Your life is *meaningful* living in this hole? I'm sure you're a really good mother, but have you given any consideration to what will become of Mattie when you go to jail for shooting me?" Ryan watched the gun muzzle dancing up and down. He inched a half step toward her. "Have you thought about how you're going to get away? Destination? Tickets? The police will nab you before you can bolt. Might even be Officer McCall, right here in Nevis. He's like a bloodhound following a scent. Investigated another murder not more than a year ago. Tenacious as hell.

"And what about James and how you're betraying *him*? Your lovely little boy—he wouldn't have wanted his son raised by a stranger . . . or his grandmother, for that matter. He'd have wanted *you.* I won't hurt either one of you. Please put the gun down."

Livia closed her eyes and bushed a tear aside. Ryan lunged for the gun, tackling her hard. They both went sprawling to the floor. He yanked the gun away and pointed it at her startled bright blue eyes. "Don't point a gun at someone unless you know what you're doing. You never took off the safety catch. Now it's your turn. Get up and talk to me." He grabbed her hand, but she jerked it lose and got up by herself.

"Go ahead. Call the cops," she taunted. "I know all kinds of things about you they'd love to hear."

"A minute ago, the manager was the best you could do. Now it's the *cops*? The last thing in the world either of us needs right now is for the cops to show up. Wouldn't you agree?"

She cut her eyes at him and pointed to the living room. When he was on the couch, she glanced once more at her sleeping son and closed the door behind her. She sat down across from him in the desk chair, one eye on the bedroom.

CHAPTER THIRTY-TWO

Framed

Ryan ran his thumb across the barrel of the cheap .25-caliber semiautomatic. "I can understand your willingness to shoot me, but you obviously don't know the first thing about guns. Who gave you this?"

"I bought it, and I would have shot you, too. You need to leave before they find out you're here."

Who are *they*?"

"Hector Young and Associates . . . the company."

"I know who they are. Is that where you got the bruises, or did you trip over another computer?"

She shrugged off the question and surveyed the damaged front door.

"Don't worry about the door; I'm not leaving you two here by yourselves. And you don't have to tell me anything else. I'm thoroughly versed in HYA's business practices. I also know plenty about you: Columbia U., overseas internship, semiengaged to James Hardy. Do you work for them?"

"There's no secret to any of that. I told Vanessa that when I first came to Nevis, so no surprises there. And no, I've never worked for them." She spat the words back at him like a pill too bitter to swallow. "My brother did."

"Your *brother*? I don't remember anyone named Williams."

"No. His name was Jackson—Earl Jackson.

All right, Jerry, you got that one right. Ryan had expected to work harder for the information, but Livia seemed quite willing to spill her guts. Her eyes kept shifting between him and the bedroom door. She couldn't possibly think he would use the gun. Indeed, it hurt to think she didn't know him any better than that.

"Earl—he gave it to me . . . for protection. And showed me how to use it. I've never liked guns."

A .25. Jeez, Earl, brother, how did you ever think she'd use this? He double-checked the safety. "You weren't too forthcoming about being Earl Jackson's sister, were you?"

"Half-sister. Shared a mom, not a household."

"Earl and I were tight," he said. "How come I never met you? In the couple years we buddied around, not once did he mention a sister."

"Earl was older. Mom remarried when he was a teen. Earl got mad and moved in with his dad. I didn't even know I *had* a brother until I was about thirteen and he tracked me down. After that, I never wanted for anything." She leaned forward in her chair suddenly and cocked her head as if listening. She glanced at the bedroom once more and then back at Ryan before easing back in the chair again. "He made up for all those lost years. I knew all about what he did for a living. Earl made certain choices, but he didn't want me to follow in his footsteps. He helped pay my way through school, including the best law school I could get into and he could afford. And when the opportunity came for me to intern overseas, he insisted I take it. He treated me like a little princess."

Ryan shook his head. "Earl was a man of integrity, but seriously, he was about as closemouthed as they come. If he was as protective as you say, he'd never have shared HYA business with you, never have involved you. Why can't you level with me? I'm trying to help you here."

She gestured to the pistol in his hand. "Maybe you could start by putting that thing away. It makes me nervous; even though I'm pretty sure you wouldn't use it on me." She began to wring the tail of her shirt into a knot. "I wouldn't have shot you, either. This isn't what you think. I'm not a bad person. You have to understand, I didn't have a choice."

He put the gun down next to him on the couch. "Everybody has a choice in life. Choices are all that separate the saints from the sinners."

"I'm not going to say I'm a saint, but I'm sure not as bad as you seem to think I am." She let go of her shirttail and started on her hands. "I'm in the middle of something I can't get out of. I went back to Geneva after James's death and finished my internship in international law. I could hold myself together to do that, and every day being pregnant was a small consolation for James being gone. Mattie was born there, and it was nice for a while, but I knew I couldn't stay indefinitely. That's where things went haywire. I asked Earl for help in getting all the papers I'd need to get Mattie back to the States. I never questioned the quality of that help. I can't blame my brother. He delegated everything to an HYA clerk. I believed it was on the up-and-up, and it got us back here, but I found out differently later. Somebody cut corners, money changed hands, and Mattie's papers are as bogus as Benjamin Franklin on a thirty-dollar bill. He's here illegally, and if I make a fuss, they could send him back to Switzerland. What mother would let that happen?"

"You're a lawyer, for God's sake!" he said, throwing up his hands. Why didn't you go get legal counsel? They could straighten it out."

"Maybe, with good legal counsel, if it didn't look so much like there was intent to deceive. We would have been separated until it all got figured out. I couldn't let that happen." She covered her mouth with a trembling hand for a moment, trying to compose herself. "Surely you can understand that, Ryan. Lawyers at HYA looked into the legality. Mr. Bishop said it was a crapshoot and the best way to play it would be to keep quiet. HYA promised they'd make sure I got everything I was entitled to. Before I realized it, I was totally beholden to them. Forget the trust fund Earl set up for us—Mr. Owens wouldn't even give me Earl's life insurance money unless I helped them. And he said they'd smear my name in the legal community . . . have me disbarred. I've never done anything under the table, but they're pros—they could make it look that way."

"Who raised a stink about Mattie's paperwork?"

"Mr. Owens. Earl set up a blind trust for us. He never discussed much about it, but he did leave a name and a phone number at HYA that I was to use if something happened to him. When I contacted them, they found all kinds of problems."

"Whose name? Bishop? Owens? Treadwell?"

"Yours. R. Thomas."

"Good lord!" Ryan said, slumping back against the couch pillows. "I never knew anything about a trust. Did you try to contact me?"

"I called the number, but they said Mr. Owens was taking all your calls. He told me the trust was in jeopardy—the way it was set up, Mattie's paperwork, even the way Earl died. They said you'd been fired from the account for mismanagement . . . and that you had a hand in Earl's death."

He slide forward to the edge of the couch seat. "Listen," he said, leaning toward her, "I didn't have anything to do with Earl's death. That's crazy."

"Owens told me the whole story. Everyone at HYA knew Earl was down here with you when things went south. If you'd given him the backup he needed, things would have turned out a lot differently."

"Knowing Owens, it's probably a great story, but as with pretty much everything that comes out of his mouth, it's pure fiction. You need to understand that you're a means to an end for HYA. I'm a big thorn in their side right now. If you had shot me, it would have solved a big problem for them. And Earl would hate to see you involved in all this. He must be rolling in his grave. You said so yourself: he never wanted you involved with HYA. But here you are, getting involved with some truly nasty people. And who'll profit in the end? *Bingo!* You should have taken what he told you to heart. It's foolish to get involved with the likes of HYA."

Ryan watched her slender hands clench into hard little fists. "I'm not naive," she said. "I want to believe you didn't sell out my brother. But *somebody* let Earl down. Why shouldn't I believe Owens's version? It was compelling."

"He's always compelling; it's what makes him such an effective liar. A while back, I was as black hearted as the rest of them. But I had my own come-to-Jesus moment, and it's changed everything. Truth is, I never even got a chance to see Earl when he came. He was working with Hector Junior. *That's* who betrayed him, not me. When I found out Earl was dead, I didn't know what the hell was going on. Hector set him up to take the heat so Hector wouldn't have to. You ever had the pleasure of meeting him? He is one conniving sack of shit. If you need something more persuasive, visiting hours at the Frederickton jail are ten till eleven thirty on weekdays."

He looked at her clenched fists. She was a fighter, but way out of her league with Bishop and Owens. He wanted to tell her that they would send Mattie back to Geneva over his dead body, but as she said, things were complicated. "There is no way I can help you if I don't know what's going on," he said in a quiet, soothing tone, leaning forward in his seat. "So tell me, what did they expect you to do here? I know they didn't expect you to come down here and shoot me in cold blood. That would be asking too much, and it's not really in your skill set. And nothing you've done or said has given me any indication that you were even struggling with the notion—quite the contrary, in fact. So, Livia Williams, why *are* you here?"

Livia avoided his eyes and wrung her hands.

"Well? Did they send you down here to keep tabs on me?"

"Not exactly."

"On Van?"

"You, but not to keep tabs. They wanted me to find out certain things about you: where you bank, how you keep your books, who you do business with—stuff like that. I'm sorry. They said you found a way to raid the trust fund and you skipped out with the money. They weren't going to hurt you, just take you to court. They promised me. Look, all I've ever wanted to do is get clear of this and make a good life for my son. I swear to God, everything I'm telling you's the truth. I've never lied to you."

"Just neglected to tell me a whole bunch of things that would have made a hell of a difference in me trusting you or not. "Benedict Point, the kiss, the flirting—was it all part of the job?"

She got up, walked to the bedroom door, and stationed herself there. "You think I came to Nevis for HYA?" She shook her head. "I came for exactly the reason I said I did: to meet Van after seeing her in the *Post.* I had no idea you were the R. Thomas connected to the trust. I didn't even know if R. Thomas was a he or a she. I took the job from you because I *wanted* to. Everything in my life was fine until a Blue Nissan pulled up beside me and a blond bitch on wheels gave me an ultimatum."

"Why did they rough you up? Didn't give them enough?"

"I haven't given them *anything* of value."

"Yet."

"Exactly. They've run out of patience. They want a flash drive they think you've hidden at the Phoenix."

He stood up. "That's of value. We can't stay here." He nodded toward the bedroom. "Go grab some things and get him up."

"Where else—?"

"Van's, to get the flash drive. It's too dangerous to keep any longer. Once it's in the DA's hot little hands, HYA'll be too busy defending its corporate and individual asses to hassle anybody."

He followed her into the bedroom. Her personal belongings had an impermanence to match the going-nowhere furnishings. She didn't need to pack anything—just zipped up a duffel and shoved it at him. As she roused her son and put his shoes on him, Ryan checked out the room. He tipped up the picture frame lying facedown on her nightstand. It was James Hardy and Livia Williams—him in a pale blue shirt and navy tie, her in white, holding pink carnations tied with yellow ribbon.

He felt a tingle shoot from his brain to his toes as a disconnected memory sprang up from somewhere. "Deep Creek Lake . . . There's a place called the Ripple Inn—a little brown shingle out front with the name and a green fish on it. When the summer breeze picks up and comes in off the lake, the shingle swings back and forth on the little iron post. A bungalow on the end looks off into a glen of hickory trees . . . gray squirrels and red birds hopping about in the understory. You know it?" he asked, searching her face.

Her mouth fell open and one of Mattie's shoes hit the floor with a thud. "HYA was *spying* on us?"

Is this one of those old-timey pictures like they take at the beach?"

"It's from the day I married James Hardy."

"Come again?" he asked, mind racing.

"James and I were married by a justice of the peace in Deep Creek Lake, right before I returned to Geneva. But then, you probably already knew that, you miserable son-of-a-bitch Peeping Tom. Why was HYA following James and me around?"

"HYA? No, never. I . . . uh . . . it brought back personal memories. I mean, Deep Creek is a lovely place. People love to get married there—happens *all the time*." He stole another glance. But the image that remained seared within him was slightly different. The way she looked that night in his pale blue shirt, and the smile beyond description, bedazzling him even now. He felt her face in his hand, her silky skin. Lover, mother of his child, wife—she had been all those things to him, and he wished he could tell her.

The feel of cool metal across his palm interrupted the warm moment as she snatched the picture from him. She brushed her fingertips across the glass and shoved it into the side pocket on the duffel bag. Then she looked at him with a trust that cut him to his core. "Please get us out of here."

CHAPTER THIRTY-THREE

War

When they pulled out of the Sleepy Time's weedy gravel lot, Ryan floored it. By now, Van would know he had gone off on Bennie and was headed her way. She didn't have to let him in; all he needed right now was the flash drive Rita had dropped off. Rita and the drive—that was where he was having a problem. They had spoken, but he couldn't remember actually reaching out and handing her the drive, sending her out the door with it. The memory was gone, or there never was one. If he hadn't given it to Rita, where in God's name was it? The Phoenix? *Somewhere* . . . in a sandwich bag that smelled like putrid crab. He broke out in a cold sweat.

The road ahead forked in two. One went to town, the other toward Frederickton. Ryan braked hard. He didn't like either choice. Tires squealed and smoked as they jerked to a halt on the shoulder, overshooting a narrow country lane on the other side. He made a tight U-turn, veered right, and headed down Sollars Wharf, an old wagon road that meandered down to the bay north of town. He had never actually driven that way, but the name had caught his attention and he asked about it soon after coming to town. Charlie Sollars told him it led down to the water and eventually wound back around toward town. At least, that was what he thought Charlie had said in between reminiscing about deer hunting and the century-old pier pilings that could still be seen of a summer tide. At any rate, the route was little traveled—a house here or there and not much else until the water's edge. There was small chance of being seen returning to town. It was perfect.

They soon began to pass gray weathered buildings—collapsed warehouses that were once stocked to overflowing with dry goods and produce bound for steamboats traveling the north-south bay route between Baltimore and Solomons Island. On a peninsula where roads didn't connect one end to the other until the 1940s, boats had been the only game in town. The old warehouse ruins meant they were close to the bay, and if he wasn't mistaken, this had to be the inlet around the bend from the pickle boat house.

He could sense Livia's eyes on him, feel her unease. He forced a smile and glanced at her small hand, gripping the console between them. He reached down and patted it. She grabbed him in a viselike grip and didn't let go. She needed him, and it made him want to protect her even more. It felt right, and he didn't fight it. He had officially crossed the unspoken line.

As if in response, the Porsche swerved violently to the left, and suddenly it was all over the road as it sped down the winding lane, nearly sideswiping legacy oaks on the far side only to shoot back across, dangerously close to fence posts strung in rusty barbed wire. Ryan pulled his hand free, but he was fighting more than a steering wheel. His body was at war with itself. He pulled right, then left, and the steering wheel swung back and forth as if to some unheard beat. The car zigged and then zagged, mowing down a swath of cattails on one side before slicing into a patch of black-eyed Susans on the other. To his horror, in the near distance, tall and stately with its picturesque center bell tower, stood a white clapboard church. It was perilously close to the road, with a few parking spaces and a handicapped access ramp out front. The Porsche barreled down the meager shoulder as if it were a grass airstrip, and headed straight for the entrance. Ryan's hands slid uselessly off the wheel as the steering froze.

"Oh, God . . ." Ryan wrenched the wheel to the left one more time.

The car veered violently and, with a loud thump, hopped back onto the road. He cut the ignition, rolled across the road, and came to rest straddling a ditch on the roadside. He was unscathed, and for the moment his mind was clear, but he knew that it wouldn't last.

"Livia," he gasped, "are you all right?"

She had her head thrust back against the headrest. Her eyes were closed, but by the rise and fall of her chest, she seemed to be physically okay. He glanced in the back. Mattie was sitting in his car seat, quiet but wide-eyed, still trying to wake up.

Ryan shook her by the shoulders. "Open your eyes," he said. "It's all right. *We're* all right. Listen to me. I need you to stay here, in the car with Mattie, okay? We . . . blew a tire. Van's house is close. I'm going to get help. As soon as I'm out of the car, you lock the door and don't open it again till I get back. All right?"

Her expression told him it was anything but all right. He squeezed her hand reassuringly. "I need you to look at me so I know you understand what I'm saying. When I come back with Van to get you, that's the only time I want you to get out of the car, not before. Got it? No matter what I say or do, not unless you see Van with me. Promise me."

She nodded, but when he let go, she grabbed his hand again. He leaned over and kissed her briefly on the lips, pulling his hand free before she could react. If he didn't try now, his chances of making it to the house were slim at best. He could already could feel the familiar pull, dragging him down as it eroded his resolve.

He flung his door open. A counterforce, like a wave of seawater, staggered him back into the car as he scrabbled at the door frame for a firm grip. He found it and pushed back through the wave, tumbling out the door into the reeds and cattails growing in the swampy ditch. Sliding on the muddy bottom, he plunged face-first into the stagnant green water before managing to crawl out onto the bluestone gravel shoulder. There he lay, wet and spent, spitting foul water as he braced for the next assault. He rolled over on his side and checked the car. The flat-tire story wasn't so far from the truth. The car sat at an odd angle in the ditch, its rear axle broken.

An overwhelming desire washed over him to get back in the car and sleep. He fought it and pulled himself up onto wobbly legs and stumbled across the road. Driving himself forward on autopilot, he moved at a sloth's pace toward the pickle boat house. He noted with indifference the weathered pilings jutting just above the surface at the water's edge—the only remnant of the quays that had once commanded the attention of all traffic on the road. The will to move forward ebbed away as his limbs seemed to obey commands that were not his, every movement a battle for control. He followed the beginnings of a swale until, at last, he saw Van's red Jetta parked along the road's edge, and her house just beyond. The car was no guarantee she was home. His head throbbed, but he pushed on. The porch appeared to sway from right to left, putting him at a loss which side to aim for. He tightened his fist—to his surprise, around Hamelin's coin, which he had retrieved from his pocket at some point along the way. He staggered to the right as his vision faded to black. Then the darkness exploded into a kaleidoscope of color as he fell forward and his knee struck the bottom step. Splinters of wood gouged his palms and embedded in his fingertips as they slid across the wood planking. The coin rolled free across the step and disappeared. He twisted around into a sitting position on the bottom step. He was within feet of the door, but it may as well have been on the moon. He could go no further.

Through his throbbing haze, Ryan looked back down the road. The Porsche was out of view. Closer, at the end of the drive, a man slouched against Van's Jetta. He looked on with an air of casual indifference, hands in pockets, jet-black ringlets swept back from around his face. Ryan wasn't surprised at the lack of help. Hamelin always seemed to have his own agenda. Maybe he was waiting for Ryan to die on his own. Maybe it would be best. He watched Hamelin's interest shift from him to the direction of the Carrera—a bystander, but far from innocent.

Ryan looked to the door behind him and noticed for the first time the carved flowers on the brass doorknob. Amid the swirling chaos, they were strangely beautiful, serene looking, and steadfast . . . until they, too, began to twist and sway with their own strange movement. The door opened as if by magic, and a woman appeared. As he slipped away, he couldn't find the words to tell her that he couldn't come inside, that the evil growing inside him wouldn't let him and that it was all he could do to keep the son of a bitch from taking control. Three feet from sanctuary, and no call for help could escape his lips. His mind swirled, his resolve eroded, and blood dripped from his clenched fist.

"Bennie, he's here," Van whispered. "Call you back." She hesitated a moment, put the phone back in its charger on the end table, and came outside. She sat down next to Ryan, but not too close.

"I didn't hear you drive up. Did I miss your knock?" When he ignored her, she began again. "I can understand if you never want to talk to me again. I deserve it. But will you at least let me defend myself?" When he still didn't acknowledge her, she dropped all civility. "For Christ's sake, if you're not going to talk to me, why are you here? Do you want me to grovel? Talk to me, damn it!" She grabbed him by the arm but quickly slid her hand down to his wrist. "My God, what have you done to your hand?" She uncurled his fingers and saw where the splinters had gouged the skin and under the nails. She looked into his blank, drained face. His eyes were open, but he didn't appear to see her. She let go of him, and he tumbled backward onto the steps, wearing the same empty expression.

Where was Charlie when she needed him? And her phone sat useless inside, on the end table. She yanked Ryan up by the shoulders. "Come in the house *now*." He offered no resistance, nor any assistance, and it was all she could do to get him to the doorway. They were almost inside when her heels hit the threshold and she fell hard backward, pulling Ryan down on top of her. His inert body sprawled across her, pinning her to the floor beneath him.

"Jean! Jean Marie. Help!" Van cried, letting loose with a shriek and a string of profanities to rival Jean at her most colorful.

Within seconds, Jean appeared, tearing up the steps.

"God in Heaven. What the fu . . ." She skidded to a halt and backed up at the sight of bodies piled and seething like a landed octopus at Van's front door. She tripped over her own feet and landed hard on her ample backside in the middle of the porch.

"Help me, Jean!"

"Oh, my God, you're alive! Call nine-one-one, somebody. There's blood—"

"Jean!" Van shrieked. "*You're* nine-one-one."

Jean scrambled to her feet. Van, with only her arms free, struggled to wriggle free from underneath Ryan's dead weight. Jean shook him by the shoulders, then smacked him hard. Twice.

CHAPTER THIRTY-FOUR

Deadlock

Ryan James awoke in a dimly lit room that was definitely not the pickle boat house. He sat up. Across the room sat a man at an oversize mission-style desk, a burgundy leathercovered book in his hands, reading under the soft glow of a silver metal extension lamp. The reader looked up, and their eyes locked. It was like looking in a mirror.

"Come over here," the other one said.

Ryan James's heart pounded. He climbed out of bed but ignored the demand and stood his ground. If this was his dream, he should be in charge. But he preferred to see the subtle expression in someone's eyes when they spoke, so he moved forward. He felt naked under the glare of the seated figure, who seemed to scrutinize his every movement.

"Where am I, and why am I here?" Ryan James asked.

The other one snapped his book shut. "Good question. If I had all the answers, you'd be here all by yourself. Seems we're deadlocked."

Ryan James frowned. He might not learn anything of value here. He said, "If this is a garden-variety nightmare, I'd as soon be done with it and wake up." He pinched his arm hard. It hurt, but nothing else changed. "Deadlocked on what?"

"You really don't know who I am or where you are, do you?" The other gave a brief smile.

"You're *me,* of course. I'm dreaming, and I suppose I'll have a sudden insight into life and then I'll wake up. It doesn't matter where this is, really."

"Of course . . . *not.* I'll be more than happy to give you some insight, but it won't be pleasant. This is *my* turf, *my* subconscious. How dare you invade my most private space!"

Ryan James studied himself across the way. "Ryan Llewellyn. You *are* Ryan Llewellyn, right? If this doesn't beat all!" He turned slowly in a circle, taking in the whole room. "Are we inside me?"

"Inside *me,*" Ryan Llewellyn corrected. "I've been waiting for a moment like this—face-to-face with the little weasel who thinks he can kick me out of my own body. And you do it so self-righteously." He tossed the book aside and stood up. "Now that you're here, stay a while. Get a feel for the place."

Ryan didn't want a confrontation, but neither did he want to appear weak. He resisted the urge to back away. "No. I have no plans to stay. In fact, I'm going now."

"Why are you assuming that it's you who should go and I who should stay? You're not going in that house. I forbid it."

"The pickle boat house? Stick it. You don't run me. I'm going there right after we're done here. But first, maybe I'll hang around a while—see just what you're up to." Ryan James pulled a book off a library shelf. "What do you do for fun down here?"

"Oh, plan ways to screw you over, and wait for you to screw up—like you're doing right now."

"Mm-m. You're not as clever as you pretend. If you had the upper hand, we wouldn't be in a stalemate, now, would we? You'd be prancing around doing something *edgy,* like selling my car or sending hookers to my place of business to embarrass me. At most, you're an annoyance. The reason we're both here at the same time is because you're not strong enough anymore to take control. I was ripe for the picking until Hamelin clued me in. He's going to drag your sorry ass to hell."

Ryan Llewellyn sneered. "Hamelin can't even drag his *own* ass to hell. That the best you can do?"

Ryan James pointed to the bookshelves.

"And I read."

Ryan James pulled out *Gettysburg,* bound in dark-green tooled leather, with gilt-edged pages. He flipped it open. "Four score and seven years ago . . . ," he began. "Where's the rest?" He flipped through the pages, all blank or nearly so, inscribed with only an occasional name or location. He pulled down a second book, the King James Bible, and began to read, but it was the same. After the first few sentences on page one, the rest of the page was blank. Scattered here and there across hundreds of pages were simple platitudes and partial phrases that he recognized but could not complete. "Why are all your books blank?"

"Here, your mind can re-create only what it already knows. If you knew the Gettysburg Address by heart, it would be in the book. Like most people, you know little about a lot." Ryan Llewellyn walked over and pulled the first book from his grasp and began to read. *"Fourscore and seven years ago our fathers brought forth on this continent a new nation, conceived in liberty and dedicated to the proposition that all men are created equal. Now we are engaged in a great civil war, testing whether that nation or any nation so conceived and so dedicated can long endure."* He put the book back. "I could go on, but you're not worth it. If you paid more than lip service to Christianity and memorized chapter and verse in Sunday school, those Bible pages would be full of ageless wisdom."

Ryan James scanned the rest of the room. Ever in motion, the space rippled and distorted in waves like heat rising from a fire. The other walls were darkly paneled—unadorned and unbroken by door or window. There appeared to be no ceiling, just endless dark space illuminated by a beam of dim filtered light. A low murmur, almost like a hum, swirled around him.

Ryan Llewellyn nodded toward the skylight. "It's talking. When you realize you'll never understand it all, you tune it out. Except when *you* talk—I never tune that out. I get all of that—all your stupid little ploys and plans with Hamelin. You know he's scamming us both, right?" He watched Ryan James for a moment. "Oh, come on. You know it's true. He's a loose cannon who can't buy into the system. He lives—if you can call it that—for the *win*. He doesn't give a shit about us. Didn't see him making any effort out there in the driveway, did you? We're as expendable as the people of Nevis."

"Hector Junior thought that, too, and you see where it got him. Neither of you can get along without the other right now. You want him free because you need a gofer."

Ryan Llewellyn shot him a disgusted look. "I don't need *anyone,*" he sneered. "Mind your own business."

"What are you hoping to win?" Ryan James said. "You do know you're dead, don't you?"

"Alive, dead—as long as I'm rotting away here and fighting you all the time, I don't see any difference. You're the only problem I've got, and I can't figure out how to get rid of you permanently. I'd love to squeeze the life right out of you."

Ryan James stepped over to the desk. "Fortunately, I don't believe you can do that. I'm going now."

Ryan Llewellyn drew alongside the desk. "You're not leaving me here."

Ryan James felt the light from the skylight warming him, tugging at him, and the room and his nemesis began to dissolve into little fragments of color. He closed his eyes and visualized the pickle boat house—the montage of pictures, the iron stair bannister, the sweet scent of Jean's mimosa tree blossoming next door, and two loved ones sitting unprotected in his car on Sollars Wharf.

He levitated toward the light even as he felt fingers tighten around his neck. Amid the hum, one shrill voice rose above the rest. "*We're not done. I forbid it. I'm going to kill . . .*"

CHAPTER THIRTY-FIVE

Sanctuary

The second slap brought tears to Ryan's eyes, but he couldn't open them. The grip around his neck threatened to choke him out as his mind sent frantic messages to his paralyzed limbs. He concentrated on the low hum in his ears until, gradually, it separated into voices he could comprehend.

"Stop slapping . . . ninny! . . . not helping. His arms, Jean—pull him . . . wriggle out."

"Van, I . . . I thought you were dead," Jean said. "You've got to get him out of your foyer. What kind of trouble is he in now? Is he drunk?"

"No . . . idea," Van said, gasping for air. "I don't smell any liquor. He was sitting on the porch, but totally out of it. I had to drag him in here." She began pawing at him. "Where's his hand? Oh, God, what a bloody mess."

"I'll call nine-one-one."

"Wait, Jean. He's coming round. Go get the basket under my sink—the one with the first aid stuff in it. Let's get him talking, and then we'll think about nine-one-one. How on earth . . . ?"

Jean scooted off to the bathroom and bounded back with a small brown wicker basket. Ryan was still on the floor, but he was alert as Van whispered to him.

"Ryan, look at me. Do you know what's going on here?" Van said. As she knelt in front of him she took a bottle and a sterile dressing out of the basket. "Who is this?" she asked, nodding at Jean.

"It's Jean, and I'm okay now," Ryan said. He pushed Van's hands away and sat up. "Where's the bag? He patted his shirt down and tried to shove his other hand into his pants pocket. "Did Rita bring you the bag?"

Van pulled his hand away. "I haven't seen Rita, and don't worry about what's in your pockets. You're going to sit right here until I'm convinced you're okay."

Ryan slumped back against the wall and massaged his neck. "I can't stay . . . I need to get back to the car with the bag."

"For God's sake, what's going on, Ryan?"

"We need to talk." He looked at Jean. She seemed torn between mopping his forehead and tossing him out with the garbage. He was fairly certain Van had never told her of his true background, and at the moment, he hadn't the time or patience to get her up to speed. "Alone."

"Sorry, Jean," Van said. "I think everything's under control. I'll catch up with you in a few minutes. Thanks for pitching in. Keep your cell on."

"I can take a hint, but unless he's drunk, I'd be thinking about dialing for help. Call me when you've sorted him out."

"Thanks," Van called over her shoulder.

After washing most of the blood off his hand with peroxide, she dabbed the cuts with antibiotic ointment and taped the dressing in place, then looked at him. "Your color's better. What's going on, Ryan? Is it HYA? Do I need to call for help? Are you drunk? Poisoned? What the hell is going on? I'm going to sit here, and you're going to tell me what's going on with you—without any shading of the facts. Otherwise, I'm going to let you die of your wounds."

He looked blankly at his hand. "You're kidding, right?"

She shook her head. "You still don't know what the heck is going on, do you?"

"I know Bennie called you. I don't get how I could be so wrong about so many people. All your sneaking and lying and half-truths . . . God damn it, you knew I had a son and you didn't tell me? I've seen him, and he's my spitting image." Ryan tried to stand up. "If you don't have the bag, it's at the Phoenix."

She tightened her grip on his hand enough to make him wince and be still. "I'm not done, and you aren't leaving this house until you tell me what's going on." She cut the excess tape off his wrist and dropped the scissors back in the basket. Is it HYA and the information you stole?"

He nodded.

She looked at him with exasperation. "Has it ever once occurred to you that maybe you can't win this one? Give up and return it. Problem solved."

"You know it's not that simple. I'm trying to do the right thing. I'm taking it all—er, taking a flash drive to the district attorney. But if Rita didn't bring it here, I have to go back to the Phoenix, and I need to go get Livia and Mattie. They were living at the Sleepy. I took them out of that shit hole, but I've already deserted them. They're stranded, alone in my car, in a ditch on Sollars Wharf."

"I didn't lie about Livia," she said. "When we last talked, I didn't even know she had a son. I saw them together on the beach—Livia and your little double, and I knew instantly he was your son. I was going to tell you everything as soon as I could prove it all. But just in case it's escaped you, you're not the only one affected by this. That's my grandson, and furthermore, I'm the only one in a position to do anything about it. You don't have any legal claim, *Mr. Thomas*."

"And when were you going to tell me she was my wife?"

"Your *what*!"

"You heard me. When were you going to congratulate me? Surely, O knower of all things, you knew Livia and James slipped quietly away and were married by the JP in Deep Creek right before he died. When were you going to spring *that* one on me? Or were you hoping it would just go away?"

Van pushed the basket out of the way and sat down next to him on the living room floor. "Did Jerry tell you that? If you got it from Livia, she could be lying—"

"Livia has no reason to lie. I saw the wedding picture on the nightstand at the Sleepy Time—the beaming bride and groom."

Van stared blankly at him. "James never told me."

Using his good hand for support, Ryan struggled to get up again, but Van put her weight against him. He gave up and sank back against the wall again. "I have to go back. Van, she's in deep with HYA. I need to go back before they find her."

"She works with HYA, and you believe you can trust her? Let's rethink that a moment."

"She doesn't work for them. She's beholden to them, and it's because of me. Look, I can't stay. My life is crazy, but I don't have time to explain it all. You need to trust me and take me back to my car. And you need to do it now." Ryan took her hand off his shoulder and pulled her closer. "This second life—it isn't free."

She took his injured hand in hers. "I'm not sure I know where you're going with all this. We've always known you couldn't squander this miracle. There's a reason."

"No, it isn't about some meaning I'm supposed to get out of all this. I'm fighting for my *soul* here."

"Soul?" She gave a skeptical frown. "Look, I don't know what you took or drank or had done to you, but a moment ago, I had a soulless, empty shell of a person dazed and bleeding on my front porch. If I didn't know you, I'd swear you were having some sort of psychotic break."

"Crazy, I can't even begin to explain. Help me. Then you can be done with me, but don't sacrifice the lives of an innocent woman and your grandson because you think my life could ever be normal. I don't have time to make you understand. Drive me back, please, I'm begging you."

"Okay. Maybe not for your sake but for Mattie's. I'll get my keys. You keep talking; then I'll decide how much to help you."

CHAPTER THIRTY-SIX

Finding Repentance

Livia twisted in the seat of the Jetta and tried to get one last parting look her son, sitting with Van in the porch swing of the pickle boat house. "You shouldn't have told her, Ryan. How do I know they'll be there when we get back? She could skip town. I feel like I'm never going to see him again."

"Calm down, Livia. I can't have you physically here and your mind elsewhere. You don't need to come with me. I'll take you right back."

"No. You can't do this alone. I'm coming with you. End of discussion."

"Then you have to keep focused on us and trust she'll take good care of him. And I didn't need to tell her. She saw you in town with him. For Christ sake, he looks just like James. She'll protect him with her life, and right now that's what you want, isn't it?"

"Just get this over with so I can get my son back."

When they got downtown and Ryan pulled curbside, the sight of the Phoenix was a punch in the gut. By late afternoon, the place was usually humming. But there it sat, lights off and front door locked.

"Something happen to Bennie?" Livia asked, peering in the window while Ryan fumbled for his key and muttered profanities.

"Bennie doesn't work here anymore," he answered. *Some dumb ass gave him his walking papers.* Firing Bennie had left no one in charge. He had to give his former bartender credit for sending everyone home and locking up the joint, even after Ryan's shabby treatment. Nothing but good had come of Bennie's interference. If only Ryan had taken a moment to cool down before mouthing off! He had banished his best friend, and Bennie would never forgive him.

"Hey, Mr. Thomas. Are you Mr. Ryan Thomas?" A thin young man dressed in faded jeans, a Def Leppard *Hysteria* T-shirt, and holey gray Converse High Tops loped across the street toward them.

Ryan stepped in front of Livia as his hand reached for the subcompact semiautomatic in his pocket. "Yes. Can I help you with something?"

"S'all right, man. Here you go." The stranger handed him a sealed legal-size manila envelope. "Consider yourself served. State of Maryland versus Hector Young. Have a great day."

Ryan flipped it over and read his name and address, typed on the white label pasted across the front. It was about time he got some good news. He tucked it under his arm, shoved the door open, and entered his silent, empty business.

Livia crowded in behind him, glanced around, and shuddered. "Wow, where is everybody?" This is spooky, and I have bad vibes. Can we pick up what you need and get the hell out of here?"

"Yeah, what's a bar without a bartender, huh? I'd cry in my beer, but we're fresh out of that, too. Okay, in and out before anyone knows we're here. We're looking for a bulky envelope with a flash drive in it."

Ryan scanned bar tops, tabletops, and all the work surfaces as he scooted from room to room. The envelope was smack in the center of his desk, wrapped in a cocktail napkin, no doubt by the ever-thoughtful

Bennie—a final act of repentance. And right behind it, perched on the edge of the credenza, sat Hamelin, going through the mail. Ryan snatched the bag from the blotter and turned to leave.

"Good man, Bennie Bertolini," Hamelin said while tearing open an envelope. "You did him an injustice. And why is *that* still here?" he asked, waving the paper at the package in Ryan's hand. "Didn't I tell you to get rid of it? Did you pick up the one from the museum, too?"

"Yes, life got in the way, another yes, and hell no." Ryan leaned closer. "Why didn't you tell me I had a son, you prick?"

"I told you I wasn't here to create a sense of obligation to Livia or anyone else. Now you know, and it will influence free will and moral decisions, as it should."

"Oh, stop the moralizing. I got a firsthand look at your callousness a while ago at Van's. You're in no position to give advice. Do you get off watching people suffer?"

"No, not at all. Contrary to what you believe, I do have a heart. Rest assured, when the opportunity presents itself, I'll help you. Plan B, remember?"

"Plan B, plan B. But that's just another diversion, like the aurascope. Why didn't you use plan B before I went into the house today? We were deadlocked. You could have had him." Ryan growled and flung the manila envelope at his head.

"No, but close," Hamelin replied as he caught the envelope and glanced at the label. He tossed it onto the credenza. "Did you enjoy your little tête-à-tête?"

"You knew?"

"It's hard to miss that kind of raging soul. No particulars, though—only the misplaced indignation of someone not ready to give up. You're becoming too effective at keeping him in check. You need to let him go, encourage him to do his own thing."

"I can't give that narcissistic miscreant free rein. Like you, he doesn't have a moral compass, and that scares me. He needs to behave long enough for me to get rid of the drive. If I let go now and your plan B doesn't work, I could get stuck down there in his miserable little library. I've got a dead lunatic threatening to kill me. There's no way he can harm anybody in Van's house, right?"

Hamelin shook his head. "No, she and Mattie are safe." He got up and glanced into the other room, then pushed the door to. His face, usually controlled and serene, was tight, the smile forced and the glow gone. "You're not taking Livia with you to meet the DA, are you? I warned you about getting other people involved."

Ryan studied his countenance. "I don't understand you. You're within an inch of dragging Ryan Llewellyn to hell, and yet, you're down in the dumps. My guess would be you're manipulating somebody. And that somebody pretty much has to be *me*. What gives?"

"Bad day. Once every eon or two, even immortals have them. Never mind. It's not important. But she doesn't have to tag around everywhere with you. Leave her here, where she's safe."

"I could take her back to Van's."

"Don't go into the house anymore. I have to wait too long for Llewellyn to regroup."

"You really think I'm going let anything happen to her now that we're together again? Now, I'm out of here before my ugly half gets uppity again. Chop-chop, off you go."

"Very well." Hamelin sighed and opened the door, then took a quick step back to avoid smacking into Livia.

"Hamelin. You . . . you're still in town." She stepped inside.

Hamelin nodded, and the tips of his ears went pink. "Final paycheck," he said, waving a piece of mail as he sidestepped her and disappeared into the kitchen. "I'm off."

"Wait." She followed him, but he wasn't anywhere in the kitchen when she got there. "Hamelin . . . ? Where did he go so fast?"

"Back door. Let him go. He's a strange fellow."

"Strange?" She shook her head. "Misunderstood, I think. An introvert, maybe. Every time we meet, he blows me off. *You,* on the other hand—you don't look so good again. Do you have what you need so we can get out of here? Maybe you should see a doctor. It's not normal to having fainting spells."

"I don't need one. My head is pounding from the stress of all this. But not for long." He dangled the bag in front of her. "It's enough to make either HYA or the DA very happy. Your choice." He dropped it into her outstretched hand.

She twirled it around in her hands, then cocked an eyebrow at him. "Back there, at the apartment, I asked if you betrayed Earl. I didn't need to ask. I answered that question the day we went to Benedict Point and every day you flirted with me at the Phoenix. It was never an act with me. If I'd thought I could solve all this by walking away, I would have. Honest to God, Ryan, I tried. After you fired me, I packed up and left town. I got as far as Duckett's Mill Bridge before I got scared and came back. I've never wanted to hurt you, but my son will always come first. Giving this to HYA is no good for any of us. They'll always want more." She handed the drive back.

"That's all I needed to know," he said. He caressed the length of her hand before taking the drive. "Let's hope it never comes to that." He retrieved the envelope from the credenza and pulled his cell phone out. "The sooner I make this the DA's responsibility, the safer we'll all be."

CHAPTER THIRTY-SEVEN

Brick Walls

Livia watch Ryan's face fall, and the ire in him rise and spread like a red flame up his neck into his cheeks. She backed up to avoid his pacing and flinched when he threw his phone against the door, punctuating the end of the conversation.

"Son of a bitch. The *Fifth*! How does he do it?" Ryan asked the ceiling. He turned to Livia. "Flanagan thinks I want to plead the Fifth. The subpoena wasn't a formality. He thinks he has to force me to get on the stand. Oh . . . my . . . God, you sorry bastard, what have you done?" He pounded his head with his fists.

Livia walked up behind him and pulled his hands away. "Stop. Flanagan doesn't want to take the drive?"

"I'm sorry," he said. He wrapped his hands around hers. "I can't explain it all. Flanagan will take it, but he doesn't trust me anymore, and he's going to make me work to get back in his good graces. I don't blame him. But the guy doesn't realize I'm making his career for him.

He's agreed to meet us down on the green in an hour, but he's not in any mood to hang around."

"Why can't he meet us at Van's?"

"I don't want anyone else involved in this. He's on a promotional dinner cruise with his photogenic family. They're due back at the dock in half an hour. We have plenty of time, but I don't think we should hang around here." He picked up the fragments of his telephone and threw them in the trash. Looking out the window, he stiffened. "Blue Nissan. That wasn't there when we came in." He pushed her away from the door. "We go *now*."

"What makes you think they aren't out front, too?"

"We're not going back out the front. We're gonna hide."

He grabbed her hand and pushed her toward the prep island in the center of the kitchen. "Get all this stuff off here. Put it on the other side of the counter seam."

As she stacked it out of the way, he reached up inside the base cabinet and flipped a latch to lock the drawer in place. Then, with one hand leveraged against the stainless steel countertop and the other pulling on the drawer handle, he eased the cabinet out from under the countertop. The cabinet rolled smoothly forward to reveal a tidy hole in the floor, big enough for a man to pass through sideways, and descending stairs.

"It's not as bad as it looks, but you have to go down first so I can roll the cabinet back in place. A few steps down, there's a light switch on the wall to the left."

Livia shook her head, and her eyes filled with tears. "Through *there*? I can't. I'll start to scream and you won't be able to shut me up. I'll find another place," she said, her eyes darting about the room."

"Liv, it's down there or HYA. Once you go down the steps, it gets bigger. You can do this, and there's no time to hide somewhere else. Please. For Mattie."

She leaned forward and eyed the black hole, gave Ryan a glare, then blessed herself and started down. When her hand found the light switch, a bare incandescent bulb in a porcelain socket came on above their heads, illuminating an old brick ice cellar. It was dry and cool, though a little close. Ryan came down right behind her. He pulled on the cabinet from the opposite direction and rolled it back in place, locking it into position with another steel latch.

"What is this?" she whispered.

"A good place to hide," he said with a wink. There was no furniture, so they settled on the floor. She huddled against him, with his arm curled protectively around her as they listened for footsteps overhead. Ryan put his finger to his lips as something scraped across the floor almost directly overhead. A chair—they were going to camp out for a while.

"They're in here somewhere. Tear it all apart if you have to. Find 'em." It was Owens, annoyed but confident. "May as well come out, Thomas. Nobody goes back to Bishop empty-handed."

Their hiding place was suddenly turning into a prison. Flanagan wasn't going to wait for them. Ryan went for his cell phone, then remembered that it was in pieces in the garbage. He tapped his wrist.

Livia checked her watch. "*Six thirty,*" she mouthed.

"Cell phone?" he whispered. She shook her head. He tapped his wrist again and leaned in until his lips skimmed the center of her ear. "Flanagan. I have to get out of here. *Now.*" He stood up, and Livia scrambled to her feet, too. He shook his head. "Stay . . . safer." She shook her head and clung to his hand.

He shook his head again and pulled her to the back of the cellar, gesturing to a dark passageway that extended from the back of the room. He had discovered the main cellar when he converted the old tomato warehouse into the Phoenix. It was preCivil War, maybe even colonial. He had allowed the workers to remove years of trash from the cellar, but that was as far as he let them go—he didn't need strangers poking around in his business. As he correctly guessed, at some point in its history, digging at the rear of the cellar had continued, creating a hidden room with an exit to the surface through a narrow brick-lined passageway—probably an Underground Railroad safe house. A historian's delight, no doubt part of a larger network scattered through Maryland. He had never told Van about the cellar. He had kept the knowledge to himself, and the wisdom of that decision was now clear. The historian in her would kill him—if HYA didn't beat her to the punch.

"This is the only way out," he whispered. "You'll never make it through here. Too narrow—you wouldn't be able to stand it. I'll come back for you, I promise." Ignoring the protest poised on her lips, he said, "This is the only way." Prying her hand loose from his arm, he backed her up several steps and sat her down on the clear plastic tote shoved up against the wall. He retrieved a flashlight out of the niche above her head and stopped for a moment to consider the liquor bottle and two glasses sitting there. He pulled the bottle out. It was Bennie's peach brandy from Mt. Vernon, half empty. Marla and Skalski had been having a little tea party. He'd hate to be the one to break it to Bennie. He put the bottle back in place and shielded it behind the glasses.

"Livia, promise me you'll stay right here till I get back."

She agreed, and he believed her. Fear would keep her right here. He kissed her lightly on the lips and turned away.

Ryan crept upright along the passageway for a dozen yards before it narrowed. He stowed the flashlight and got down on hands and knees. His back throbbed, and the uneven floor sent biting pain through his abraded palm. He was not claustrophobic, but it was tight, worse even than the CAT scan he had undergone when he dislocated his shoulder. Only someone in desperate straits would tolerate this closeness for any length of time. He had come down this way only once, and only far enough to verify that it indeed led to the shed. He had promised himself he would never do it again unless he had no other choice. The timber shoring had seemed solid enough at the time, but if someone had moved things around in the shed and covered the exit hole, he would be forced to crawl backward all the way, without turning around. He wasn't sure he could do that, and Livia was in no position to help.

The air was cool, but sweat trickled through his close-cropped hair and into his eyes. He kept his eyes closed as he inched along, softly humming Mozart's Symphony no. 40 in G Minor. When he finished it, he opened his eyes to pitch darkness. His ears throbbed with the hammering of his heart, and his breathing accelerated as the walls seemed to close in around him. He let out an involuntary whimper. He was about to spiral into panic, when he heard a moan and heavy breathing just behind him. "Livia?"

"You're stuck! Oh, dear God in heaven, you're stuck." More moaning followed and soon began to rise into a full- throated scream. We're gonna die, Dear G—"

"*Shh!*" he hissed. "Livia, be quiet, for God's sake. I'm not stuck. Jesus Christ, what are you doing? Don't you ever listen to a damn thing anybody tells you?"

"No-o-o," she said, her voice thin and strained. "Only when it makes sense. I can't stay back there. They'll find me." And again her voice took on that breathy, panicky edge.

"Slow down. I'm not stuck—just frustrated. Keep your eyes closed. Count to ten. Come on, I'll count with you." He listened as she counted. Her breathing slowed, though it was still labored. Thank heaven she had backed off the screaming. "You're such a hardhead. You would have been perfectly okay back there, or I never would have left you. Now, come on. Couple more minutes. Can you keep going, or do we have a new problem?"

"I . . . can do this. I can do this."

He could hear her moving again. He said a silent prayer and pushed forward, this time humming an angry theme from Prokofiev's *Peter and the Wolf.* His left hand splashed into a puddle up to the knuckles. He jerked it back and sniffed—just mud, thank God—then wiped it on his shirt. The rest of the passageway had been stone dry, so they must be close now. Despite the throbbing pain in his knees and back, he crawled on, tapping the ceiling of the tunnel now and then, feeling for the planks of the escape hatch door. The floor was now one continuous puddle, and he began to rue his impulsive decision use the tunnel. Flanagan would still be DA tomorrow. They should have played it safe and stayed hidden in the cellar.

He cracked his head into a wooden beam—the shoring at the end of the tunnel, now grown slick and rotten. He said a silent prayer and pushed against what he supposed was the trapdoor above. Fear gave way to relief as it lifted up, broke apart, and rose away from the hole. He climbed out and pulled Livia up after him, and they collapsed muddy, cold, and exhausted, on the floor of the shed.

Ryan lay motionless until his knees stopped throbbing and his heart slowed. He looked at Livia and thought he could see a slight smile on her lips. She was enjoying the adventure . . . and, apparently, him. His eyes returned to the roof of the shed. Her pluck and her attraction to him kindled a warmth and contentment he had experienced only with Van. She was going to be a distraction, possibly a dangerous one.

"Livia, if they're out and about looking for us, we may not make it to the green," he said. I have a plan. There *is* another copy of the information: a CD I squirreled away near Van's old train station, in a metal shed next door. I want you to go to there, off Second and Bayside, and bring it to me on the green. If something goes wrong or things don't look right out there, I want you to hightail it down to the post office next to Fulmer's Market—you know, down on Seventh Street?—and mail it to Flanagan at the County Courthouse. Can you do that? Does it all make sense?"

She nodded. "It makes sense."

"Good, because I don't want you changing in midstream on me. I'm depending on you. Liv. Don't desert me now, okay?"

She nodded again.

"The shed's padlocked, but I hid a key under the top left corner of the mat in front of the door. It's full of carousel horses. Look for the white one with flowers all over it. I don't know flowers— they're pink, I think. Whatever, it's the fanciest horse and it's on the end farthest from the door. Pry the top of the saddle up. The CD should be inside the cavity. And here . . ." He handed her his pocketknife. "You'll need this."

Then he grabbed her, kissed her full on the lips, stood up, forcing himself not to look back. Slipping out the shed door, he bent as near to the ground as his aching back would let him, and headed for the fence.

CHAPTER THIRTY-EIGHT

Enough

The green was much closer than Van's warehouse, but undoubtedly the riskier trip. How HYA had known he was ready to pass off the drive was a mystery. Bugging a young mother's motel room was certainly not beyond them. At any rate, Mattie was safe, and his mother was heading off in the opposite direction from the trouble. That was the limit of what he could control. If she could just follow his directions, she would probably be okay. He, on the other hand, couldn't get across the green without attracting watchful eyes. Flanagan hadn't specified where on the green—probably not far from the dock. If he was hanging around the near end, Ryan could engage before anyone could stop him. And if the Flanagan family was about, all the better.

A drop in the summer humidity had drawn the town walkers out in force, and he could hear squeals and the high-pitched shouts of kids still playing hard before darkness forced them home for the evening. He passed a young beach guy, blond hair cut high and tight, waiting for his black designer dog to pee on one of the town azaleas, and fell in line behind an older couple strolling hand in hand. He would go with the flow until he caught sight of Flanagan. Make the handoff, and he would be out of here. Up ahead, the green was a hive of leisure activity—townspeople out on a warm evening. It was great for cover, bad for spotting the DA. No one looked like a blue-blood family getting off a yacht. He walked closer to the public dock and scanned more carefully. *There.* A small family group crossing the green. The two men locked eyes. Flanagan stopped, kissed the woman at his side, and pointed the family toward the parking lot across the green. He made a show of checking his wristwatch and walked back toward the dock.

"Hey, Ryan, I haven't heard from you!"

The woman's voice, calling from behind, startled him. He didn't recognize the sophisticated blonde in the little black dress until he had worked his way down those long legs to the scarlet Louboutin heels. Before he could open his mouth, the hooker was shoving a white toy poodle at him.

"Sorry, hon, but I can't keep her." She nodded toward the smartly dressed banker type watching her closely from farther down the pier. "We're off on a cruise. No dogs," she said with a shrug. She gave Hoffa a kiss and a coo and toddled off on her four-inch heels.

Fast though she was, she didn't escape Flanagan's attention. "When you're done settling up for your playtime, it better be good," he said, taking in Ryan's soiled shirt and muddied pants. "I don't waste family time."

Ryan stroked the dog and tucked her under his arm. "She found my lost dog. What a nice lady! Believe it or not, she wouldn't take any money." He took a quick look around, reached into his pocket and pulled out the baggie. "Names, dates, and account numbers—enough to cause trouble. There's more if immunity's involved." He handed it to the DA.

"Maybe *trouble* is enough" Flanagan said, studying the bag. The crease between his eyebrows deepened and when he looked up, his eyes were full of fire. "Ignoring my phone calls, torpedoing the Young case, pleading the Fifth—"

"Maybe *being district attorney* is enough," Ryan said, his eyes smoldering. "And anyway, why would I want to do all that? And where did you get the idea I'm pleading the Fifth? I've spent more days trying to get you guys to move on this case than I have working at my own pub!"

"Schizo son of a bitch . . ." Flanagan caught a whiff of the bag and made a face. "When do I get the rest?"

"When you can assure me I get immunity."

Flanagan shook his head. "No promises."

"Excuse me, do you know the time?"

It was the blond beach guy with the black ornamental doggie. He didn't wait for an answer. The pistol silencer showing underneath the *County Gazette* said it was whatever time he wanted it to be.

"Give me the bag and we're done . . . both drives," he said as Flanagan held out the bag.

"There's only one drive," Ryan said, shifting Hoffa out of the line of fire. Flanagan, uncharacteristically speechless, nodded in agreement.

The guy took a look around and dropped his dog's leash. "Up on the boat," he said, motioning with the paper toward the catamaran *Lady Mary,* moored at the end of the pier.

Ryan stood his ground. "No way I'm leaving land."

You got all of it," Flanagan blurted, "unless you want money. Look, you can have everything . . ."

He fumbled for his wallet, and Ryan did the same.

And then, for a split second, everything blipped to black. Ryan redirected his attention to the man and intensified his focus. His vision blipped again, longer this time. It was that distinctive pull, and it demanded his attention and control. He might keep Ryan Llewellyn at bay here on the green, but on the boat he stood no chance.

Shit. Now he must add to the mix Livia, blithely crossing the green toward him. How had she gotten back so fast?

Blip, refocus, blip, refocus, blip. He refocused again and shook his head. "We have money. Let's talk here."

Beach Boy pointed the newspaper at a wharf piling twenty feet away, and Ryan heard a soft *zip* as the gull perched there gave a low squawk and fell clumsily into the lapping water below.

"We can do this all day. But why bother all these nice, innocent people? Boat."

"No harm in hearing what the man has to say." Flanagan grabbed Ryan by the arm and guided him toward the pier, his grip tightening the closer they got. Ryan felt weak-kneed, but there was no use struggling.

For whatever reason—restocking food or off having a rum punch at the Phoenix, maybe—there was no crew on the luxury yacht. Beach Boy probably couldn't sail it away, but they were isolated enough for whatever he had in mind.

Dizziness and blackened vision swept over Ryan in waves. He allowed Flanagan to pull him up the length of the gangplank, but when he stepped onto the deck, he clutched the railing with his free hand, and refused to be dragged any farther. At this point, a bullet was the lesser evil. His vision blipped again.

"Hand over the second drive—now."

"Only one drive," Ryan insisted as the world tilted around him.

"Only one, honestly," Flanagan repeated. The DA had been in contentious situations before, but his darting eyes gave him away. He was ready to pee his pants. Then suddenly, he changed from cautious milquetoast to manic lunatic, flailing wildly about. "Officer McCall! Evening, Officer McCall!" he yelled to the beat cop making his nightly rounds down the boardwalk.

To Ryan's surprise, Beach Boy didn't shoot anyone. Instead, he spun around, sprinted down the gangplank, dodged the elderly couple walking hand in hand, and was a quarter of the way across the green before McCall sorted out who had hailed him.

And then adrenaline kicked in and drove Ryan Llewellyn back to the murky depths. In the moment of confusion, Ryan shoved the poodle at Flanagan and ran after Beach Boy. Beyond the retreating figure, he could still see Livia and a handful of kids playing tag. The gunman had homed in on her and was closing in at a dead run. Ryan was the faster runner and was gaining ground, but he had no chance of catching up in time. He motioned frantically at her, but Livia just smiled and waved back and continued in the same direction and pace. At the last second, the assailant, in a baffling move, veered to the open ground on the right to avoid her. Even more baffling was Livia's response: she stuck out her foot and tripped him. He hit the turf with a grunt and rolled right back up to his feet before Ryan could make an open-field tackle. The guy pivoted, gun out, and Ryan saw it, in his eyes and stance: the impulse to blow them both away—if for no better reason, then simply for the annoyance factor and maybe the humiliation of being bested by an unarmed slip of a woman. But he hesitated a moment, perhaps uncomfortable with the number of potential witnesses, most of them children. Tucking the weapon into his waistband, he turned right toward Fifth Street and disappeared.

"What kind of fool stunt was that?" Ryan asked, hands on knees, breathing heavily.

"I thought you wanted to catch him. I slowed him down for you. "

"That would have been helpful when I thought he was coming for the CD. When he changed directions, you should have let him go and not gotten involved. He was going around you, for cripes sake! He's seen your face now."

Ryan looked back across the green and saw a hubbub of activity at the pier. There was Flanagan, talking to Officer McCall, who was cradling Hoffa in his arms like a baby.

"Come on," Ryan said, pulling Livia in the opposite direction, down Sixth. "Let him have the drive. We go this way, then double back as fast as we can . . . You find it?"

"Yeah." She reached in her jacket pocket. "Right where you said."

"Don't pull it out," he said. "Come on. I need to sanitize a few things before I turn it over. No need for *everybody* to go to jail."

CHAPTER THIRTY-NINE

Hubris

They crossed the quiet residential street, and Ryan stopped. They needed a plan. His burst of adrenaline on the boat had all but dissipated, and Ryan Llewellyn was fighting him hard. Every decision he made now was challenged by the tiny but growing presence, pounding away at him.

"Where do you think, Liv?" Ryan asked. His vision blipped and he plunged into momentary darkness again. He started again. "Can't go near the pier—too much going on, too many eyes. That leaves straight ahead, or right and away from downtown. Either way, we're eventually going to be alone on the street—not all that appealing. What do you think?" Another round of vertigo seized him. He let go of Livia and vomited on the sidewalk as, inside, he spun and sailed out of control, flashing through light and darkness, power passing back and forth between his two poles. Every little movement of his head sent him sailing in a new direction.

"My God, what's wrong?" Livia held his shoulders and rubbed across his back. "We're going back to Van's. You look awful, and I need to be with Mattie." Her eyes began to dart, and her hands kneaded his back a little too hard.

He pointed to the right, bent over, and heaved again. "Next block down, another quick right to Sixth Street . . . best way back. A minute, okay?"

No sooner had he made his decision than another voice in his brain began to torment him. *You need to let him go, encourage him to do his own thing.* It was Hamelin's admonishment, looping on continual replay. *No, I need to get back to the pickle boat house before he eats me alive. Where's your plan B now?* The voice in his head replied, *It's time.*

Ryan straightened up. The air had grown stifling, and little yellow butterflies were everywhere, fluttering around their heads and lighting on their clothes.

"Hamelin?"

And there he was, across the street, leaning against a sycamore tree and watching them.

Livia saw him, too, and instinctively started toward him. "Hamelin, help! Does he have a car, Ryan? He can get Van's car."

"No, Livia . . . wait. You don't understand." Ryan James clasped her hand and tried to pull her back, but his other hand pulled at their entwined fingers as Ryan Llewellyn tried to pry them apart. Ryan James swung back and forth between light and darkness, going under and resurfacing as the series of events that could only be Hamelin's plan B unfolded in a sort of slow-motion time warp. Livia stepped off the curb, a blue Nissan hurtled forward, and Hamelin, shimmering in unearthly light, streaked across the street toward them. This time, Ryan put his trust in Hamelin. He let go of her hand and himself.

Ryan Llewellyn seized the opportunity. In his most violent outburst since the front porch of the pickle boat house, he shoved Livia from behind, straight into the path of the Nissan. The impact sent her arcing up into the air, and she smacked down on the sidewalk. Drawing himself up to his full height, he took a step back from Hamelin, standing inches away.

"Thought you had me? That's proof enough you have no business here. He'll give up now that he has nothing, and you can't touch me."

"No, but I can."

The smirk froze on Ryan Llewellyn's face as the indistinct figure of a man, shimmering in golden light, bore down on him from behind and clamped tight his arms to his sides. A white bolt of energy flashed through Ryan Llewellyn, from the top of his head to the soles of his feet. His frame began to vibrate and quiver as he lit up like an X-ray. His eyes rolled back in his head, and steam rose from his shoes, which scorched a perfect impression of his feet into the sidewalk. He stiffened and crumpled to the ground as the air around him crackled with electricity and the acrid smell of ozone.

CHAPTER FORTY

Relativity, Promotion, and Fissionable Offenses

Ryan James opened his eyes to an evening sky. Someone had knocked the wind out of him, and his toes were prickly with pins and needles. A strange burnt smell filled his nostrils. Rough, lumpy asphalt pressed against the back of his head, but it didn't look like Baltimore International Airport, and the long-term bus was nowhere in sight. The throbbing in his head changed to a pounding in his chest as he recognized Hamelin leaning over him, reaching for him.

"Get away from me!" he gasped. Hamelin stepped back and moved away.

Ryan James sat up. Several feet beyond, Livia lay sprawled on the sidewalk. Hamelin stood next to her, watching for a moment before stooping down beside her. "Livia . . . Oh, God, no. Let her be, you demon." He struggled to get up, but pain shot through his right leg, and he collapsed back onto the pavement.

Hamelin glanced indifferently at him, sat down next to Livia's crumpled body, and, to Ryan's horror, reached out and took her hand. Her fist relaxed, and the fingers uncurled and grasped the big, gentle hand, its thumb making little circles on the back of hers. He leaned forward and whispered to her while the air around the two shimmered so intensely, Ryan could scarcely keep his eyes open. Livia's grimace softened into the peacefulness of sleep, and every line of pain and worry in her face seemed to disappear.

"I can't move," Ryan murmured. "I'm paralyzed, aren't I?"

"No. Relax. Time is relative, remember? I'm allowing you to experience this, but in your sense of time, it's but a blink of an eye."

"They let you do that?"

Hamelin shrugged. "I'll be here a few moments more."

Ryan's face burned as hot tears streamed down. "Are we going to die?"

Hamelin shook his head. "You're safe now."

"My evil twin . . . he's gone?"

"Already burning in his new home.

"Did you ease his transition?"

"What do you think?" A cryptic smile flitted across Hamelin's lips. "Let's say Ryan Llewelyn Thomas is very sorry for all the evil he carried out in this world, and leave it at that."

"He pushed her. As soon as I let her go, he *pushed* her." The sensation of her hand sliding out of his kept playing over and over again. Ryan's eyes returned to Livia. He could hear the wail of sirens off in the distance. "You could have saved her. How can you exist knowing that you not taking your job seriously got her killed? Why didn't you do something sooner?"

Hamelin shook his head slowly but said nothing.

"If I had known she was part of plan B, I never would have let her go."

"She was a routine plan A, never plan B."

"Plan *A*? Wait . . . *what?* Oh, my God, it was her all along! You were never supposed to save her. That's why you wouldn't shake hands with her?"

"After she arrived in Nevis and the chess pieces were all accounted for and began to move, I knew it would come to this. Her time had come—a simple, routine plan A. You just witnessed a twofer."

"Twofer," Ryan repeated, sobbing. "I put my faith in you. God, I let go of her hand because I *trusted* you. God Almighty, there has got to be a place worse than hell for people like you, you greedy bastard. Playing with people's lives and emotions . . ."

For the first time, Hamelin looked up from Livia. His eyes were calm and gentle as he spoke. "Settle down and understand. As I've told you, I don't control any of this," he said with a sweep of his hand. "I'm here to make sure it all works out in the end. It is, and it will. No more Ryan Llewellyn Thomas, and little Matthew will be raised by his father . . . and his grandmother. Everything is as it should be. She can move on now, and you can stop searching for answers. This is your purpose." His gaze returned to Livia.

Ryan flung his arm across his eyes and tried to stem the flowing tears. "He pushed her. I saw—felt—him push her toward the car. Why would anyone . . ."

"She was the key," Hamelin said, not looking up. "With your deep emotional connection to her, your life was coming back full circle to what you were before you died in the car crash. Ryan Llewellyn understood that. He was going to annihilate you. He went for broke, as I did. Fission went according to plan B: you came through unscathed, and the other party was dispatched along his appointed journey. In a rare moment for me, I followed the rules and everything worked out—with a coworker's assistance, of course."

"But, for God's sake, you can't take her to hell. She doesn't deserve *that*."

"No, don't be ridiculous—to the good place."

"But you don't *do* heaven."

"Promotion. It seems even I am not immune to St. Peter's principles." For a moment, the shimmering around Hamelin intensified.

"They could demote you. You're already back to breaking all the rules to suit yourself."

"In that case, pray it's not me that comes for you. I have to clean up my act—new responsibilities, expectations to live up to." Hamelin pushed the hair back from Livia's face. "She's already at peace, can you see? That's my gift. Whatever ill you think of me, at least give me that. It's why I'm here: to give comfort—even to you, if you'd just let me." He reached over and placed his fingertips on the pulse point of Ryan's wrist.

Ryan flinched. "Are you killing me?"

Hamelin smiled but didn't remove his hand. "Hardly. You're safe with me. She's reviewing her life. Would you like to share a few memories?"

"Don't you just handle pain and suffering?"

"No, I see everything from her life. There is so little regret and darkness here. She's serene, with enormous faith and lovely memories. The memories may be painful for you now, but not in the long term. It's up to you, but it'd be a shame to waste them. Little Matthew would appreciate them someday."

Ryan nodded.

"My pleasure. He held both their hands, gently leading one soul forward while holding the other back. As he spoke, his face was kind and his eyes never left her face. "We're not dwelling on regrets, but on the lovely, all-encompassing love she's walking toward."

The memories were bittersweet—comforting in their love for James and Matthew, but heartrending in that she didn't know that the one who shared those feelings was here as her life ebbed away. The memories weren't enough. He wanted her to know he remembered the Ripple Inn—the blue shirt she wore, the heady scent of Chanel on that last night they spent together, the night Mattie was conceived.

"Robert Johnson," Ryan blurted.

"What about him?"

"Hamelin, tell me, how long did you know him? A couple of hours? You've known me a lot longer than that—years, if we go back to your first stalking episode. We have a rapport, strange as it is."

"Time has no meaning for me."

"Exactly. Make a deal with me."

Hamelin cocked an eyebrow. "I'm listening."

"I can see compassion in your eyes for the first time. Embrace it, Hamelin. Don't take her now. Sixty years. Come back in in sixty years. If it has no meaning for you, why would you care? Six decades is nothing in eternity, but it's a lifetime for her. Please."

"And in return, what? Robert Johnson gave the gift of music. You'll give me a lesson in skimming, graft, and peddling inebriation?"

"Self-esteem. If you had taken Ryan Llewellyn when you were supposed to, she wouldn't be lying here in the middle of the sidewalk, her life ebbing away. Right now you have a chance to right your mistake. I don't know anything about your existence, the connections you make in the other world, but I know that misty longing in your eyes—you have feelings for her. That night at the Phoenix when I introduced the two of you, you were totally checking her out. The boat in the bottle—a buck fifty at Mac's—you could fool her, but I know who gave it to her. Connect with her right now by giving her a long, happy life. You owe it to her."

Hamelin shook his head. "I form no connections; I have no home. We've been over this before. The notebook is my guide," he said, nodding toward the book in his pocket. "I do what is bidden, and then move on in the world. I am what they need me to be. I took chances when I was at the bottom of the heap. When you haven't really bought into the system, there's nothing to lose. But now . . . now they're giving me a second chance, and more is expected. I can't let them down, and I can't go back to being a snuffy. You understand, don't you, about second chances?"

For a brief moment, Ryan sensed an opening in the conversation as Hamelin spoke candidly about his new role. "You'll never go back to that, because you have something now you didn't have before: compassion. It's in your grieving eyes. Sacrifice for someone else, Hamelin. It's a brief moment in eternity. They'll never catch you. Averaging is a beautiful thing, remember?"

Hamelin shook his head. "It's too late."

"No, it's not," Ryan said, struggling to sit up. "Be bold. It's not about them telling you what to do and you doing it. You need to exercise judgment, based on compassion. Just because you're here doesn't mean you have to take her. It can be Disney World all over again. You didn't take me, and you don't have to take her. Give us a life together. Go to the next person on your list. Please."

"You know I didn't change your fate in Disney World," Hamelin replied, his voice low and quiet. "That power resides elsewhere. I need to go where they send me when they send me. There's no need for compassion there. I am sorry. You're pleading with the wrong person. I'm not the decision maker." He fixed his intense gaze on Ryan once more. "For now, you need to sleep, Ryan James. When you remember, don't think too harshly of me."

"No. You can't get away with this. I can fight you. You're—"

"I'm precisely what I need to be," Hamelin repeated, sounding every bit like the company man he had become. "Someday, I'll be back for you and you'll be ready. Grieve, but be comforted. God's hands are broad and gentle. Sleep now."

Ryan struggled to free himself from Hamelin's grasp, but it was a purely mental endeavor, useless. Hamelin's face remained compassionate and calm as he resumed watching Livia, his grasp firm, the shimmer around them intensifying. Ryan closed his eyes, and then he knew no more.

Hamelin let go of Ryan's hand and pulled out the notebook. He skimmed several pages and then flipped to the last tab before returning it to his pocket. With a smug smile and eyes brimming with compassion, he looked into Livia's serene face. He let go of her hand.

CHAPTER FORTY-ONE

Courting Favor

It was one of those crisp fall days without a cloud in the cerulean sky. Ryan wondered how the world could keep turning when it was full of so much pain. Being robbed of life at age 24 seemed like punishment enough, but now the universe wanted to keep punishing him every single day for the rest of his second life—his son, too. In the past weeks, his world had gotten smaller, shrunken away. He felt like an old man, but without the wealth of memories from experiencing what life had to offer. He tried to think back on the last words they had spoken. Were they memorable? Could he see Livia's face, her reaction? Had they connected, or did he squander the precious moment on banal conversation—throwaway words lost in the vastness of a meaningless existence? He couldn't say. He knew only that he was left empty, yearning to take it all back and make sure it counted this time. He wanted to sleep it away, but his deepest thoughts and fears would only churn and rise up in nightmarish visions.

From the top stair of the Frederickton courthouse, he looked out and surveyed the sea of cameras down below. A lot of PR machines were working overtime: the DA's office, HYA, and the *Frederickton Journal,* all busy spinning their take on the verdict. Innocent. A jury of Hector Young's peers had refused to convict, and he was a free man. How many had voted with their conscience, and how many with their wallets, was anybody's guess.

Surprisingly, District Attorney Flanagan was a happy man. With his tough stance on crime, he still had a good public image, and he had no doubt set his sights on a bigger arena than this little bayside county.

He tapped Ryan on the shoulder. "Thank you, Mr. Thomas. This isn't over yet. My office will be in touch." He held the handshake while cameras flashed. Then he drew in close. "Might want to clear out now. Young will be making a grand exit shortly, and then on to the Maldives, we think. No extradition there. If he's smart, he'll stay put there. If not, we'll take another crack at him with the new information. In the meantime, you might want to lose yourself in a little cabin in the woods somewhere." He clapped him on the shoulder once more and descended into the throng of reporters.

Ryan wasn't going to hole up in the woods, but running into Hector was not in his plans. He skirted around the crowd outside and outpaced the few reporters who dogged him to his car. Moments later, he found himself totally alone as the press stampeded for the building, where Hector Young had just emerged, flanked by several high-powered attorneys. Ryan watched as Hector scanned the crowd, stopping for a moment to stare in Ryan's direction. *Hector, I know you can't see me, you bastard.* And anyway, if Hector wanted to talk, he could swing by the Phoenix. If not, a second trial could bring them back together, and a sweet little gift of immunity would allow Ryan to testify without prosecution. He pulled away from the curb and headed back to Nevis. It might not be a cabin in the woods, but as the treasury of all his memories, it would always be his haven.

CHAPTER FORTY-TWO

The Mulligan

Ryan sat on a chair in the kitchen, watching Van put dishes away. Every time he started to speak, he realized it wasn't going to come out right, and kept his mouth shut. And he had kept it shut about plenty. Whether it was Hamelin's doing or merely a part of the trauma of losing Livia, he hadn't spilled a word about Hamelin and what happened. But silence didn't make their problems go away, and neither of them was ready to acknowledge the elephant in the room. Where did they stand with each other? Their relationship didn't seem to be based on anything other than loss, and only a fool would try to create something out of that. He felt like a can of warm soda, shaken and about to explode.

Van didn't seem to be faring any better. Her face was drawn, and dark circles shadowed the skin below her eyes. She dried her hands on a red-striped dish towel and draped it around the refrigerator door handle. "Bennie coming back?"

"Don't think so—at least, not right away. I don't think it's anything personal. I called him and apologized."

"How much did you tell him?"

"Not enough, but he did graciously accept my apology. You know Bennie; he apologized, too. He feels obligated to stay a while at Martin's, the guy that hired him. He gave me the name of a friend who wants a change of scenery. Good man according to Bennie—very hands-on. Can't get any better than a recommendation from him. This guy's interested in brewing his own—might be a good time to venture into that. And the distributors want to do business again now that HYA's backed off of 'em, so everything should run smoothly.

"I've got to step back for a while, you know?" He choked, and tears threatened. He put his hand over his chest. "I remember her." And then he pointed to his head. "And I remember her here, too. No picture, no prompt, they're real memories—*my* memories. They're coming from inside *my* head, not someone else's. For the first time, there's a *me* in here.

Van smiled at him, and there was a misty tenderness in her eyes. "I know. It'll take time. Time will make it bearable." She turned away. "Have you heard any more about Mattie through any of your *friends*?"

Ryan turned away, wiped his eyes. "He's still with Child Services. No legal briefs have been filed yet other than yours. It would be a surprise if Earl's parents filed. They're old and not in good health. I have it on best authority they'll rule in your favor. Then we can work it out from there." He walked into the front room and pulled open the café curtain. "I don't know. The pessimist in me says we have a slim chance of getting him back if . . ." He dropped the curtain. The face was gaunt but unmistakable. "It's him. Richard's here . . . doesn't look like he's getting out. Nice new car."

Van glanced at Ryan but didn't speak. She scooped her purse off the table and lifted her keys from the brass hook by the back door. "We'll be in touch. Can you lock up? It . . . it would look strange for you to walk out with me."

Ryan nodded and watched her go as far as the door. "What are you going to do?" As he had expected, it sounded desperate and needy.

"The right thing," she said without turning around. "I can't deal with this all at once. I *will* be back. Sometimes, moving on requires taking a step back. Do you really think I could let him die alone?"

"Going back to him shouldn't be about obligation."

"Who said anything about obligation? I do still love him, you know. Not the same, but it's there. Forgiveness soothes a lot of wrongs—something you might want to think about." She eased the door open and slipped out.

The door pulled to. Ryan's breaths came in little shallow gasps as she descended the porch steps and crossed to the car. She was a contradiction—a force of nature on the outside, swirling around a fragile inner psyche. He watched as her normally effortless grace transformed into a thoughtful, measured gait that left undisturbed the fallen scarlet oak leaves beginning to carpet the front lawn. Her determination spoke louder than any words. She would stand by Richard when he needed her most, either holding his hand as he beat the cancer or kneeling before his coffin if he didn't. It was what better people did.

Van gave her ex-husband a smile and an awkward half wave. He got out of the car and gave her a pat on the back before opening her car door. Before she ducked into the car, she paused and looked back at the window where Ryan stood inside. He searched her face for indecision, but if she felt it, she gave nothing away. She slid in and closed the door.

Richard had lost weight. He moved with the caution of an old man. Ryan felt a pang of guilt, and it surprised him. He moved away from the window and looked around the living room. He couldn't read Van right now, and it was possible he might never be in here again. He walked through every room and leaned on all the windowsills and took one last look from each window. He caught Jean next door, staring out the window at the goings-on. She gave him the finger before closing her curtain. He couldn't blame her. With Marla still out there somewhere, Bennie was all she had. Van thought she would follow him to New York, and that would probably make them both happy.

Last stop was the bathroom. He pulled off his field boots and climbed into the claw-foot tub, reclining until the back of his head rested against the cool enamel. He tried to picture all the baths he had ever taken in his grandparents' house. As expected, he couldn't recall a single one.

When he was done, he locked up and walked back toward town, turning to take a long last look at the house. He had no clear idea where he was headed. He just kept moving. Farther down the street, he felt compelled to veer left, and he headed toward the shore. He could make it short, satisfy the need to feel the vastness and majesty of a power greater than himself.

He found a free space along the railing of the crowded pier. Minutes went by, his mind busy with nothing much. Surely, there was somewhere he needed to be, things that must be done. But there was nothing, nothing but the passing of time. And he knew that time was not his ally but, rather, a measure of something painful and heartbreaking taking flight and soaring just far enough away that he could not call it back to soothe it, or seal it away until a brighter day. He slipped the document out of his back pocket and gently unfolded it, running the back of his thumbnail down the folds to smooth it out. "The State of Maryland," it read across the top, and then came all the particulars required to legally bind two individuals as husband and wife. He touched his and Livia's signatures—signatures of two people who had lived and loved and no longer existed, their lives played out in the never-ending drama that the universe had been staging since time immemorial. He could never be James again, and she was, well, wherever good people existed after they won the game. To be with her again, he, too, needed to learn how to play to win—however that was done, even if it took forever.

Ryan clung to the beach railing and tried to send his spirit across the bay to Kent Island—to fly like the birds, gliding and sailing along the bay currents. It was something Livia would have done. Her memories that Hamelin had given him told him so, and he felt her passion. He could feel it, but he couldn't hold on to it. He felt it drifting away, drowned out by the revving of an outboard motor—a twenty-something decked out in a dark blue sailor's jacket, white linen shirt, and dark colonial breeches, backing a Whaler away from the dock. His girlfriend, a shapely brunette in a red tank top and jean short shorts, sat cross-legged in the bow, her wispy hair blowing free around her face. She stretched out her long, tanned legs and called out to the pilot, her high clear laughter carrying across the water. It wasn't the sound that mesmerized Ryan, but her lovely face and crystal blue eyes the color of calm tropical ocean. He felt their intensity meld into the core of him, and a thrill ran through him. In a hundred lifetimes, he could never forget such eyes. He fumbled for his cell phone and tried to snap a picture of the boat as it turned, picked up speed, and headed out into the channel. He worked his way through the throng, to the railing at the end of the pier and snapped one more shot, trying to capture the port of call. By then the boat was indistinguishable in the flotilla of bobbing pleasure craft clustered around a majestic full-rigged colonial tall ship in full sail.

"What's that boat?" he asked an old guy in a brown John Deere ball cap, leaning against the nearest piling.

"Son, there's about thirty of 'em out there. Which boat we talking about?"

"Sorry, the blue tall ship in the center there."

"That'd be the *Kalmar Nyckel.* They're showboating it around after the reenactment."

"What reenactment? Does it dock here somewhere?"

The man frowned and started again. "The 1814 Battle of St Leonard's Creek? Whereabouts you from?"

"New York. Does it dock here?"

Naw. Only a damn fool sails a blue boat on the bay. Docks up in Delaware. They can do whatever the hell they want up there. We're waiting on the *Pride of Baltimore.* It's yellow."

Ryan pulled the photo app up on his phone. The first picture was a great one of the boat, but the registration numbers were out of focus. He tried the last picture, enlarging it again and again until the lettering on the bow was legible. And then he laughed loud enough to turn a few heads. The craft was the *Mulligan Two,* out of St. Peters, Maryland.

Dear God, Hamelin Russell. I take back every nasty thing I ever said about you. He understood all about second chances. He put the phone back in his pocket and studied the smaller boats maneuvering around the ship, trying to find the Whaler. He failed, but that was okay. It appeared that *forever* was farther than the eye could see on a crystal clear day, yet close enough to visit—right across the bay in a little burb called St. Peters. Nothing happened by chance. With the apparent blessing of an immortal who was never wrong, everything would somehow work out just fine.

Livia, I will find you and help you understand, he promised.

Made in the USA
Charleston, SC
15 September 2015